D1016814

Hurts So Good

OTHER ELLORA'S CAVE ANTHOLOGIES AVAILABLE FROM POCKET BOOKS

Lover From Another World

by Rachel Carrington, Elizabeth Jewell,
& Shiloh Walker

Fever-Hot Dreams

by Sherri L. King, Jaci Burton,
& Samantha Winston

Taming Him

by Kimberly Dean, Summer Devon,
& Michelle M. Pillow

All She Wants

by Jaid Black, Dominique Adair,
& Shiloh Walker

Hurts So Good

Gail Faulkner
Lisa Renee Jones
Sahara Kelly

POCKET BOOKS

New York   London   Toronto   Sydney

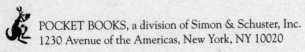

POCKET BOOKS, a division of Simon & Schuster, Inc.
1230 Avenue of the Americas, New York, NY 10020

Library of Congress Cataloging-in-Publication Data is available

ISBN-13: 978-1-4165-3613-0
ISBN-10:   1-4165-3613-2

This Pocket Books trade paperback edition April 2007

10 9 8 7 6 5 4 3 2 1

Contents

Hurts So Good

Romeo

GAIL FAULKNER

To Char for her insight. Thank you, Patti, for your expertise. Allen who knows no limit to patience. Patricia Roxanne for inspiring me and enjoying the way my inspiration turns out.

"I SHOULD WARN YOU ABOUT my cousin," Carla stated casually as she flew down the flat expanse of highway. After turning off Interstate 20 the road was virtually empty, a perfect opportunity to push the new Nissan 350ZX Turbo boy magnet she'd just given herself. This was the first real chance Carla had had to open it up and both girls were enjoying the speed and freedom the little car embodied.

"The fact is you're exactly his type—a delicate thing who's china-doll pale with big blue eyes and black hair. Of course, he's older than we are, the first child of the oldest son and all. He probably has six chicks on a string anyway. Likely, you don't have to worry. He'll be busy."

"Worry? Why would I worry? He's not a rapist, is he?" Lauren asked, laughing at her friend who seemed serious about the warning. Until now it had been a relaxed, girls out kind of trip. For Lauren it was an even greater step into independence than most, a welcome chance to get completely away from her loving yet stiflingly protective family. This little taste of *Thelma and Louise* was just the ticket as far as she was concerned. She was unwilling to let anything ruin the carefree weekend as they cruised down the road with the windows open. The sage and sun-laden air felt and smelled like sweet freedom.

"No, no, nothing like that. It's just that he's so 'in charge' about everything. He's the stereotypical tall, dark and handsome cowboy," Carla grumped as her long body shifted uncomfortably behind the wheel. "He's really bossy, dictatorial and a general pain in the ass. I'm only going to the ranch because all my other cousins will be there, and, well, I'd like to see his reaction to you."

"Me? Why me? He's seen a million of me according to you," Lauren commented in growing concern.

"Yeah, but he's never met you. The original Ice Queen is what you are and you know it. I know I should have told you about him sooner, but I was afraid you wouldn't come," Carla confessed. "I've told everyone else about you and they can hardly wait to meet you."

"What? Who is 'everyone' and why are they so eager to meet me?" Suspicious and irritated, Lauren slid around to face her friend.

"The cousins. They, um, well . . . I told them you'd turn a cold shoulder on him for sure. They're sort of anxious to see that," Carla confessed.

"I see. You're selling tickets to a show, Carla? That's low. You're right. I wouldn't have come if I'd known what you're up to. It's not fair to me and certainly isn't fair to what's his name."

"Aw, Lauren. He's an arrogant, never been wrong, never been turned down jerk," Carla responded. "His name is Romeo."

"You're kidding," Lauren scoffed.

"Nope, seriously not kidding. Sick, isn't it? He's rich, good-looking and named Romeo. You can hardly blame us for wanting him to get a little taste of humble pie. You're just the ticket. The woman of his dreams who's never gonna be interested." Carla's attractive face twisted in a grimace while her wide hazel eyes sparkled with mischief. High energy radiated off her long, lean body even after several hours of tedious driving. In almost every way the two girls were exact opposites. One tall and in constant motion, the other petite and surrounded in an almost palpable calm. Their instant friendship was a mystery to most until you got to know them.

"Carla, I came as a favor to you. You begged me to come because you'd be so 'bored.' I didn't agree to be the main attraction. You know I've never been on a ranch before and that alone makes me uncomfortable, with all the large, stinky animals and things. You promised it'd be fun. Now you spring this convoluted tale of what—revenge?" Lauren frowned darkly.

"Come on, be a sport. You don't have to do anything differently than you normally would. I didn't actually lie. The ranch is a blast when Romeo isn't hanging around making up a bunch of rules. He really is a pain in the ass," Carla continued.

"What do you mean, a lot of rules?" Lauren asked.

"You know, no running at the pool, no cannon balling each other, no playing bumper horse, it's endless," Carla explained.

"Sounds like reasonable safety stuff to me. Are the cousins

a bunch of teenagers?" Lauren wanted to know, doubtful now that she'd heard the complaints.

"Oh, we're all around our age, twenty to twenty-five now. Last time we were all at the ranch I guess we were teenagers." Carla laughed. "Oh, well, he deserves it. The man lives a charmed life, I swear. He needs shaking up."

"I hardly think my visit will relieve all the angst I hear in you, Carla. It's more like you and your cousins need therapy over this guy. Good grief. Those rules were an attempt to keep you all alive to reach your twenties. I doubt he'll give me a second look anyway. You'll be disappointed again and the little chip on your shoulder will just get bigger," Lauren predicted. "In any case, I don't intend to perform like some dancing bear. If it weren't such a long way back, I'd make you take me home."

They were three hours and forty-five minutes into the trip. Turning around now would be another three hours and forty-five minutes of being mad at each other as they drove back. Yuck.

"Yeah, I knew you would. Part of why I didn't work up the nerve to tell you 'til just now. Come on, Lauren. You know I love you. You're the one who got me through that whole Philip fiasco. I wouldn't do anything to hurt you. The Romeo junk isn't that important. I just thought I should warn you," Carla sheepishly added.

"I have a feeling it's the only important thing about this trip, Carla. I detest subterfuge. You know that. Tell me about your other cousins. The wild monkey ones," Lauren demanded. "I get the feeling I'll be the odd one out anyway. What the hell is 'bumper horse' and is it as dangerous as it sounds?"

Laughing at her city friend, Carla proceeded to explain bumper horse and various other activities. Soon Carla turned into an imposing entry gate and drove up a long, winding road to the Texas ranch her cousin owned. The drive was long enough for her to get through a short history of the ranch and its present bad-boy owner.

The ranch was the original family homestead, but now it was owned and operated by Carla's oldest cousin. His parents had died tragically young in a private plane crash. He'd been seventeen, an only child. His grandparents had still lived at the ranch then so they'd been his guardians. By the time Romeo turned twenty-two, they'd both passed away. He'd been sole owner and completely in charge for fifteen years now. His aunts, uncles and their families visited often. Somehow, he'd managed to retain the ranch as the family hub for the entire clan.

Privately Lauren was intrigued, although Carla told the whole story in an offhanded manner. Carla was not impressed with the man who'd been forced into the responsibilities of adulthood so young. As far as she was concerned, he'd been an ass forever.

As they pulled up to the sprawling ranch house, Lauren grinned. It looked like a scene from a western movie. The main house was a prominent feature but surrounded by barns and outbuildings in easy walking distance. A massive operation if you went by the number of barns, Lauren decided. A porch wrapped around the rambling house, which had obviously grown through several decades and styles. The resulting massive structure retained a relaxed casualness expressed in the comfortable rockers and porch swings distributed along the entire veranda. The landscaping surrounding the house was gracious and welcoming, as was everything about this large working operation.

Lauren stepped out on the far side of the car while Carla sprang up from behind the wheel to greet a number of young people. Lauren took the few seconds she remained unnoticed to glance about. The tang of cut hay mixed with animal scents drifted up from the barns. It wasn't unpleasant, just a sort of fresh outdoors smell she wanted to inhale into every part of her. It was a smell she'd never experienced before in a life filled with sterile interiors. Her gaze drifted to the side of the house to see a huge dog race around the corner. Following the dog sauntered a large man using a battered cowboy hat to beat the dust off his body. The man was tall and moved with the loose-limbed grace of muscles honed and developed through hard use. His rolling gait was simply the cowboy stroll at its finest. His dark head was bent as he whacked thick thighs with the hat. The shirt stretched interestingly across his heavily muscled chest might have been white or beige at one time, now it was mostly dirt-red and sweat-stained. The soft material moved with him to mold a flat abdomen then disappear into low-riding jeans. Slim hips seemed emphasized by the powerful long legs below them.

The man glanced up at the commotion and while his face didn't change, Lauren received the impression of a grimace as his eyes slid over the sporty little car they'd arrived in. His dark, lazy gaze traveled to the boisterous crowd and suddenly he looked directly into her eyes. Lauren blinked at the shocking intensity of that gaze and glanced down at the stampeding dog again. Coming from the side made its path a direct line to

Lauren first. The dog was completely okay with the arrangement as he managed to doggy-grin and wag his tail while pounding across the lawn. Lauren weighed a hundred and ten pounds—the dog had her beat by at least seventy and showed no signs of slowing down. Lauren considered jumping in the car again but that just seemed too cowardly. No one else appeared concerned. They wouldn't let a killer dog run loose, would they?

A plump lower lip sucked and white teeth clamped down on it as she watched the thundering approach. Abruptly a low whistle pierced the air and the dog stopped, turned in a flash and rushed back at the man. Lauren's eyes shot up to him and a hint of a grin met her gaze. He kept moving toward the group as a whole but looked only at her. His focused attention was just beginning to feel uncomfortable when Carla called her name and waved her around the car to start introducing Lauren to the boisterous gang. Smiling and greeting each one with seeming undivided interest, Lauren still knew exactly where the cowboy was at all times. He stood back and watched, the dog squirming at his side. The feeling that his eyes never left her was unsettling, but at least the dog didn't leave his side either.

ROMEO WAS CONTENT TO wait while Carla introduced her friend around to his cousins. It gave him a minute to enjoy the view. His first look into those liquid blue eyes had sent a sharp bolt of heat straight to his cock. From this slight distance, he drank in a long look at the rest of her and experienced the sensation of his life flashing before his eyes. Bachelor days were over. Heat surged up from his crotch like a swarm of angry bees. It enveloped him with stinging awareness. He'd been attracted to compact little women all his life, but he hadn't known there was a perfect one out there. This curvy feminine being with her flawlessly beautiful face was the one he'd been looking for.

Her every feature seemed painted with perfection. Huge, dark blue eyes, full inviting lips, a shining cap of soft black curls tumbling around her head. She was barely five feet four inches tall, but no one could mistake her for a child. The gentle slope of breast and hip drew the male eye like a magnet. His absolute awareness of her femininity overwhelmed him for a moment. Her delicate bones, the graceful way she tilted her head and smiled at something one of the idiots said. Even the way her body shifted as she turned to another member of the family captivated him.

He was damn glad to hear her name wasn't Juliet. That would have been just too much. As it was, he'd have a hell of a time not jumping her in the next ten minutes. It was surprisingly difficult to control the elemental drive to claim what he considered his already. This aggressive need to possess her wasn't even remotely rational, he realized in amazement. Romeo wasn't comfortable with the conviction that this was his woman. He wasn't arguing with it, just startled by it. Yeah, that was probably the biggest understatement since "Houston, we have a problem."

She stood there and changed his world by merely existing. Making up his mind swiftly was both a curse and a blessing, but that's how he'd always been. This time it shoved him off the edge of the planet into an unknown universe. His future suddenly stretched before him full of things he'd thought were a long way off. Now he could hardly wait to get there. He'd imagined feeling trapped when some crafty female finally made him contemplate walking down the aisle, not this overwhelming drive to propel her there as fast as possible.

Her wide-eyed look at Edgar told him large animals intimidated her. She also looked tired. He noticed tiny lines of strain around her edible mouth. Schooling his features not to frown at that, he waited for Carla to get around to him. The primitive monster that was his need to protect and control a loved one's environment reared its head. The need to cosset and pamper infiltrated lust with searing urgency, shoving aside all other considerations as he studied those telltale signs, which were chillingly familiar. He wanted to whisk her off to a soothing environment, to personally ensure his overactive family remained at bay until she felt better. He ruthlessly wrestled the possessive monster into submission and consciously projected civilized urbanity.

Romeo stepped forward as Carla finished with everyone else. "Hello, hellion," he greeted her warmly.

Laughing, Carla went up on tiptoes to peck his cheek while warning him, "Don't you touch me, Romeo. You're filthy."

Lauren had known who it was. No way to miss the air of quiet authority draped across the wide expanse of his dusty shoulders. He might look like a ranch hand, but his presence said "master of the domain." His above-six-foot height made him imposing, but it was the dark intensity of aristocratic features that told one of his Spanish ancestors mingled with the tough Texan survivors of a bygone age. It created a sinfully handsome man with thick black hair, which now fell over his brow in Rhett Butler rakishness. From the top of his glossy head, down his chiseled nose to the cleft in his perfect chin, the man was just ridiculously handsome.

Carla turned to Lauren. "This is my friend Lauren. I knew you wouldn't mind one more this weekend."

"What?" Lauren sputtered, grateful for a good excuse to drag her eyes off his unbelievable face. "You didn't tell him you were bringing a guest?" she demanded of Carla. Oh great, just great. Not only was she the dancing bear for half this crowd, she was an unexpected guest to the other half.

"Romeo doesn't mind. Do you?" Carla insisted.

"No, not a problem. Nice to meet you, Lauren, I hope you enjoy the ranch." His low voice seemed to vibrate down to her bones as he held out a hand to her. Placing her slender hand in his large grip shot that vibration right back out again with an electric jolt to her system. Damn, not a good indicator for the Ice Queen expectation.

"I'm sure I will," she managed in a steady voice as she pulled away from his gentle grip. "Sorry if it's an inconvenience," Lauren added self-consciously.

"Don't be silly," one of the young men assured her. "Another beautiful face is always welcome, right, Romeo?" The young man turned to Carla. "Hot car, hellion. You didn't say you'd gotten a new one. Can I drive it?" Lauren decided the family resemblance was most pronounced in the high energy radiating off each one of these cousins. All of them tall . . . well, anyone was tall compared to her, but the family seemed to breed tall and good-looking right down the line. The constant motion thing would have marked them though. In a group, they were like a force of nature.

Before Carla could answer, Romeo's deep voice interjected smoothly. "Perhaps the girls would like to take their bags in and relax first, Steve. It's a four-hour trip down here. Pop the trunk, Carla." His tone was low and quiet, but there was no suggesting about it. Those soft directions were commands. Lauren immediately recognized the attitude that drove Romeo's cousins nuts.

A little smile snuck up her face and she had to look down to hide the amusement. When she glanced up again, Romeo shot her a questioning look. He'd seen her instant amusement and questioned it with a raised brow. Lauren pretended not to see the brow as she reached into the now open trunk for her one bag. A large hand closed over hers from behind and gently moved her hand aside as Romeo lifted out her bag.

"This it?" he questioned softly, his tone intimate in the midst of the crowd. Around her, Lauren felt watching eyes and avid expectations. He now stood beside her to curve his large body over hers for the bag. His scent of fresh-cut hay, pine and just pure male enveloped her in a slightly dizzying fog of strange new hormones she didn't know what to do with. No, no, no. These vultures were not going to read anything from her interaction with Romeo.

Being careful not to breathe in too deeply and lose all hope of rational thought, she resolutely turned slightly away from him. "Yep, and the rest are Carla's." Lauren smiled brightly and intentionally looked over at Steve. "You look like you're into weightlifting, Steve, they should be no problem for you." Her flirty joking blended into the ribbing and diffused the attention off her and Romeo.

Steve and his younger cousin Jason grabbed Carla's bags

and commenced to loud groaning at the weight. Carla smacked both of them on the back of the head in playful protest and everyone moved toward the house. Somehow, Romeo was right beside Lauren with a large hand at her back as she went up the steps to the porch. She moved away from him quickly, trying to be casual as the group entered the house to greet more family in the form of aunts and uncles.

The large entry, which had probably been the front room at one time, was crowded with Monteros and it was almost difficult to see the casual comfort that made this rambling structure a home. There was a fireplace off to the side, beside it were long rustic benches for removing boots and coat racks at each end so clothing could be shed right at the door. No stuffy pretension of a formal entry existed.

Through several archways one could see the various rooms and a hallway leading off down both sides of the house. Directly in front of them was the oversized living room whose casual seating arrangements fed naturally into what appeared to be a den, complete with a pool table. In the opposite direction off the living room an archway led to a large dining room. Beyond that appeared a doorway that probably led to the kitchen since there was also a pass-through in the wall and cabinetry barely visible in the other room. Every room boasted its own fireplace, which seemed to draw the rustic past into the present. The fireplaces were large and welcoming with wood stacked neatly by each one, even in the middle of summer.

The introductions over and general pandemonium continuing unabated, Lauren suddenly felt a warm rush of breath wash over her ear from behind. "Come on through here, I'll show you where you can relax a moment." His low voice sent a shiver down her spine.

It would have been nice to turn down the invitation, but at this moment, her head was pounding and her legs had just started trembling. Lauren really wished she wasn't physically desperate for a few seconds' peace. She should have told Carla about her little problem before accepting this invitation. It's not like the condition was transmittable or contagious. It was just a pain in the ass, as Carla would say.

Lauren's head turned slightly to him and nodded. Immediately his large hand spanned her back again and guided her backward. With tender insistence, his hand remained on her back as he turned them down a hallway.

At the end of the hall he opened a door, ushering her into what immediately felt like a soothing space. But Lauren couldn't be sure anymore—she needed her medication as the pounding in her head grew louder. Romeo stepped past her to deposit her case on the bed. In that moment when his back was to her, Lauren let herself grope for the chair at the wall beside the door. She sank into it while shaking hands fumbled with her purse.

He seemed to sense her distress and glanced back at her even before he dropped the bag. Sharp eyes took in her collapse onto the chair and shaking hands.

"What is it?" Romeo demanded as his big body moved across the room in a second and he sank to his haunches before her. Steady hands took the purse from her and delved into it. "What am I looking for, Lauren?"

"Prescription," Lauren breathed, her head relaxed back onto the tall chair and her eyes closed gratefully.

"Let me get you a glass of water, just a second." He bounced up and was gone. Then she felt a glass pressed into her hand and a pill to her lips. She opened for the pill and drank the water gratefully.

Opening her eyes a slit, Lauren found him in front of her on his haunches again, studying the prescription bottle. He read it carefully then plucked her purse off the floor and started digging through it again. "Are there more?" he asked tightly.

"No, just that one for headaches. I'll be fine in a few minutes. It's only a migraine," she assured him. His casual commandeering of her purse was something she didn't have the energy to deal with right now. However, it highlighted his in-charge attitude. Lauren was aware enough to be relieved she'd put the immunosuppressive drugs she'd now be on for a lifetime in her case. His nosy ass would have had a field day with those. Aaarrrrggg, even snorting silently hurt.

Romeo dropped the purse and looked into her eyes. "Why?" he asked bluntly.

"Because I get them?" Lauren attempted a feeble joke to distract him.

"I'm asking why you get migraines? People who get them this bad know why, Lauren. Tell me." There was that commanding tone again—it was beginning to wear on her.

Lauren smiled weakly—he really could be a pain in the ass. "It's stress. That's the trigger. Relax. I'll be fine soon."

"What caused this much stress, Lauren? You've only been here ten minutes. It takes much longer than that for this sort of thing to build. You were already shaking and couldn't see very well, could you?" Romeo pressed her with surprising knowledge about the condition.

"You really want to know, Romeo? You won't like it," she warned him tiredly and leaned back, closing her eyes again. It took too much energy to look at him and argue.

His hands settled on her jean-covered thighs and rubbed up and down in a soothing caress. "I already don't like the fact you get them, honey. I really don't like the fact that the doctor on your prescription is a heart specialist. What's one more thing to dislike?" His low tone was an auditory smile as he murmured to her encouragingly. "So tell me why you have the headache, then tell me about your heart."

Shocked at his perception, Lauren managed to lift an eyebrow. "What makes you say it's a heart doctor?" Lauren asked.

Before he could answer she opened her eyes and frowned at him. "Look, Romeo, we just met a few minutes ago. I'm an unexpected guest in your home so that entitles you to some answers about a near collapse. It does not give you the right to demand my life story," she informed him firmly and removed his hands from her legs.

"I see," he mused, allowing her to remove his touch but now resting both palms on the chair arms on either side of her. "Then tell me the part it does get me."

"I am feeling stressed because of your cousins. The reason Carla invited me this weekend is not entirely what it seems. I found out in the car outside your gates. That's what gave me the headache," Lauren stated and closed her eyes again.

"Really?" Romeo's voice was a gentle murmur. He straightened up and bent to scoop her into his arms. Before she could react to being in his arms, he deposited her on the bed and adjusted the pillow behind her. Immediately turning to the tall windows, he pulled the drapes, submerging the room into a dimly lit environment that did calm her. The bed she lay on had to be a queen, its width covered with a muted forest green down comforter that pillowed her entire body in welcome softness. The room seemed to flow around them in tranquil tones of well-polished natural wood and plush woodland colors.

Fetching water again from the attached bathroom, he held it to her lips until she drained it. Then he was sitting on the side of the bed and leaning over to take her hand in his. "Now tell me the real reason you were invited."

Lauren huffed. He was good, very good. He'd done everything possible to aid her recovery, waiting on her hand and foot, and then asked for information. She felt obligated to tell him. She took a deep breath, trying to ignore how gorgeous this dominating, caring man was, and began her explanation.

"Carla said she convinced me to come this weekend because she wanted to see your reaction. She has also told your cousins what a cold shoulder I'll give you and now they're watching our every move. She thinks I'm the Ice Queen. They can hardly wait to see me put you in your place," Lauren said resignedly.

"Why does she think you're an Ice Queen?" Romeo asked.

"Because I hardly ever date, and when I do, I don't . . . um, she knows I don't put out," Lauren finished determinedly. He wanted details, might as well be blunt.

"Ah, Carla doesn't know about your weak heart, does she?" Romeo surmised.

"I do not have a weak heart. It's perfectly fine!" Lauren defended herself.

"But it wasn't fine before, was it? Tell me what happened, Lauren. It's better if I know to begin with. That way we won't have any nasty surprises later." His gentle tone made him sound perfectly reasonable. Until you thought about what he was saying. The weasel wouldn't give up.

"My heart is fine. It's the rest of me that's, ah, not what it could be. However, I am not in danger or an invalid. So stop with all the concern and let me rest a minute. I'll be up soon and everything will be normal," she insisted. Lauren determinedly closed her eyes and decided ignoring him was the best method of getting rid of him.

Firm lips briefly brushed hers then were gone. Her eyes blinked open as he straightened and smiled down at her. "I need to clean up and then I'll be in my study when you get up. It would be a good idea for us to have a chat about this little plot my cousins are trying to involve us in." He strode to the door and turned. "Don't worry. It was right to trust me with the truth. You'll come to find I'm a dependable guy."

Romeo Montero moved down the hall frowning. The little female he'd left in the darkened room disturbed him on every level. The first thing he needed to know was what her condition really was. A photographic memory gave him the doctor's number from the prescription bottle. He'd known the name anyway. He knew what the man did for a living and it worried him.

Looking at a frail form lying in a darkened room wrenched him back in time. The flood of helpless anger was familiar and not welcome. His mom had been a tall blonde but slender, easily exhausted and often suffered the same migraines. Intellectually he knew it wasn't his fault she had been sick. It wasn't his fault she and his father had died so young. Emotionally it'd been hard to deal with. Losing his parents and grandparents in a short time span left side effects that lasted a lifetime. It had created a deep fear of losing loved ones. His natural protective instincts kicked into high gear at the first sign of danger.

After a quick shower and change, he headed across the house. Entering the den on his way to the study, the din of laughing and talking quieted suspiciously as his six cousins looked up at him.

Carla glanced around. "Hey, where is Lauren?" she asked.

"I showed her to her room. She seemed tired," Romeo answered tersely. He was sure Carla didn't know her friend had been or was gravely ill. That didn't excuse her from obviously losing track of her for this long, much less not noticing the white lines of strain around Lauren's mouth a few minutes ago.

"Is she all right? Should I check on her? I thought she'd share my room, where did you put her?" Carla wanted to know in her usual rush of both questions and information.

"She's in the green room. She said she'd be out in a few minutes. I doubt she wants anyone checking on her," he responded.

"She's cute, isn't she?" Carla insinuated as if it'd just occurred to her.

"Beautiful," Romeo agreed casually. "But she seemed a bit prickly to me." Six sets of eyes lit up at his comment. The whole group was obviously in on this just as Lauren said. That required some attention—right after he took care of the important stuff.

"I've got work to do. I hope you guys are old enough to refrain from killing yourselves or one another." With that, he headed off to make a few phone calls.

Shortly thereafter, Romeo had all the information he

needed. Lauren was a heart transplant recipient. Her surgery had been two years ago. At the age of ten she'd been in a serious car accident, which had nearly killed her. That's when they'd diagnosed the heart problem. She'd spent years waiting for a new organ and the injuries from the accident complicated her condition. Consequently, her life up to a year ago had been very sedentary. The doctor explained she now had a healthy heart but her body was trying to catch up.

The doctor also divulged that Lauren belonged to a very protective family with three older brothers and father who were all still uncomfortable letting her go. They'd spent too long with a sweet little girl on the edge of death. The doctor laughed as he commented she'd be pissed if she found out he was telling another protective male about her condition. But Romeo and the doctor were old acquaintances. Their relationship went back too far for the request to be denied. Especially when Lauren was at Romeo's place.

Leaning back in his chair, Romeo realized the house felt very quiet. Lauren hadn't shown up in his study and he began to have a bad feeling when he realized how much time had passed. Rising, he went in search of her. She wasn't in her room, the pool area was quiet but down at the corral there seemed to be a commotion. Romeo frowned as he headed in that direction.

ALL SIX COUSINS WERE appalled when Lauren confessed she'd never been near a horse, much less on one, at their suggestion of a ride before supper. Carla assured her it was a blast. She had to learn to ride, it was just wrong to be a native Texan and not know how. So wearing her brand spanking new cowboy boots and jeans, Lauren stood beside what looked like a giant of a horse and petted it nervously. Steven was the one who brought it out of the barn and "tacked up" for her. Now Carla was insisting she "mount" it.

They were standing in the wide, long corral directly off the horse barn door designed for a large number of horses to be tacked up at the same time. It was actually big enough for the private rodeo shows Romeo and the hands occasionally put on for visiting groups of schoolchildren.

"You're sure it's gentle?" Lauren asked for the fifth time.

"As a lamb. It's the most boring horse Romeo owns," Carla assured her. "Now put your foot in the stirrup and swing the other leg over."

"I can't reach the thing, Carla. I haven't got the mile-long legs you have. Is there a stepladder I could use or something?" Lauren questioned as Carla laughed and the big beast swung his head around to eyeball the two women. Lauren stared back at it and could swear the thing was laughing at her. Could horses laugh? This one could apparently.

"Shouldn't there be, like, padding? Or helmets? A hockey uniform to ride these things?" Lauren wanted to know. Up close and personal put a new perspective on riding and it wasn't a nice one. How could anyone consider the insisted precaution of wearing boots protective clothing? Carla had made a big production out of the appropriate attire for riding, making Lauren go change before they came out here. Dang, that whole irritating clothing scene seemed woefully less than adequate now. The horses were mammoth.

"Jason," Carla called. "Come over here and help Lauren

up. She's too short to reach the stirrup." At barely twenty and the youngest cousin, he was all energy and action on a whole new level it seemed. Jason grabbed Lauren around the waist and easily lifted her slight form up on the animal in what seemed to Lauren an abrupt motion giving her no time to prepare.

Lauren found herself perched atop a shifting mountain of muscle. Fear shot through her and she froze. Unaware of her friend's momentary bout with terror, Carla untied the horse from the rail to lead it to the center of the corral so she could teach Lauren the basics of riding. At that moment, Steven emerged from the barn with the horse he intended to ride. It was a magnificent, prancing beast. As far as Lauren was concerned it snorted fire and had a death wish for every other living thing. It reared and screamed, broke away from Steven and charged down the corral at top speed, straight at Lauren and her huge horse.

The horse under Lauren had no problem deciding what to do. It whirled and jerked to get out of the way. The swift, unexpected movements made it seem to simply step out from under her. She didn't have a good hold on it and her feet weren't even in the stirrups yet. Crashing to the ground from that height was not Lauren's greatest concern. It was the black hooves of death thundering toward her as she lay in the path of the screaming devil horse.

All she could do was roll over and bury her head in her arms. There was a lot of action around the corral as people tried to yell instructions, but the two seconds between Lauren's hitting the ground and wild horse being upon her didn't allow escape.

Only one hoof hit her with a glancing blow to the back of her upper thigh. The way it moved her and her cry of pain made it appear to the horrified eyes watching that she'd been trampled with every fall of the steel-shod hooves. Romeo's huge body vaulted the fence and came skidding to his knees beside her prone form. Large hands hovered over her, afraid to touch, afraid not to. Lauren groaned and lifted her head to check the location of the satanic beast.

"Oh, God, you can move? Don't move! Where does it hurt? Is it your back, your neck? Don't move!" he commanded again as she attempted to roll over and look at him.

"Why not? I need to get out of here," Lauren stated belligerently. "That damn beast wants to kill me. Getting on the other side of the fence seems like a really good idea to me."

"He could have seriously injured you. We have to be careful moving you. Now tell me where it hurts! Please, Lauren, don't move," he begged her desperately.

The panic in his voice made Lauren twist her head around to look at him. The Romeo kneeling beside her was a pale, tortured man. It was an emotion she recognized immediately. She'd seen that face leaning over her hospital bed on countless occasions—she'd seen it as they wheeled her into surgery. She was tired of that face.

"I'm just bruised from the fall. The devil beast didn't manage to actually trample me. It got me once on the thigh, which hurts like hell, but I doubt it's a fatal injury. Now help me up. I think I'm lying in poop or something. It smells like poop down here." Lauren started to push herself up. Strong hands stopped her and pressed her back down in the dirt.

"You're sure? We can fly straight to the hospital. But it's so important not to injure you further. If it's an internal injury we may not know right away," he insisted.

"Romeo! Let me up!" she demanded. "I told you I'm fine! Stop with all the commanding shit and let me get out of here."

"Okay, okay, but go slowly. It's better to be sure," he insisted.

As Lauren rolled over, she found herself looking up into a ring of faces. Romeo on his knees beside her was running a clinical hand over her body while every one of the cousins gathered around. Lauren frowned fiercely at all the attention and the stricken look on everyone's face.

"If all of you are staring at me, who is keeping the wild beasts away?" she demanded.

For the first time Romeo glanced up and realized they were all there. "Put the horses away," he barked. His low voice held lethal command. Everyone jumped into action immediately. Looking back down at Lauren, he sighed deeply. Her shirt was ripped at the shoulder and several scratches could be seen on the back of her shoulder and upper arm, her face and hair were covered in dirt, but she seemed whole otherwise.

He slid his arms under her and lifted her to his chest as he stood up and headed for the gate. Over his shoulder, he issued orders in terse statements. Lauren felt the immense body carrying her shudder as he lifted her and knew it certainly wasn't the strain of her weight that bothered the big lug. He was feeling a reaction to fear. Somehow, she always seemed to make big men feel helpless when something happened to her. She knew she wasn't as delicate and fragile as they liked to think she was, but the look on his face had told her he'd thought the worst when he saw her hit the ground. Her arms slid around his neck and her head came to rest on the broad shoulder beneath it. One hand crept into his hair to massage his scalp while the other patted his back. She always felt sorry for them when she saw that look.

"It's okay," she whispered to him, trying to ease his burden. "I'm not really hurt."

Striding away from the confusion in the corral, he whispered back to her, "Well, I'm not okay. You scared the goddamn life out of me, baby. Don't do it again!" The sight of her being trampled was burned into his brain with ghastly clarity. He'd almost lost her before she even knew him. Losing another person was unacceptable. Losing her would be an event he couldn't survive. Never mind they'd shared less than an hour's acquaintance. She might not know it yet but she was his woman.

The simple fact that her shirt was torn and he could see blood on her body was intolerable on a cellular level. The unexpected shock of watching her fall shook him to his core.

"It wasn't my fault, Romeo," she murmured defensively, mistaking the stark terror in his tone for reprimand. "It's those beasts. They went crazy."

"It's Steven's fault," he informed her. "He had no business taking that animal out! Of course, all of them were behaving like irresponsible imbeciles again. You've never been on a horse before, have you?"

"Well, no. It seemed like a good idea until I got right next to one. They are much bigger than they look on TV," Lauren commented seriously.

Romeo barked out a laugh at that. They entered his private apartment. He carried her through his bedroom to the bathroom. Sitting her down carefully on the vanity, he started unbuttoning her shirt.

"What are you doing?" Lauren demanded.

"Undressing you. We have to treat the scratches on your shoulder and you need a shower before we do. It'll help wash out the wound and you smell like poop anyway," he teased softly, trying to appear harmless and altruistic.

Romeo's need to possess would not allow him to let her out of his sight to take care of the injuries. He knew this level of intimacy was neither normal nor called for, but it was unthinkable to do anything other than see to every one of her needs himself.

"No." Her hands came up to cover his and stop the action.

"Look, baby. You've got to take care of those scratches right away. I know you want a shower so why not take it now?" he argued gently.

"I'm not undressing in front of you, Romeo. Let me go to my room and I'll take care of it myself," she stated calmly.

"Aw, don't worry, Lauren. I've seen a woman before. There is no need to be embarrassed, honey. Now let's get this done. You'll feel better afterwards," he insisted.

"I said no, Romeo. Are you going to force me?" she asked quietly.

"No! Good God! Why would you even think that? I just want to be sure you're all right." His concerned eyes searched her face. Something else was going on here. The way she looked at him was old. Way too old for the twenty-three he knew her to be. It wasn't embarrassment on her face, it was— armor. Her face was a mask he couldn't see behind.

"What's going on, Lauren?" he asked quietly. "Why is undressing a hot spot for you? Did someone hurt you? Did something bad happen?" His serious face turned hard and a deep flush swept over it. "You can tell me, sweetheart. It's okay. We'll just deal with that, too."

"No, nothing like you're thinking happened," Lauren quickly responded to his tight look and shuttered eyes. It didn't consciously occur to her that they were reading each other on an intimate level. She simply knew exactly what his dark mind had come up with. "But I've spent a lot of time in hospitals. People treat you like a piece of meat in there. They undress you and bend over you in groups examining you. They discuss you and forget to pull the sheet back up. Sometimes you can't do it for yourself. It's all done 'for your own good,'" she explained in a tight voice. "I am not going to be the only naked person in the room ever again. If you want to undress me, you'd damn well better get naked first."

He smiled. Already knowing her history, the problem became crystal clear. "Sure, I can do that."

HIS CLOTHES HIT THE floor in an amazingly short time. Suddenly straightening before her was a gloriously naked man. Her eyes traveled over his wide, muscled chest, the torso below undulated with ridges leading her to narrow hips and the fascinating equipment between them. She'd never actually seen a naked man before. Pictures and movies did not prepare her for the reality.

Her gaze centered on the heavy erection and she couldn't look away. He stepped up to her again and returned to unbuttoning her shirt. She sat there dumbly and just stared at him. Her shirt and bra disappeared and he took a moment to look at the line down the center of her chest. It hurt him just to see it. He didn't worry she'd notice him examining it. She still hadn't lifted her eyes from his cock.

"Never seen one of those before?" he asked quietly as he lifted her slightly to slide jeans and panties down over her butt.

"Not in person," she admitted. "Does it hurt?"

He frowned as he squatted to remove her boots and slide the pants off. "No, why would you think that?"

"It's sort of red and swollen. It looks like it hurts," Lauren stated as he stood up. She looked into his face. "It also looks much too big to fit where it's supposed to. Are you bigger than most guys are? Because if that's normal, I'm not sorry I've said no anymore."

In the back of her mind Lauren knew getting naked with a virtual stranger should have been utterly shocking. Something about this man and his need to take complete control of her care made it feel natural. His gentle tone of voice and competent, matter-of-fact handling hushed the panicking virgin. After his clothes hit the tile floor, it had been impossible to think about anything else. *Apparently, in the right circumstances she was a brazen hussy*, the virgin within sniffed in disdain.

"Lean over, baby, I need to see the bruise on the back of your thigh," he directed as his big hands helped her sit on one hip so she leaned to the side and he could look at the back of her leg. The large red mark was already beginning to darken. A deep, ugly bruise would quickly appear.

"It fits, sweetheart," he answered her question as seriously as she'd asked it. "I don't know what most guys have. Don't make a habit of looking," he stated casually as he lifted her off the vanity and moved them over to the big shower. He adjusted the temperature and stepped in with her. Gently placing her under the water, he carefully rinsed the dirt and grime out of her hair and off her body, paying special attention to the abrasions on her shoulder. Shifting her out of the water again, he grabbed the shampoo and started massaging her hair, carefully keeping the soap from the cuts.

"I'm glad you've said no, too. A little thing like you requires special care, honey. A man has to prepare you really well before it'd be a pleasurable experience for you. If you let the wrong guy touch you, you'd be scared for life." He rinsed her hair and soaped up a washcloth. She let him bathe her with an absentminded acceptance. Her eyes were still glued to the stiff, red-knobbed cock and heavy balls below it. He gingerly patted the scrapes on her shoulder and she barely winced. That small pain made almost no impression on her. He supposed it wouldn't after what she'd been through.

The conversation, her wide-eyed innocence and his overwhelming sense of possession drove him hard. She'd given him nothing but acceptance once his clothes came off and the gift of her trust sang through his soul. Touching her intimately became a necessity. He hadn't meant to do it now, but the need to show her how precious she was to him wouldn't let him stop.

Romeo put down the washcloth and soaped his hands. "Now I'm going to wash between your legs, honey. This is how a guy should touch you."

Wide eyes shot up to his. "You are? Ah . . . I . . . um . . ."

His soapy hands slid down her body from both sides as he stood to her side, her uninjured shoulder pressed into his chest. The position gave him complete access to every curve and crevice. Callused fingers separated her bottom and moved down the crack. They almost distracted her from the hand in front 'til he glided fingers over plump folds, pressing up to insert them into the deep grooves. Gently he rubbed her sweet cunt and rimmed the rosebud ass behind her.

"Oh," Lauren moaned. "That feels so good." She sounded surprised.

"It's supposed to, now relax and let me show you how good it can be." Knowing fingers found her clit and stroked over it gently. Slowly he added pressure to the bundle of sensitive nerves. Behind her, his middle finger slid into her ass shallowly, working in and out with gentle thrusts.

Lauren felt dazed and awash with entirely new sensations. Letting Romeo touch her like this wasn't the hardship people who knew her might think it was. Being an Ice Queen was a defense mechanism for a helpless little girl trapped in a hospital bed. It protected her from the ones who worked the white corridors only for a paycheck. It shielded her when the ones who really cared moved on to a new floor and another job. She'd spent formative years hiding behind it. Now it was a habit.

Besides, she reasoned to herself, *if you were offered the opportunity to learn from the best, who wouldn't?* According to Carla, Romeo had a vast amount of experience and the women involved seemed happy about it. It was embarrassing to be a virgin at twenty-three. This was the perfect chance to change that.

Lauren clutched his thick forearm in front of her as heat spread through her body. It burned in a tingling rush up her legs as the fire in cunt and ass intensified. Dazed eyes turned up to Romeo and he dipped down to claim soft lips. Unable to be gentle with his kiss, he plunged into her depths with the hard push he needed so desperately elsewhere. His hands remained tender and patient, insistently guiding her into passion's inferno.

The luscious little body in his arms started to tremble and he increased the pressure on her clit and thrust deeper into her tight ass. She exploded, jerking and thrusting on his hands as he swallowed her moan of release and kept eating her mouth. His fingers manipulated her unrelentingly—thrusting into her bottom while two rough digits gripped her slippery clit and pinched down, shooting a new fireball up her body.

Lauren screamed and collapsed against him, no longer able to support her own weight as her body came a second time before the first was complete. As the trembling subsided, he lifted his mouth and smiled down at the panting woman in his arms while his fingers still petted both cunt and ass.

"Oh, Lord, that was an orgasm, wasn't it?" she gasped.

"That was two orgasms, baby," he corrected proudly. His hands reluctantly moved up her body. The one in front drifted to her breasts to stroke and cup dainty mounds. His thumb rubbed over her nipple firmly and she shuddered. "Those can't be your first?" he questioned softly.

Lauren laughed shakily. "First ones like that. Stop," Lauren sighed. "That feels way too good already. I can't do that again so soon."

"Yeah, you can," he growled with a smile in his voice. "But we need to get out and dress your scrapes first."

"No. What about you?" Lauren asked, recovering swiftly as she turned to face him. "You need a shower, too. I get to touch everything you got to touch. That's our deal."

Romeo grinned at her earnest face. "I love the rules. I'm all yours."

Lauren had to stand on tiptoes to reach the tops of his shoulders so he picked her up and held her against his body as little hands smoothed over him. Sweet mother of God, this was torture, he decided. A breathtaking torture he'd be willing to endure for the next sixty years or so.

"Hand me the shampoo," she directed—he complied. Washing his hair while suspended off the floor was tough. Especially when he kept trying to nibble on her neck, her nose, her ear, anything he could reach. Lauren wrapped her legs around his waist for leverage so she could lean back.

Romeo groaned and dropped his head to her shoulder, just where she needed it to get the back. Suddenly she became aware that the big red part of him was positioned at the narrow pink part of her. Lauren froze. Romeo chuckled softly into her neck.

"Don't worry, baby. You're not ready for that yet. Are you done with my hair, because I can't take much more of this." His hips moved shallowly and the bulb of his cock caressed the damp folds of her pussy.

"How do you know I'm not ready?" she panted.

"I know because I haven't tasted you yet. You are done with the hair," he decided for her and let her slide down his body. Her hands immediately went to work on the rest of him. Apparently, she could be easily distracted with a hard body. Except those busy hands eventually found their way down to the throbbing erection and tight balls she couldn't stop looking at.

She tried not to hurt him while exploring his long shaft with gentle, soapy hands. She didn't quite believe something so swollen, throbbing and reddened was not hurting him. He groaned in a deep rumbling sound as soon as she touched him. When his hips jerked, her worried eyes went to his face. It was set in a grimace.

"Oh, sorry. Did I hurt you?" Lauren immediately let go. "I'm so sorry, I didn't mean to."

"Lauren, touch me. Keep touching me. It doesn't hurt." Romeo growled as his hands took hers and brought them back to his shaft. "I like it, baby. This is not pain on my face and when my body jerks it's because I like it even more."

Worriedly she looked down as he wrapped both her hands around his thick erection and then let go of her. "Show me what to do, Romeo?" she asked.

"Do whatever you want, Lauren. I like it," he breathed.

"Just show me! I don't know how to please you. I'm afraid I'll hurt you or something," Lauren demanded.

His hands came back to hers and closed around them to tighten the grip, he moved them up and down. "Like this, oh, yeah, nice and tight. Now on the up stroke run your thumb over the head. That's it. Do it a little bit harder. Yeah, just like that, don't stop." He panted, his eyes were closed and his body thrust into her fists with each stroke.

While Lauren watched in fascination, the erection in her hands expanded even more as the head turned an angry-looking red. Each time her thumb swept over the bulging head, she found a silky substance she wished she had time to investigate. His body was thrusting, every muscle clenched and defined. His massive thighs propelled each plunge and he groaned deeply. She saw his flat abdomen tremble and he gasped, "I'm going to come."

White ropes of hot liquid shot out of his cock up over her breasts and stomach. Romeo grabbed her and hugged her against him in a fierce hold as his body continued to shudder and rub in powerful thrusts. He barked out an exclamation that wasn't a word and gulped in air harshly. It looked like a pain reaction to her. But he'd said it didn't hurt so she kept caressing him.

"Enough," he gasped. "Stop."

Her hands stilled, his head dropped down to rest his cheek against the crown of her head. He held her tightly as her hands now caressed his ass in an attempt to soothe him.

"You okay?" she ventured cautiously. His swollen cock was still hot and pulsing against her stomach and he was barely able to breathe.

"Honey, the only way I'd be better is if that happened inside you," he murmured.

"Oh," Lauren frowned. Well, that was very instructional. If she couldn't even wrap her hand around the thing, what made him think it'd fit inside her? Now she knew virginity was not the worst option. It was a damn good thing this happened with a guy who was very sexually active elsewhere. No need to worry about his wanting to try the other with her. They weren't even a dating couple so he would not assume she wanted to anyway.

Romeo stepped back and put them under the water again. Reluctantly he let go of her to rinse his cum off her breasts and abdomen. He still felt dizzy—her little hands wrapped around his cock was better sex than pounding most women into the mattress. Seeing her splattered with his seed was a visual that moved him in an elemental way. Oh yeah, keeping her naked and covered with his cum felt right. Suddenly he understood the urge to mark a woman in the most primitive way possible. He wanted his cum in her, on her. It stated ownership on a cellular level. His drive to establish ownership of this woman was a base animal response that would not be denied.

He ran the soapy washcloth over her then shut off the water. Stepping out of the shower, he immediately grabbed a towel and dried her carefully while he dripped on the bath mat. He didn't get his own towel until he'd wrapped hers around her and secured it. Drying off quickly, he purposely tossed his towel back on the rack. Letting her be the only clothed person in the room wouldn't fix past hurts, but it was something he could give her. Maybe it would help deal with that old pain.

Sitting her on the vanity again, Romeo grabbed supplies to dress the scratches on her shoulder. She turned for him and he prepared to swab the area. Neither of them commented on the clothing issue as she watched him tend to her.

"How am I going to get clean clothes?" she asked. "I can't walk through the house like this. They'll all know exactly what we did."

"I'll go get your bag in a minute," he responded. "If they see me, I'll just say you're in the shower. It'll be fine. Besides, they know better than to talk to me after this."

"It wasn't anyone's fault, Romeo. The horse is evil and it went nuts." Lauren tried to reason with him. Strangely, she felt the need to curb his wrath before he went face-to-face with his cousins. "I'm not even hurt that bad, just a scrape and a few bruises. Let it go."

"Honey, this is letting it go. If I think about what could have happened, things would get ugly real quick," he responded quietly as he pressed a large square adhesive over the injury. Helping her off the vanity, he led her into his room. "Why don't you lie down a minute while I dress and get your things? How's the head? Any sign of another headache?"

"No headache, but I could lie down. It's been a busy day," Lauren confessed tiredly. She went over to the bed and took off the damp towel. Draping it over the side of the bed, she crawled in, sliding under the sheets naturally. Even an averted migraine left her drained. Trying to hide it took an even greater toll. The events in the shower added an amazingly warm and fuzzy layer of tired on top of that. After what had just occurred, sliding into his bed for a tiny minute didn't register as anything but a necessity for Lauren.

Romeo watched her as he dressed and a smile spread across his soul. He didn't dare let it show on his face. Seeing her settling into his bed while he moved about the room quietly felt good. Fully dressed, he stepped over to her and dropped a kiss on her forehead. "I'll be back in a bit, baby," he whispered and she grunted. Her eyes didn't even open as he slipped out of the room.

It was already after six and everyone was gathered at the big kitchen table having supper when he emerged. Walking into the room brought a hush to the table. Romeo almost felt better when he saw the worried faces.

"How is she?" Carla asked immediately.

"She's resting," he responded in a quiet voice. Cold black eyes cut around the table as he looked at each face. "Did you know she'd never been on a horse before?" he asked the group. All the heads nodded. "I see." His lips turned down as he regarded them. Even the uncles didn't say a word as the aunts sat back and watched.

"I won't waste my breath on how stupid that stunt was, Steven. You and I will talk later. Carla, how long have you known Lauren?" he asked as he pulled out a chair and started loading his plate.

"About a year now. Isn't she going to eat? Should I take her a plate?" Carla wanted to know.

"No, I'll take her one later. She's sleeping. How did you meet her?" Romeo started eating as he waited for a response.

"She volunteers in the children's ward. She and I hit it off when I was doing a rotation in there," Carla told them. "She seems to really understand the kids. I don't know why she's not going into a medical profession. She'd be so good at it."

Romeo raised his eyebrows and looked at her. "You ever ask her why?" It made perfect sense to him. Of course, she'd volunteer there. She knew exactly what it was like to be little and trapped in a bed.

"No, I guess I haven't. We met when I was going through a rough patch and we never have gotten around to talking about that," Carla mused.

Romeo nodded and went back to his meal.

"Are you going to tell me if she's hurt?" Carla demanded. "I am the one in pre-med. I think I should look her over."

Romeo lifted his eyes slowly to Carla. The black depths weren't cold anymore. They burned with the anger he'd been holding in. Carla gasped and sat back instinctively.

"No. She's had about enough of your care. Perhaps you should work on your medical observation and diagnostic skills, Carla. Because when you're a real doctor, I'll expect you to be able to tell when someone has had a HT in the last twenty-four months," he bit out.

"No shit!" Carla gasped.

"And I'll also expect you to know when they're showing signs of a migraine," he continued. "It's the little white stress lines around their mouth and eyes. Of course, the trembling and difficulty seeing is a dead giveaway, too." Romeo suddenly clamped his mouth shut. Lauren was going to kill him. He knew Lauren hadn't wanted everyone to know about her condition. She wanted to be treated normally after being an invalid so long. If Carla didn't know about her physical problems yet, she'd probably been hiding them.

"What's an HT?" Jason wanted to know.

"Heart transplant," Carla told him shortly. She was frowning as she registered all Romeo was and wasn't saying. "She had the migraine when we arrived, didn't she?" Carla asked quietly.

"Yeah," Romeo replied. Looking around the room at the somber faces, he sighed. "Look, guys, don't treat her like an invalid. She'd hate that. Obviously, she didn't tell Carla because she wants to be treated like everyone else. Her new heart is fine. But she doesn't have the stamina everyone else does. Do me a favor and try to be adults about this." He frowned darkly at them. "And back off the Ice Queen shit. That was beneath you and you know it."

He stood up to leave the room, no longer interested in food, but turned back to them. "I'm going to marry that woman. I hear one of you give her a hard time about not turning the cold shoulder to me, I'll give you the hiding I should have when you were kids. And believe me, mommy and daddy will not lift a hand." He glanced at his aunts and uncles, raising his brow at them. They all smiled and shook their heads. Romeo stalked into his study to gather some papers he needed to go over.

Back in his room, he made himself comfortable on the other side of the bed and started doing the paperwork a ranch and investment portfolio the size of his entailed. He needed to get a lot of it done. He intended to be busy doing other things in the near future.

LAUREN WOKE UP TO a dimly lit room. Directly in her line of vision sat Romeo. Pillows against the headboard propped him up. His long body stretched out as he studied a paper he was moving forward and back again as he tried to read it. His other hand held the file he'd gotten it from and he frowned fiercely at the defenseless paper.

"Where are your reading glasses?" Lauren asked quietly.

He didn't even look at her as he scowled at the paper. "In the old man store where I'll get them when I'm an old man."

"Ah, perhaps you should visit the 'Seriously in Denial' store and see if they have something to tide you over," she suggested.

Romeo stuffed the paper back in the file and laid it on the nightstand. "Hungry, brat?" he turned to her and asked.

"Why are you naked?" Lauren wanted to know. It certainly wasn't a complaint as her eyes wandered over the long, lanky length of him. Romeo naked was a visual delight of honed muscle covered with a dusting of dark male fur that begged to be stroked.

Romeo grinned. "I'm a 'follow the rules' kind of guy." He rolled off the bed and reached for a pair of shorts at the foot of it. "I'll be back in a minute with a tray." He tugged on boxers and the shorts he'd left on the bed.

"No thanks." Lauren turned over and stretched.

"Uh? You're not hungry?" he questioned.

"Yeah, I am. What time is it?" She slid out of bed. "Did you bring my clothes?"

"Over there." He pointed at the closet. "You don't have to get up, honey. I'll bring you something," he offered again.

"I don't like trays in bed. I'll just raid the fridge and get out of your hair," she stated casually as she pulled her bag out of the closet and grabbed the first clothes she came to.

"I was hoping you liked being in my hair," his low voice rumbled. He leaned up against one of the bedposts, crossed bulging arms over his bare chest and watched her dress.

Lauren shot him a glance and smiled. "You know I did. It's time I went back to my own room though. You've got things to do I'm sure."

"Nothing more important than convincing you that this is now your room," he murmured.

Lauren tucked her shirt into shorts and noticed they didn't go together. A lot like this situation. "This room is taken. The one you gave me seems free. I'll keep that one, thanks."

"I'd like you to stay, Lauren," he stated directly.

Lauren faced him fully and cocked her head to the side as she studied the seriously imposing man looking at her. Wearing only shorts and leaning casually against the four-poster bed, he was a pinup advertisement for tall, dark and sexy. "You've been very kind, very, ah, educational. I'm grateful for both, but I think it's clear I'm not in the same class as you. Heck, I'm barely on the same planet with you when it comes to experience. I'm not able to be casual about sex, certainly not with a stranger. And particularly not while there is an audience outside just waiting for something to happen. I'm sorry if I somehow implied I could do a weekend fling."

"Okay, sweetheart," he said after staring at her a second. *She takes this seriously*, he thought. "We'll start at the beginning. I don't want you to be uncomfortable with this relationship. We'll do the dating dance. We'll go to movies, have picnics down by the river and drink wine in front of the fireplace. You'll fall head over heels in love with me. I'll ask you to move in with me. Then I'll get you drunk in Vegas and you'll wake up married to me. How does that sound?"

"Seriously, Romeo," she sighed. "I don't want to be a plaything. I thought I wanted experience but as it turns out, I'm okay with being a nerdy little virgin."

"There is nothing in this conversation that I'm not serious about," Romeo countered. "I'm not looking for a plaything. We need to spend some time together before you're ready to commit, honey. We can do that starting right now. What I don't want is to see you walk out that door. We're not strangers, Lauren. You can't deny we have the kind of chemistry that starts fires. The people outside that door have nothing to say about what happens between us."

"Romeo, this is your home. Do you usually bring a woman here? Are they used to seeing cohabitation with someone you met the same day?" she asked incredulously. "Carla told me I'm exactly your type, but that you usually have six women on a string. It's the type you're attracted to, not the person. I don't want to join a long line of others. I just can't do that right now."

"Carla talks a lot of shit," he spat out. "There are not six women on a string. Yes, I have been attracted to women who look like you all my life. But I know the difference between a body that gets my rocks hot and a woman I want to spend the rest of my life with, Lauren. I'm not a kid chasing after his dick. And if it makes any difference, I have never brought a woman here. You're the only woman outside my family who has stepped foot in this room."

Romeo straightened from the bedpost and stalked over to her. His hands came up slowly to fold her into his embrace. He moved slowly so she'd know she could stop him at any time. She didn't. "This is what we have, Lauren." He brought his lips to hers and licked along the seam of her closed mouth. Her hands clutched his biceps—he slowly kissed his way into her mouth, gently, leisurely invading her this time. When her lips parted to accept him, he took the time to explore her teeth, the soft interior of her cheeks and finally stroke her tongue. He insidiously turned up the heat, pressing her along the length of his body. One hand went to her bottom, cupping it to bring her into him while the other cradled her head as he sucked her tongue into his mouth.

Lauren knew he was going to kiss her. She even knew he'd make it the best damn kiss ever had on the planet. He'd do it because he could. She just couldn't dredge up the will to stop him. His declaration that she was the only woman to have ever stepped foot in the room was so convincing. She decided wanting to believe something too good to be true had to be a sickness. It made you let the guy who could make an Olympic sport out of kissing kiss you. It made you wrap your legs around his waist and rub his cock into your wet pussy as well, apparently.

Romeo turned to the bed and laid her down on it gently. Those gorgeous legs wrapped around his waist kept his cock crammed right where he wanted it to be. With her beneath him, he could keep teasing her sweet pussy with his cock and use his hands for further convincing. His whole body rubbed sensually over her as he ate her mouth. His hands gravitated to those delectable breasts and hard fingers plucked the little pebbles atop them.

Her body knew it liked this now—it exploded into flames as soon as he touched her. Every inch of her wanted his caress and every one of those inches was determined to ignore the logical virgin shrieking at them from her brain. The only plans her body was willing to hear about were the ones that let him do whatever he pleased. But he wasn't doing it fast enough. He hadn't loosened a single button, zipper or snap. How were they supposed to get her clothes off if he wouldn't follow the program?

Romeo lifted his head and looked down at the moaning, undulating woman in his arms. Her hands were clawing down his back, her knees in his armpits and willing written all over her. Romeo took a deep breath and focused on the long-term goal. "Sweetheart, if I just wanted to nail you, I'd be doing it now." He gave her a minute to open her eyes and realize they'd stopped the lovemaking.

Lauren frowned up at him in confusion and Romeo continued. "I want you to understand that I mean what I say. When I tell you I want a long-term commitment that means I'm willing to do whatever it takes to get one. So, I'm going to confess some things that will make you mad as hell at me. I'm doing it right now because we need to get everything out between us. And because I'm sure you'll find out soon anyway and be even madder if I don't tell you."

Lauren tried to ignore the sheepish little boy tone in his voice. That dark-eyed, dark-haired scamp peeked at her guiltily as he confessed he knew she'd find him out. He was such a cutie she had a hard time frowning seriously up at him as she waited for the dreadful confession. He held her pinned beneath him, but most of his weight was supported on his elbows. "Are you going to let me up to hear this?" she asked.

"No. I might need to remind you what we are together. I can't risk it," he stated tightly.

"Well, get on with it," Lauren prompted when he hesitated again. He really was afraid to tell her whatever it was he thought he'd done. That amazed her. He was supposed to be the experienced man of the world. The guy who was fully in charge at all times. This hesitation gave her the first real indication that he was truly sincere when he claimed his feelings for her were genuine. You couldn't be afraid of a "throwaway" person. By all accounts, Romeo wasn't afraid of anyone.

"I called your doctor this afternoon," he started. "I actually know the man. My mother was his second heart transplant surgery. So, it's not like he was telling a stranger your case history. I know about the accident you and your mother were in when you were ten. How your mom died in your arms while you were trapped in the car. The serious injuries, how they had to rebuild your pelvis, that they discovered your heart problem then. How long you waited for a donor, the heart surgery and the migraines. I also know you have three older brothers and your father is still living."

He paused to study her face. She watched him calmly without a flicker of emotion. That in itself was disturbing and he swallowed roughly. "I'm sorry if you think I was prying. I had no idea he'd go into such detail when I told him you were here and I was worried for your health because of the headache. But I didn't stop him either. I wanted to know," Romeo trailed off quietly.

"Is that it?" Lauren asked.

"Ah, most of it," he hedged.

"There's more?" Her eyebrows rose.

"Yeah, at supper I got so mad at that bunch of irresponsible children that I told them you'd had a HT twenty-four months ago and the migraine when you got here. I sort of ripped into Carla over being a piss-poor doctor for not knowing this stuff." He paused again. She waited. "It just fell out of my mouth. My choices were that or see to it they all carry the same bruises you do. As it is, I still have Steven to deal with. He deserves a thrashing for bringing that particular animal out like that."

"I forbid you to touch him, Romeo," Lauren stated quietly.

"Forbid me? What the hell kind of statement is that? No one forbids me. I understand you're pissed at me, but you can't go around forbidding me." He frowned into her eyes.

She didn't respond, just watched him as calmly as she had for the last five minutes.

"Look, Lauren, let's get this out in the open between us. Be mad at me. Tell me exactly what you think of my overbearing, interfering and generally controlling ways. You can swear at me, kick me, whatever. But you can't forbid me. No one forbids adults."

"There is no point in any of that, Romeo. You are well aware of what you did. You know exactly how intrusive I find your meddling. You wouldn't have been afraid to tell me if you didn't." Her tone was still calm and even. "The only thing I can change is the future. I forbid you to touch him. If you ever want me to forgive you, that's what it'll take."

Romeo popped up off her as he realized what was happening. His big body paced across the room and turned to face her again. Lauren propped herself up on her elbows to watch him.

"You'll forgive me and then what?" he wanted to know. His eyes narrowed as he studied her. She was playing a power game with a master strategist. The fact she held all the bargaining chips didn't escape him. So maybe it wasn't a game but a test. Would he bend to her wishes? It really depended on what she was willing to give for the concession on his part. If it was just a tiny bit of what he wanted, it was a game. If she was willing to let this go and start over, it was a test. Oh, God, he hoped it was a test. A test meant she wanted to trust him, wanted to believe him.

"Then we start over and get to know each other," she responded.

"Starting tonight? You'll stay with me?" he pressed, unable to believe it was actually going to be that easy to get around what he'd done.

Lauren got up and paced to the other side of the room. At least she was farther away from the door, he noticed.

"I spent all of my teens in and out of a hospital or going to a therapist because of the way my mother died. I want to date, Romeo. I want to experience some of what I missed. Go to a movie with my boyfriend and neck in the back row. I want to make out behind the barn. Get flowers on Valentine's Day. To know what it feels like to get a call at two a.m. just because he misses me and wants to hear my voice. Or when he takes me to the beach, so he can look at me in a bikini. I want to have fun." Lauren turned and stared out the window into the starry night.

"I'm also really unsure about sex with you. I know exactly how big that thing is and I think it's going to hurt. I'm afraid. I know I'll disappoint you. I know all the stuff I want are things you did a long time ago. It's got to sound lame and stupid to you," she ended softly.

Romeo was across the room in a lunging move she didn't see. Pressing himself up behind her, he wrapped his arms around the forlorn little figure she made. His head dipped down to press his lips against her ear. "I want to take my lover to the movies," he whispered. "And neck in the back row. She won't have panties on so I can make her come with my hand and no one will know. I want to take her out behind the barn to the back woods and go skinny-dipping in the pond. We'll make out on the bank as we dry off. I want to send her flowers on Valentine's Day with a diamond in the center of every rose. I never want to call her at two in the morning because I miss her. I want her to be right there beside me so I can lick her awake because I need her. I want to make love to her in the backseat of a limo after we do dinner and a show in London. I want to take her to a private beach in the Caribbean so she won't have to wear a bikini at all. I want her to have fun. I want to play with her."

Lauren turned in his arms and looked up at him. Tears dripped slowly down her cheeks. He licked them off and continued. "I will never do anything to hurt you, Lauren. If I can't make you beg me to put it in you, and then you enjoy it all the way to your womb, I will not do it. You can tell me to stop at any time and I will. I swear, honey, you'll like it."

He'd just taken what she felt were silly little-girl wishes and made them beautiful, sensual adult fantasies. He promised the moon and she secretly suspected he could give it to her. Where did this man come from? Was it possible he was telling the truth about everything? Could he really have decided so abruptly that they were made for each other?

"I'm still not comfortable with the audience out the door. I know it's old hat to you, but this is a big deal to me. I can't relax and stay here tonight, Romeo. I'd never, um, it'd be . . . I can't," Lauren wailed softly into his chest.

"I took care of that already, Lauren." Romeo glanced away and frowned. "I guess I threatened them all with a hiding if they said one word to you about being an Ice Queen or not turning a cold shoulder to me. I, well, I told them that mommy and daddy wouldn't lift a hand while I did it either."

Lauren's mouth dropped open as she stared up at him. "You threatened them with a spanking?"

"Yeah," he acknowledged.

"You can't say that to adults!" she scolded emphatically.

"Well, if they act like children they deserve to be treated like children. I also told them I intend to marry you. No one is going to say one word to you if you stay here tonight. And if they do, I will take care of it in the manner they deserve," Romeo threatened darkly.

"Romeo, I forb—"

"I know, I know, you forbid me to touch them," he interrupted. "All this forbidding better come with some conceding, honey." He was still frowning as he held her against him.

"What kind of conceding?" she wanted to know.

"The kind where you agree we're an exclusive couple," he told her. "And you agree to stay with me tonight." She opened her mouth to interrupt but he laid a finger over it. "We don't have to do anything, baby. I know you're still a bit shaken up. But I want you to sleep here with me. Tomorrow we can deal with the others. Just stay," he pleaded softly.

Lauren's arms crept up around his neck. Her fingers sifted through his hair as they gazed at each other. A smile bloomed across her lovely face as the big man in her arms held on tightly.

"You want to be my boyfriend?" she whispered.

"Oh, yeah," he breathed.

"Good. My first boyfriend needs to be a big guy who won't be so intimidated by my brothers. They are a mean bunch and have been scaring men off for a couple years now. I thought I'd be a virgin for the rest of my life." Lauren stretched up on tiptoes—he helped her by lifting so her lips brushed his as she spoke. "And then there is my dad, the ex-Marine. I don't even want to think what he'd do to a little guy." The sentence ended as her lips sealed against his and he opened under the firm licking of her warm, soft tongue.

Romeo reached down and grabbed her thighs to wrap her legs around him again. It was easier to kiss her when she was riding him. He suspected her father might be a valid issue, but he didn't have time to deal with it right now.

Lauren pulled her mouth a breath away from his and continued. "My oldest brother just retired from pro football this year. So he's old and you probably don't have to worry about him." She dived back in for another long suck on his tongue. Pulling back a millimeter, she continued with the list. "The next one owns a boxing gym. He doesn't compete professionally anymore so that makes him old, too." Lauren licked down his jaw to suck on the tender spot between neck and shoulder.

"The youngest one is a race car driver. He's away a lot. You can probably avoid him." Her licking tongue traveled back to his mouth and they kissed deeply for several long minutes.

While still kissing her deeply, Romeo carried her over to his nightstand. His hand reached down and he dialed the phone without looking, only pulling away from her mouth to put it to his ear when someone picked up on the other end.

"Yes, this is Mr. Montero." He spoke smoothly into the phone with his eyes locked on hers. "I'm reserving the honeymoon suite for tomorrow. Yeah. We'll be in around four. Sure. That will be fine. Thank you." He hung up and went back to kissing her.

Lauren pulled back and sputtered, "What did you do? Where? Tomorrow?"

"I reserved us a room in Vegas for tomorrow." He turned and headed for the door with her still wrapped around him. He kissed her neck down to her cleavage as she tried to avoid him and get some information from the growling heathen who was easily carting her across the house to the kitchen.

"What about dating? You haven't asked me to move in with you. What happened to all that? We can't get married tomorrow. You don't even know, well, we don't know if . . ." Lauren glanced up as they entered the kitchen and her voice trailed off. Oh, damn, she'd been nearly yelling at him, every one of the people in the kitchen had to have heard every word.

Romeo lifted his head from her chest to answer and saw the surprise in her round eyes. Following her line of vision, he turned swiftly to see what she stared at. All six cousins were seated at the kitchen table with two loaves of bread and every condiment known to man spread across it. It was after midnight, he should have known they'd be in here. They all gaped at him walking in with Lauren wrapped around him, yelling about not getting married tomorrow while he licked her chest.

Carla recovered first. "I see you're feeling better, Lauren. Is he being a pain in the ass and trying to order you around?" she asked hopefully. "I warned you, girlfriend."

Romeo turned and walked over to the table, only releasing Lauren when he had a chair to sit her in. People shuffled and moved over quickly so he could slide another chair in beside her.

"I . . . ah . . . no, I mean yes, he's a bit, ah . . . decisive, but . . ." Lauren trailed off in embarrassed confusion.

"Hand me the bread and some of that stuff, guys," Romeo asked. He swiftly started making two sandwiches.

Carla continued. "What's this about tomorrow? You're planning on getting married tomorrow? Don't you think Devin might have a problem with that?"

"Oh, um, we're not . . ." Lauren floundered.

"Yeah, we are. Her family is made up of trained killers and I have to be married to her before I meet them. They might let me live then. Which one is Devin?" Romeo asked as he plopped a sandwich in front of her. The faces around the table grinned at this amusing turn of events.

"They are not," Lauren defended. "Well, two of them are, ah, maybe three of them. The fourth one is just fast."

"Devin is her wanna-be boyfriend," Carla supplied. "The one who has been puppy-dog infatuated and saintly patient for months now. He's the guy who gets to hear how she's not ready to settle down all the time."

"Carla!" Lauren gasped. "We haven't actually had an opportunity to discuss that quite yet," she stated sharply.

Romeo put down the sandwich he was about to bite into and looked at Lauren. "I guess we can refer to Devin Dufus as your stupid ex-boyfriend now. Right?"

"Well, he's not really stupid. He's a surgeon. I think I should—"

"Let me give him a call after we get married and tell him to shove off," Romeo interrupted. "Then we'll call him your nerdy, stupid ex-boyfriend if you like."

"Ah, what I was going to say is that he deserves an explanation, Romeo," Lauren stated firmly. "I have no idea what that explanation is, but I think I should give it to him personally. He deserves at least that."

"Oh, man!" Steve hooted. "Can I come? I'd love to hear how you go from casual no-commitment dating to married to someone you just met in less than twenty-four hours." Leaning back from the table balancing on two legs of his chair, Steve continued to chuckle over this tale.

"Shut up, Steve," Romeo barked. "The only reason you're not in the emergency room right now is she forbade me to touch you. That was over the horse incident, she hasn't said a word about your wise-ass mouth."

Steve's chair slammed down and his mouth dropped open. "She forbade you? Shit, Lauren, I think I'm in love with you. You're obviously a magical being or something. Would you care to consider another proposal?" Laughter erupted around the table at that.

"Careful, pup," Romeo warned. "I don't feel benevolent about this. Lauren is busy for the next sixty years. If I die before she does, she's still not available."

"Cut it out, guys," Lauren demanded. "You're enjoying this little show way too much. I'm about to revoke the other thing I forbade him to do." Lauren pushed away from the table. "I'm done discussing this in front of an audience." Romeo grabbed their sandwiches and stood up with her.

"Hey," Carla called after them as they headed for the door. "What was the other thing?"

"Spanking each one of you," Lauren shot back over her shoulder. "I fully understand the urge to do so."

"There's a private patio off my rooms, we can eat there," Romeo murmured as he sort of herded her back toward his wing of the house.

Lauren glanced at him and sighed. "No one said you weren't determined, I suppose." He wasn't about to let her go back to her own room. Now a whole bunch of new junk was cluttering up the original disagreement and they were nowhere near a compromise. One thirty in the morning and it looked like a long night ahead of them.

His private patio was a walled-in oasis complete with a stone waterfall into an inviting hot tub. Lush shrubbery made it a perfect private garden of delight. The table's umbrella was folded so they could see the stars as they sat on the padded chairs and munched through the sandwiches. Both remained silent. She suspected mostly to be sure she ate. He watched like a hawk 'til the last morsel disappeared.

They both sat back and looked at each other. "What now?" Lauren asked quietly.

"We go to bed and get some sleep. I'm beat," Romeo sighed.

Lauren smiled. "Good plan."

LAUREN AWOKE TO A rough hand caressing her thigh while a very gentle mouth sucked and licked at one of her nipples. Groaning, she stretched while the mouth remained attached to her breast and the hand slid between her legs to lightly cup her intimately.

Romeo lifted his head and grinned up at her. "Need the bathroom?"

"It's morning, doesn't everyone?" Her sleepy face scowled up at him.

"Ah, not a morning person." His wicked grin widened. "I'll be here when you get back, honey."

Closing the door behind her, Lauren frowned at the lavish surroundings and headed for the toilet. Afterward she turned on the shower. His ass could just wait. She knew what he wanted. She still didn't think it'd work between them and she wasn't about to rush back in there and see how badly that scenario would turn out.

Just as she turned her head up to the warm spray, the door behind her opened. Of course, what made her think he'd stay in bed like a good monster? Two hands slid around her to cup her breasts.

"Did you not get that I'm a nasty grump in the morning?" Lauren asked as one of his hands wandered down her abdomen.

"Hmmm, the nasty part is good, the grump part is my responsibility," he mumbled into her shoulder while dragging his tongue across it. Firm fingers plucked her nipple then rubbed across the swollen nub. The other hand was pushing between damp folds, petting them softly. "If you're still grumpy when we're done," he continued, "I'll agree that you get to tell Dufus to take a hike."

"And if I'm not?" she questioned distractedly, his hand between her legs making it difficult to think as it strummed and caressed without giving the firm touches she was beginning to want.

"We fly to Vegas this afternoon," he mumbled into her other shoulder.

"That's it? All I'm agreeing to is a visit to Vegas?" Lauren questioned as she turned in his arms and slid her hands down his torso to grasp his cock firmly as he'd shown her yesterday.

"Oh, God, easy, baby," he gasped. "Ah, yeah. A visit," he agreed. "I want your agreement on the marriage thing. But I'd never make a deal over it." Romeo groaned as she stroked him steadily, not easing up one bit. "Slow down, I'm not the one who needs help getting turned on. Let me pleasure you," he pleaded as her hands worked him, one hand kept stroking and the other slipped under his balls to lift and roll them between curious fingers.

Lauren leaned forward and dragged her tongue across a male nipple then immediately sucked it into her mouth, pulling hard. Romeo's hands left her body to flash to the walls of the shower stall steadying him as his body clenched and jerked in response. "Lauren! What the hell are you doing?" he barked out.

She ignored him and reattached both hands to his erection. Suddenly her lips let go of his chest and she melted to her knees. Romeo only had time to look down in amazement as she held his cock securely between both hands and fed it into her mouth. Her lips sealed around him as her hot, wet little tongue slithered across and down. Gulping desperately, he watched her head start to move. The firm suction she applied with each pull removed all coherent thought from his brain. He braced bulging arms more firmly against the walls and hung on.

Her fists worked the thick root of him as she slurped over his inflamed head with increasing speed and pressure. The fire of release streaked up his body with white-hot explosions, she drew the fluid from his soul as her greedy mouth pulled and swallowed every drop that erupted out of him. She worked him hard 'til he slumped back against the wall in trembling shock, drawing his cock from her mouth.

He gazed down at her blankly as she regarded him from her knees. Slowly she rose while he slid down the wall. When he sat on the floor of the shower looking up, she calmly stated, "Don't challenge me in the morning. I told you I was cranky." She raised one brow and stepped out of the shower.

Romeo thought his brain might explode. If that's what

happened when she was cranky, he needed to hide the coffee. Perhaps sprinkling crumbs in the bed would do it? Maybe leaving his socks on the floor? Whatever it took, her cranky sent him into another stratosphere. Gathering himself off the floor, he shut off the shower and stumbled out.

Lauren was brushing her hair at the vanity, already in panties and bra. "You gonna get over it and get dressed? I need coffee and I'm not facing that room full of vultures alone after last night."

Romeo grinned. She was still cranky. He'd lost the deal he'd been so confident of, but aw hell, she made the sexiest cranky person he'd ever seen. Sauntering over to her, he dropped a kiss on her head. "I'll be just a second, angel face," he murmured and grabbed his razor. Once again he stood there naked, seemingly unconcerned while she was partially dressed. Swiftly done with the shaving, he quickly dressed. Lauren was standing by the door leading to the main house tapping her foot.

"Where'd you learn that, honey?" he asked quietly as he held the door open for her. They moved across the relatively quiet house.

"You taught me," she answered shortly.

"Damn, seems like I'd remember that," he mused as a wicked twinkle sneaked into his eyes. She was getting crankier—apparently talking was a struggle before coffee. "Just yesterday you'd never seen one, this morning you operate it like a professional. How does that work?" he pressed.

"Movies, books, ability to extrapolate. Coffee?" Lauren demanded as she stepped into the big, empty kitchen.

Romeo chuckled. If he'd had a few more steps, he could

have pressed her with enough questions to reduce her responses to one word or grunts. "Have a seat, I'll get it going," he offered.

"Now, Romeo, do it now," she demanded and followed right behind him as he got the materials.

"You can sit, baby," he insisted as she stood at his elbow while he measured granules into the coffee filter.

"Want to know where it is," Lauren murmured as she watched the first drips appear in the empty carafe.

Romeo shook his head and laughed. "Now that I know the paramount importance of coffee, we'll have a coffeemaker in our apartment. Don't worry. No one will withhold it."

Lauren's eyes darted to his. "Good, withholding would be suicidal, Romeo," she warned darkly. "Grounds for divorce!" she added for good measure.

Romeo's grin widened. If she was threatening him with divorce, she expected to marry him. Hell, he'd go pick the beans himself if need be, there was never going to be a shortage of coffee in this house. Well, except for certain early mornings when he couldn't help himself.

"Not a problem, baby," he assured her.

When the carafe was half full, Lauren grabbed it and filled the cup he'd slid in front of her while she stared at the dripping nectar of the gods. Adding two sweeteners, she took a sip and slumped against the counter. Romeo picked her up—careful not to spill a drop from the cup she clutched and gently sat her in a chair at the table. His own cup in hand, he settled beside her.

When she'd gotten to the bottom of her first cup, Lauren glanced around. "Where is everyone?" she questioned.

"It's only seven thirty. They won't be up 'til after nine," he answered. "Which is a good thing because we need to talk, sweetheart."

Lauren got a second cup and sat down again. "Okay, talk."

"When are you going to call Devin and take care of that?" Romeo asked.

Lauren raised her brows as she regarded him. "I thought I'd see him Monday and have a chat with him then."

Romeo frowned. "You're a hard woman, Lauren. Is this how it's going to be? I demand and you just do whatever you please?"

"Pretty much," Lauren responded and took another sip.

"It's how you handle your family, isn't it?" he accused.

"It is now," she confirmed.

"I don't like it," he growled.

"You're going to put up with it, aren't you?" She smiled at the big scowling man beside her who'd just realized little did not mean helpless. She might be brand spanking new to the intense relationship scene, but there was no reason not to start like you meant to go on.

Romeo turned to her and swooped down, fastening his lips over hers. His kiss invaded her forcefully. Sweeping into her mouth, he sucked her coffee taste deep into his body, stroking over tongue, teeth and soft tissue with masterful demand. His hands gathered her upper body against his, pressing into her hard. Her arms wound around his neck and she groaned into his mouth.

Insistently he drew on her, his hands roaming her body. Plucking and squeezing her breast, gliding down to her ass, he filled his hands with it and roughly cuddled it. Suddenly he grabbed her hips and swung her up to straddle his lap. Slamming her down on the rock formation in his crotch, his hands returned to her ass. Her body undulated under his urgent direction, rubbing both cunt and tits into him as he kissed her desperately.

Romeo broke away from the kiss and stared up at her. "You're doing it again!" he accused.

"What?" she gasped.

"You're meeting me more than halfway in this physical stuff. I can barely keep up with you, honey. What happened between last night and today?" he asked softly as she continued to rub against him.

"You happened. You told me you'd make all my wishes and desires come true. You told me you'd stop if I wanted to. I haven't wanted to yet," Lauren purred. "Is it a problem? Am I too much for you? Are you tired of it?" Her face turned worried as that occurred to her.

"Oh, God in heaven, NO," Romeo assured her. "I'm a bit confused but happy as hell, sweetheart."

Lauren still frowned. "Now I feel uncomfortable." She sighed deeply and stepped off his lap to pace across the kitchen.

"No, no, no." Romeo watched her move away from him. "I'm an idiot, baby. Don't think this isn't what I want. I need to understand where you're coming from, that's all. I don't want to scare you or shock you. I asked because it's important you're comfortable emotionally as well as physically."

Lauren leaned against the counter and folded her arms as she looked at him seriously. Another little frown skittered across her brow as she thought about what he asked. She wasn't sure she wanted to examine her physical responses. Intellectually she felt hesitant and uncertain about moving into the new ground a full sexual relationship entailed. However, as soon as he laid a hand on her she became some sort of wild woman who couldn't crawl into his pants fast enough.

"You know I've never had a sexual relationship, right?" Lauren questioned.

"The very reason I've been cautious, baby," Romeo answered.

"You also know I've been cooped up in a hospital or under the protective eagle eye of my family from preadolescence until recently. Suddenly you happen and you're everything forbidden and dangerous. You turn me on and know what to do about it. You say you want a long-term relationship with a reasonable amount of believability. That gives the good girl in me freedom to let the bad girl out. I feel like the gloves are off. I'm suddenly liberated from adolescence with a walking, talking 'He-Man from Castle Grayskull' who wants to show me everything Ken would never do to Barbie. If you really want to go on with this, be prepared to deal with a woman who can't get enough of this.

"You asked what's different between last night and this morning. What's different is I woke up beside a naked, sexy man who wanted to touch me. I woke up in an adult situation with a fully developed adult who intends to share it. I feel brand new. I want to try everything. What happened in the shower was just flat-out going for it. It's how I wanted to express what I felt. You understood it. You knew I was feeling defiant and independent. I needed to push back on the physical level. You let me. You let me be an adult who can make her own choices and you let my choices mean something to you.

"Just being free to make a choice is a new and exciting activity for me. When you're that sick and that damaged by circumstances, you have no choices. Everything from what you eat to how or when you sleep is regulated to improve your chances of survival. Survival becomes the decision maker in every aspect of your life. I know this sounds really horrible—they worked so hard to give me this chance to live, but being the baby girl in a family of strong men already cuts into your choices. When you're sick and on the edge of death, well, you have none. They didn't even know what taking me to the mall would have meant.

"You're right. I'm different, I intend to stay different, Romeo. You can hardly say you knew me before, but does this change things for you?" Lauren asked.

Romeo cleared his throat and swallowed. The gorgeous woman standing across the kitchen from him just declared she intended to go wild. She'd literally broken out of the cage and given herself permission to try everything. He was damn sure that if he didn't get on board, she'd find someone who would. There was no way he'd let her take her brand-new self out that door to go wild in someone else's arms.

"The only thing that's changed is my urgency about getting to Vegas, baby. Whatever you want to try, we'll try, but I want you to know you're going to be trying those things with me." Romeo stood up and stalked over to the counter where she stood. Resting his hands on either side of her body, he leaned into Lauren's face. "I'm the guy who broke open the box for you, darling. I am the only guy who's going to show you what fun it is to play with the big kids."

66 / GAIL FAULKNER

Romeo sealed her mouth with his. Immediately her arms went around his neck and her mouth opened to suck him in. He gathered her willing body to him and plunged into her with barely restrained lust. His body thrust into yielding feminine curves that pressed back at him. She turned into the wild, moaning sex maniac she'd warned him about. Now that he knew where this came from, he encouraged her abandon with hands and body.

At the doorway to the kitchen, Carla groaned loudly. "Oh, for heaven's sake. Can you two please get a room? People need coffee. Besides, I'm too young to see this. You're going to scar me for life. I'll never be able to face this kitchen again without wondering, damn it."

Romeo lifted his head and laughed. Lauren buried her face in his chest and echoed Carla's groan. His little wild woman was embarrassed at being caught crawling up his body. She'd had one leg wrapped around his hips just when Carla interrupted them. Two minutes more and Carla wouldn't have had to wonder. Lauren would have been balanced on the edge of the kitchen counter with both legs wrapped around him, with nothing but a condom separating them. An interesting possibility, but not where he wanted her first time to be.

"Oh, yeah, I intend to get us a room, and you can be damn sure about every surface in that place," he growled as he gently moved the two of them away from the coffee machine.

Lauren smacked him on the arm. "Romeo!" she hissed. "I said I wanted to be a bad girl. I didn't say one word about public displays and general announcements!"

He grinned at her red face. "Well, tell the good girl that I fully intend to make a general announcement and as big a public display as I can manage of our marriage license. So give me back that nasty little bitch in there. I want to show her what bad boys do first thing in the morning." Romeo swung Lauren up in his arms and headed out of the kitchen, leaving a bemused Carla staring after them.

They reached his rooms in a lust-induced fog. Unable to resist her mouth long enough to get there, he'd been kissing her deeply all the way across the house. Neither knew if anyone else saw them. Neither bothered to look.

Romeo put her down at the foot of the bed and whipped his clothes off. Fully naked, he yanked her back into his arms and fastened his mouth to hers again. Lauren's hands wandered his body as he fumbled with buttons and snaps on her clothing. Getting the shirt and bra off first, his mouth latched onto a plump nipple as soon as it became visible. He gave up on the clothes and simply grabbed her shorts at her hip bones and ripped them in half.

Lauren gasped as the sound of rending clothing penetrated her brain but his mouth didn't give her any time to analyze. Her panties suffered the same fate as her shorts. His mouth was now on her tender belly as he sank to his knees. His large hands palmed her ass and held her hips still as he moved lower. The licking, kissing man in front of her was actually growling deep in his chest as he buried his face in the springy curls at her crotch.

Lauren's legs started trembling when his tongue snaked out to flick over her swollen clit. The damp caress sent her staggering back against the bed. Romeo lunged after her as her ass hit the bed. He grabbed her thighs and shoved them wide while his face returned to the plump folds between them. The low rumble in his chest hitched a moment then returned to a contented growl as he licked up a deep groove and down the other side.

Lauren felt burning waves of heat radiate from her center as his relentless mouth sucked in each fold and bathed it carefully. Her body fell back on the bed as she gasped in great gulps of air. Suddenly his hot, twisting tongue plunged into her opening—thick fingers held her cunt lips open while he pressed into her. He didn't withdraw but remained buried in her, licking and rubbing sensitive tissue that had never known this kind of attention. Lauren groaned and flexed her hips up into his face. It felt so damn good, so dark and nasty. He didn't thrust—he entered and stayed to investigate every millimeter he could reach.

The blood rushing through Lauren's body gathered at cunt and breasts. Her nipples ached and throbbed as he flattened his tongue to stretch her narrow passage. Lauren thought she might die as her body twisted to get more of him inside her. Her hands went to her breasts to rub the ache away.

Romeo finally pulled his tongue out of her, pressed it against her engorged folds and dragged it up to the puffy clit beckoning him. He gently licked around it, circling slowly while he glanced up her body and watched her fondle her breasts.

His avid tongue snaked over her clit and her whole body jerked. He lifted his head and looked down at the open cunt beneath him. His fingers came up to investigate as he watched. Sliding over flushed folds gently—he prodded her clit with light touches. His other hand moved down to press a thick digit into her contracting passage. Her body pushed up at the dual stimulation, the finger in her cunt disappeared to the knuckle and she groaned loudly.

"That's it, baby," he breathed. "Are you ready for more?"

"Romeo, don't talk!" she gasped. "Can't talk!"

Romeo chuckled as he watched her writhe on his fingers. "Oh, yes we do, sweetheart. I tell you how beautiful you are and you let me." He slipped another finger into her tight opening and ducked down to lick around his knuckles.

"Oh, God!" Lauren gasped. "You're a talker? We're doing this and you want to chat about it?"

Romeo slurped at her as his fingers thrust in and out gently, he lifted his head to watch again. "Yes, I want to look at you, taste you, feel you, eat you and tell you exactly how wonderful and beautiful it all is."

Lauren moaned as he thrust a little harder. Her tight channel contracted around his fingers. "I can't . . . You can't expect me to . . . ah . . . Oh, yes, just like that. More, I need more."

"See, talking is good," he crooned as he thrust into the pretty cunt harder. Lauren moaned and undulated to the rhythm he set.

"I love how you look, baby. Looking at you is almost my favorite thing," he continued.

"Okay," she gasped. "What is your favorite thing?"

"This," he stated as he head dived down and his sucking mouth fastened over the clit he'd been tormenting. He sucked hard as her body fought through the firestorm that swept up her.

Just as the burning pleasure ebbed to glowing warmth, he grabbed her under the arms and hauled her up the bed with him. When her head reached the pillow, his heavy body settled over her and he started kissing her again. Romeo reached down, hooked his arms under her knees and brought his hands back to her breasts. The slow motion adjustment to her position didn't register until she found herself spread and unable to move as his heavy erection slid down her dripping cunt to stop at the gaping entrance.

She sucked in a breath as he pushed into her insistently. Thick inches squeezed into her slowly. He lifted his head from her lips and watched her face carefully as he pressed in. Her eyes rounded as hot steel invaded her. She kept waiting for the pain. It never came.

"Oh," Lauren gasped as he settled his groin onto her fully impaled cunt.

"Am I hurting you, baby?" he gasped as his body began to tremble.

"Ah, no," Lauren whispered.

"Do you want me to stop?" he questioned again.

Deep inside her body, the thick head of his cock nudged her womb. She could feel it burning her from the inside out. It felt hot, hard and so good. "NO. Don't stop, Romeo, please don't stop!" she groaned.

"Oh, God, thank you!" he moaned and his hips pulled back marginally, pushing in slowly. The shallow thrusts caressed nerve endings that seemed connected to every possible body part.

The incredible fullness robbed her of rational thought. The pike between her legs wasn't moving fast enough. Her calves tried to wrap themselves around his forearms for leverage so she could push back harder. He wouldn't let her.

"More!" she demanded.

"Wait," he responded and kept inching in and out of her slowly.

"No!" Her nails raked his back to make her point.

"You need more time!" he insisted shortly.

"Fuck. Me. NOW!" Lauren screamed at him.

"Damn it, woman! I'm trying to make sure you like it!" he groaned in exasperation.

"I LIKE IT. Fuck NOW!" Lauren grabbed his ears and held his face directly in front of her. "NOW!"

"Oh, baby, I can't wait!" he bellowed as his hips suddenly jerked back and slammed into her. He let go of her breasts, grabbed the backs of her knees and held them straight-armed out to the sides. His knees came up and he crouched over her bent body, pounding his thick cock all the way in her with a force and speed that sent her spiraling off into the universe. Screaming her release didn't slow him down one bit. He pounded through her clenching cunt with mind-numbing power. As her shudders wound down, he suddenly pulled out of her.

Lauren felt strong hands grip her torso and flip her over. "Kneel!" he snarled at her. She complied, dazedly gazing down at the bed. From behind, he thrust into her channel with full body–powered ferocity. Each slam of engorged cock into the wet inferno between her legs wrenched a guttural grunt from him. Lauren's arms collapsed and she was suddenly on knees and elbows.

He knew he was fucking her hard and rude. He couldn't stop. This little woman stripped away his control with the demand he fuck her. The simple male animal that needed this could not be appeased with only one orgasm from this cunt.

He needed her cum dripping down his thighs before he'd let her up. One of his hands released her hip to slither around to her swollen clit. Thumb and forefinger clamped sensitive flesh between them and began milking it like a nipple.

The rough handling sent her into a ruthless, grinding climax. Her body thrashed as white-hot explosions shot through her. Lauren screamed and tried to arch away from those callused fingers. He wouldn't let her.

"Please . . . Oh, God, please, Romeo. I can't take anymore!" Lauren begged.

"Yes," he growled. "More." Romeo threw his head back and squeezed his eyes shut. The sensations thundering up his body demanded a base dominance. He needed her to know him for her mate. How fucking her 'til she passed out was going to do that remained a mystery, but he couldn't stop.

Her body shuddered weakly under him again and Romeo finally let the orgasm take him. It felt as though his body liquified and simply drained into her. The hot jets of seed kept racking his entire form with harsh intensity as he slammed into her. When it subsided, he collapsed on her back. She lay limply beneath him.

Gradually it dawned on him she hadn't moved. Romeo rolled off her and came up on an elbow to look down at her. Her head was turned away from him and all he could see was the gentle rise and fall of her back with each breath. He frowned.

"Lauren," he murmured as he ran a hand down her back. She didn't respond. "Honey, are you all right?" Nothing.

"Lauren, baby. Please talk to me. Please, sweetheart. Did I hurt you? Are you in pain?" He tried to brush the hair off her face but she turned it into the pillow and brought her arms up to clutch it tightly.

"Oh, Jesus, baby. I did hurt you. I'm so sorry. Oh, God, please, baby, tell me where? Okay, you don't want to talk to me. I understand. Should I get Carla? Would you be better if I got Carla?" He scrambled off the bed.

"No! Get back in this bed and calm down," Lauren's muffled voice demanded.

"Ah, yeah, sure. But, ah . . ." he trailed off as he gingerly sat back down on the bed. Her little hand reached up blindly and came to rest in the center of his chest. She pushed gently and he allowed her to press him back down on the bed. "Uh, honey, what's going on?" he asked cautiously.

"I am trying to recover from a full-body meltdown," she huffed from the pillow. "I've just been had by the world's wickedest lover and I need a minute to handle it. Please refrain from calling an audience!"

"Oh," he responded blankly, and then what she'd said sank in. "Ohhh," Romeo purred and gathered her slender body next to his. "No problem, sweetheart. I'll just be here amusing myself until you're ready to talk." He started dropping kisses down her spine. At the slope of her ass, the kisses turned into licks with little nips scattered among them. He couldn't resist and since she still hadn't moved, he opened his mouth and sucked gently until he was sure he'd left a hickey. Levering up to admire his handiwork, he saw her body start to shake.

"Did you just mark my ass?" she questioned around muffled giggles.

"Damn straight I did," Romeo responded, and licked over the cute red mark already glowing against lily-white skin. He decided the other cheek needed one also, just for balance, you know. Leaning over her, he licked that globe 'til he found the perfect spot and again sucked gently. This time the mark was right on the underside of her cheek where ass met thigh. As he sucked, her bottom lifted off the mattress and her legs drifted open.

He saw no reason to lift his head when she obliged him so sweetly. He lapped up the juices on her inner thigh. Her legs shifted again and he licked higher. Now she was squirming under his questing mouth, trying to center him where she wanted attention. He gently lapped up all the remnants of their lovemaking before nudging her legs farther apart. She complied swiftly, spreading herself as wide as possible for the man who was now lying between her legs.

Romeo grinned as he surveyed the bounty before him. The puffy little cunt was red and sloppy. Above it, her rosebud ass innocently clenched as his finger rimmed it. Have mercy— this dog had gone to heaven. He lowered his face to take a long swipe. Starting at her clit, he dragged down over plump folds, briefly he dipped into her tender opening then up the delicate membrane separating it from her ass.

Lauren squealed and rolled over to face him. "Romeo, what are you doing?" she demanded.

"Getting your attention," he innocently responded.

"What? You don't think you have a woman's full attention when she spreads her legs as wide as possible for you?" Lauren demanded.

"I wanted you to talk to me," he defended himself. The almost petulant response made her laugh outright.

"I thought men didn't want to talk after." She gasped as he

crawled up her body, dropping a kiss on each nipple as he passed them.

"You thought wrong," Romeo mumbled into her neck. Her legs shifted out as he settled his big body over her.

"Hey," Lauren sputtered. "We're talking, remember." His cock rested on the damp folds of her as he shifted himself around to get fully comfortable. Most of his weight was supported on his elbows but his lower body sought nature's cradle between her hips. His powerful legs adjusted out, spreading hers even wider to accommodate him.

"We are talking, baby. I just need to be sure I have all your attention." Romeo grinned down at the suspicious face she turned up to him.

"Okay, what are we talking about?" Lauren wanted to know. "I have the distinct impression you're pinning me down to tell me something you're afraid to again."

"Yeah, well, you know me too well already. I just thought we should discuss the fact that, well, I lost my mind a few minutes ago." Romeo sobered as he regarded her. "I'm sorry, baby. I should have been gentle the first time."

"Ah, you're apologizing because you think you should protect me from an experience like that?" Lauren questioned.

"I'm apologizing because I behaved like an animal. It won't be like that next time, I promise. Even if it kills me, I'll go slow, sweetheart. Please give me another chance."

"Is it always like that for you?" she asked.

"No." Romeo glanced down and swallowed roughly. "I, ah, I've never quite felt like that before. I don't know what came over me. I've never lost it and gone berserk. Honey, I'm really sorry," he ended sincerely.

Lauren grinned up at him. "Never?" she pressed.

"No." Romeo frowned as her slender legs slowly slid over his to wrap around him.

"I'm the only woman who's ever made you lose control?" she purred softly as her fingers threaded through his hair.

"Yeah, and you can stop that right now," he warned as her body shimmied under him. The motion moved his dick to the opening of her cunt. She had to be sore—he knew he couldn't have her again so soon.

"We have more talking to do, woman," he stated firmly as he readjusted away from temptation. "The thing we haven't mentioned yet is, I didn't, ah, I lost my mind as I said and didn't, ah, there wasn't—"

"Condom," she interrupted him. "The word is condom. Nope, you didn't put one on, did you? Is that a regular omission for you?"

"Shit NO! I've never entered a woman without one before. Never! I mean, it just doesn't happen." He rushed on as she opened her mouth. "I want you to know that the doctor told me about them having to rebuild your pelvis. I know you weren't physically a virgin because of all the surgery. I also know you can't deliver a baby because of the pins in your hip bones. Honey, I think it's too soon to have kids, but if there is one, we'll handle it together. You have to believe that. Do you?" he questioned worriedly.

"Am I allowed to talk yet?" Lauren raised her brows.

"For God's sake, talk!" he demanded.

"First, my doctor talks a hell of a lot, but I forgive him this time. Second, I'm relieved to hear I'm the first. Third, I'm on the Pill."

"The Pill?" Romeo repeated darkly. "Why?"

"Well, I was dating someone, for quite a long time actually. As we can both attest to, you can't ever be sure of when emotions are going to explode. Naturally I thought it might be a good idea to take precautions," Lauren explained.

A growl rumbled up Romeo's chest. "Yes, well, isn't it lucky Carla got you out here in the nick of time?" he bit out.

Lauren cocked her head. "Are you mad that I'm on the Pill?"

"No," he snapped.

"Then your fists are clenched in my hair because . . . ?" Lauren trailed off as she watched him visibly try to relax.

"I am not mad," Romeo stated. "I'm tense."

"Oh, I see. The big difference between those two escapes me at the moment. Explain it to me," Lauren invited.

Romeo huffed and glanced away from her. "I am tense because you thought about sleeping with that man."

"Excuse me!" Lauren gasped. "Correct me if I'm wrong, but aren't you like the embodiment of sexual experience? Can you even count the number of women you've actually nailed, much less thought about?"

Romeo pressed his pelvis into her as she started to squirm out from under him. His hands gripped her head as he turned her angry face to his. "You're right, Lauren. I am the last person on earth who has any right to say that. I'm not proud of it. You asked me a question and I answered honestly." His sincere face mollified her and she stilled beneath him again.

"Honey, I'm going to start apologizing right now. I am jealous of any man you look at. I am not rational about it. I will try to control it, but as of right now, I hate it that you thought about sleeping with him. I'm sorry if that offends you," he ended quietly.

Lauren smoothed a hand down his face. "Do you have a little black book, Romeo?" she asked quietly.

"Ah, no." He frowned.

"List of numbers on your computer?" she pressed.

"Sort of, my address book is in my hand-held," he confessed cautiously.

"What do you suppose I think about that?" she asked.

"I don't know. I guess you don't like it either. But honestly, I'm not involved with anyone. Even if I was, it'd be over now. This is the relationship I want," he stated firmly.

"Do you want me to trust your word on that?" she asked.

Romeo frowned. Slick little girl had skillfully cornered him with his own words. Regardless of his answer, he'd have to extend her the same trust he wanted from her. Romeo shifted and looked away from her, spitting out a vile curse before he met her eyes again.

"You're a damn dangerous woman. Just so we get all the cards on the table, let me list my faults—I am obsessed with protecting the people I love, obviously that makes me controlling, bossy and now the brand-new fault of jealous. I do not wish to be rational about this but you're gonna make me, aren't you?"

Lauren smiled serenely. "It's time to let go of that old fear, Romeo. You know it is. You can do it and I have faith that you'll understand how it makes everyone else feel."

Romeo scowled and rolled off her. He stared up at the ceiling and shook his head. "You're going to tell me, aren't you? The part about how everyone else feels."

Lauren moved to rest an arm across his chest and her chin sat on it. She grinned at the pout on his face and assured him she would. "Oh, yes. Each and every time."

He couldn't resist touching her for long. His hands glided up and down her slender back as he looked into those laughing eyes. "It might take a while to rehabilitate me," he stated darkly.

"I am willing to invest the time in you," she promised seriously. "I have faith in your ability to learn. Given the right incentive, that is." Lauren knew the play was taking a huge step into commitment. It wasn't really the risk she'd thought it would be. He'd convinced her somewhere in the kisses and phenomenal lovemaking that this sort of thing didn't happen very often.

His eyes crinkled but the smile remained hidden on his lips as he continued. "It's taken me fifteen years to get this way. I'm sure correcting old habits will take longer than acquiring them."

"Mmm, so you're saying we can't be sure for another fifteen years?" Lauren frowned.

"Nope, I think you need to double the time to get rid of something. Then it's a good idea to be cautious for another twenty years at least. Yeah, this could take as long as fifty years, sweetheart."

Lauren laughed. "I suppose you'll put me up for at least that long. Do you think you can find the room?"

Romeo rolled her over and kissed her long and hard. When they were both gasping for air, he raised his head and grinned down at her. "Sorry. Not an empty room in the house. You'll be bunking with me."

Lauren cradled his face with her hands, her smile faded as she gazed at the striking bad boy leaning over her. "I need to be sure about this. The feelings between us are new and untested. I need you to keep your promise, the one about dating. Can you do that?"

Romeo searched her eyes. In them, he found a scared little girl who wanted to trust him but still wasn't sure she could. There was the woman who'd taken her first steps into intimacy and didn't know what to do next. Primarily there was a sweet, giving spirit that he wanted to gather into his body and protect at all costs.

"Lauren, I will keep every promise I ever make to you or die trying. We'll take all the time you need, baby. As long as we are both clear that the relationship between us is exclusive and intimate, I'll probably do any damn thing you want. What I will not do is leave you. Do you understand what that means?" He kissed her palms as her hands drifted down his face to rest on his broad shoulders.

"Explain it to me," she invited.

"Wherever you are, that's where I'll be," Romeo explained. "If you need to be at your place near the specialists, that's where we'll live. If you'd like to move to the ranch, that'd be great. We don't have to get married right away but, honey, I want my ring on your finger. Can you do that for me?"

Lauren smiled into his serious face. "Aw, how sweet. You want to mark your territory."

Romeo grinned back at her. "Damn straight. I hope you're willing to lift weights 'cause the rock on that little finger is going to weigh you down. If it can't be seen at twenty paces, it's too damn small."

Lauren chuckled. "Careful, big guy, don't make me a target for muggers and desperate criminals."

"Oh, you'll have all the security you need, angel face." Romeo dipped down to sip at that smart mouth because he couldn't resist it. "I'll be right next to your luscious body at all times. They want the rock, they have to go through me."

"Mmm, so now you're a bodyguard?" Lauren teased as she twirled a lock of his hair in her fingers.

Romeo was licking down her neck when he grinned into her flesh. "Guarding this body has just become a career for me. I'm very serious about my duties. Don't interrupt me, woman."

"Well," she murmured. "I've heard about your guarding me, wanting me, being jealous of me, marrying me and moving in with me. There is one thing I haven't heard."

Romeo looked up sharply, his eyes narrowed as he surveyed the lovely face watching him so carefully. His body slid off to the side of her as he considered this turn in the conversation while sitting up slowly.

Lauren sucked in a breath as he voluntarily removed himself from bodily contact. He sat back against the headboard and gazed out the window. Lauren didn't move as she waited for him to speak.

Taking a deep breath, he started talking in a quiet voice. "I was a fully self-sufficient man until you stepped out of that death trap Carla drives. I'm the one whose world came to a screeching halt the first time big blue eyes met mine. You were looking at the dog. I'm the guy willing to beg just for you to sleep in the same room with me. You wanted to call it a fun time and be done with it."

He turned his head and looked down at her with a gentle

smile. "I'm not complaining, baby. It's not your fault—you didn't do one thing to trap me. The fact that your little hands hold my world, that you are as necessary to me as the air I breathe, is my problem. I haven't told you I love you because I couldn't live if you looked at me with doubt or worse, pity." He grabbed her hand and squeezed it as she opened her mouth to respond. "No, let me explain this. You don't have to say anything."

Lauren frowned but nodded.

"I'm a confident guy, sweetheart. But that doesn't mean I'm not scared shitless every time I look at you. You're a beautiful sparkling spirit who's suddenly discovered the big wide world. What if you decide you want to explore it by yourself? What if being your first means you want to know what the second would be like? I'm not strong enough to say 'Go play, I'll be here when you decide to settle down.' I need you too much. My heart has spent a lifetime searching under every rock and around each corner for you."

He brought her palm to his lips and kissed it. "When I hand you my heart on the 'I love you' table, I'd like to be reasonably sure you want to exchange yours as well. I'm willing to earn that from you. I'll do the time it takes to get you to look at me, not the dog."

Tears streamed down Lauren's face. "You've got to admit, the dog is scary. How could I know the guy who owns him is *actually* the big bad wolf?" she whispered. Looking into his serious face, she saw a man who'd protect and guard forever. He'd try to hide it for her, but there was no doubt in him over what he wanted. She considered her meager experience with men. It wasn't like several hadn't indicated interest, she'd just never been interested back. Not enough to do anything about it at least. This tidal wave of emotion he drowned her in, was it the real thing?

All she had to judge it by was the practical knowledge that love was never selfish or mean, or thoughtless. He'd passed that test with flying colors. He not only passed but also added dizzying sexual hunger and a freaking astounding ability to satisfy it. Was she willing to walk away from this? *NO* echoed through her mind with resounding finality. If this wasn't the real thing, she'd no desire to figure out what was. It couldn't be better than this.

Romeo laughed softly. "Perhaps you should pay more attention to the drool on my chin, baby, I'm the one salivating over you."

Lauren blinked and grinned with him. "When do you suppose we can sit down at the 'I love you' table? I'm not sure I can do the time to earn it. I've just discovered the big wide world, you know, it's hard to walk past it without touching."

Romeo closed his eyes and leaned his head back against the headboard again. "If we go there, Lauren, I'll never let you go," he warned her quietly.

"Aren't I a lucky girl," she purred. "First time out of the gate and I get the grand prize." A curvy little body slithered up the expanse of tense male sitting on the bed. Firm thighs straddled his hips as she situated herself in his lap. Round breasts pressed against the hard planes of his chest when arms wrapped around his neck. Butterfly kisses peppered his face. His hands couldn't remain at his sides. Suddenly steel bands wrapped around her and he was crushing every inch of her into him.

"I love you, Lauren." Romeo groaned as he buried his face in her hair. "Please let it be enough, baby."

The world shifted as she turned her face into his neck and felt her soul sink into its new home. He completed her in ways she'd never known were incomplete. He was tingling excitement and the perfect serenity of a safe harbor. There was no doubt or fear, just a sigh of intense pleasure as the future filled with every fantasy the little girl had missed opened before her. How could she ever have thought she wanted to do them alone?

Lauren laughed shakily. "I love you, Romeo. Now don't make me get rough with you. I need a lot more instruction on the care and maintenance of the big bad wolf. Between the two of us, you're the one most likely to get bored."

"Okay," he agreed. "We'll start with the 'Worship Him' lesson and move right into 'Obedience and Compliance.'" He was already lowering her to the bed, kissing her deeply.

"Start wherever you want," she whispered as his lips moved down her throat. "We'll still end up in the shower eventually. Don't forget what happens when I get pissed."

"Sweet Jesus, I live for your little cat fits," he agreed reverently.

Hurt So Good

Lisa Renee Jones

Prologue

SHE WANTED HIM, AND she planned to have him.

He oozed sex and power. Tall and dark with shoulder-length black hair. The minute he'd entered the clinic, her eyes had locked with his. She'd felt heat rocket to her thighs, burning a path to her core. Raw with blatant sensuality, his eyes dropped to her cleavage, lingering and then lifting. She knew he wanted to fuck her.

Her brow lifted. A silent challenge. What was he willing to do about it? He smiled at her. A bring-it-on kind of one-dimple job. And she knew the only cure for the sizzling need this stranger evoked was hot, behind-closed-doors sex.

It was only minutes later when she knew he was alone in his room that she acted on her need. Entering his examination room, she shut the door and leaned against it. Watching him watch her. Her eyes dropped to the crotch of his pressed black pants. She could see his cock pressing against his zipper. As hard as she was wet, it was clear they both felt the power of nameless, potent lust.

She'd never seen him before today. Somehow, it only made the encounter more erotic. A forbidden interlude was what they would share. Her body pulsed with sensations she knew he could easily turn to ecstasy. And he would. It was in his deep, blue eyes . . . a sensual ability to please.

Eyes glittering with intent, his gaze slid along the lines of her body, lingering at her hips and breasts. Her nipples tingled with anticipation, pressing against the lace covering of her bra. His perusal was bold and hot, as if he'd touched her with his hand rather than by sight.

Her lips parted slightly, a long, blond strand of hair falling over her cheek. His shoulders were wide, his chest impressive as it stretched over the rippling muscle she would soon have beneath her palms. Pressed to her body.

"Hard to believe a body like yours is injured," she said, a husky quality to her voice. "I might not be able to take away the pain, but I know how to make a hurt feel oh, so good." She paused for effect. "I promise."

He pinned her in a stare, eyes narrowed with questions but still hot with obvious interest. "Who are you?"

"I'm your physical therapist."

His eyes narrowed. "But you're not in scrubs. You're dressed like a nurse."

The tip of her tongue slid along her bottom lip. She reached for a button on her white blouse and slid it free. And another. "Darn," she said, "wrong outfit. I better take it off." Buttons came free until there were no more. Pushing open her neckline, she knew what he saw. High, full breasts barely covered by sheer lace. But she didn't stop there. Her shirt fell to the floor. Her bra came off next.

The hungry look in his eyes turned her on, and her nipples ached as they tightened, begging for his hands and his mouth. But yet, she loved this little game they were playing. "Like what you see?" she purred.

"Yes," he said in a deep, low voice, his gaze lifting to hers. "Show me more."

Pleased to comply, she reached behind her, sliding her zipper down before letting her skirt drop to the floor. That left her standing before him wearing white lacy panties and thigh highs.

She stepped forward, ready to feel his hands explore her body. Positioning herself directly in front of him, she reached for his shirt. He sat there, unmoving as she undressed him, shoving his shirt over his shoulders, hands trailing over the muscles. The move thrust her breasts closer to him, the warmth of his body and the power beneath her palms making her burn with anticipation.

Her hands settled on his shoulders, but he still didn't touch. Then he surprised her. The control became his.

"Tell me what you want," he ordered.

Eyes locking with his, the fire of lust was almost too much to bear. "Touch my breasts," she whispered.

"Whatever you want," he said, a tease of a smile on his lips as he filled his hands.

She sucked in a breath as he squeezed and then pinched her nipples. "Yes," she whispered. "Lick them."

He pushed the full mounds together, and his tongue lapped one and then the other. Teeth scraped. Mouth suckling. Her hands went into his silky hair, her moans begging for more.

"You like that, do you?"

He was looking at her, tweaking her nipple roughly, but oh so perfect. She bit her bottom lip with the pleasure of the moment and nodded.

"So do I," he said, lowering his head to taste her again. "So do I."

Suddenly, he stood up and she found herself bent over the examination table, her ass in the air and his warm hands exploring. Without warning, his fingers slipped beyond the silk barrier between her thighs, pressing into the slippery proof of her arousal.

"Damn, you're wet, woman," he murmured, hunger in his voice. His finger slid inside her, but she knew he was unbuttoning his pants. She could hear him and feel the movement.

"Yes," she whispered, arching as he hit a sweet spot. "I want you inside me."

His hands went to her hips, her panties yanked down her legs. She kicked them away, wanting what came next. His fingers slid along her sensitive flesh, preparing to enter her. And then he was there, his cock sliding inside her body, pushing deep to her core. She cried out.

"Ah, yes," he half groaned, moving from side to side as if he could get an inch deeper.

Then he pulled back, lingering with just the head of his cock inside her. She cried out, frustrated, needing him inside her. And then he thrust hard and deep. "Yes!" she cried out. He felt so damn good. So hard. She closed her eyes, arching into him. And then he was over the edge, pounding her with stroke after stroke of breathtaking pleasure. Pleasure swirled in her center, the tiny beginning of orgasm pressing close.

But then a loud beeping noise made her freeze. He started to pull out of her. "No!" she screamed, needing him, needing this. He was so hard, and she was so close.

And then everything was black. But the noise kept ringing in her ears . . .

KELLY MARSHALL BLINKED, THE sound of her alarm clock inching into her mind with the reality of a new day. "Oh, hell," she said, feeling the wetness slick between her thighs. "Not another sex dream!"

Beating the pillow, she rolled to her side. What in the heck was wrong with her? She never, ever, acted like she did in those dreams. She hadn't even had sex in damn near two years.

She frowned. Was this some way her body and mind had teamed up on her to tell her she had gone too long without a man?

"H<small>E ASKED IF HE</small> could kiss my feet."

Kelly's fork stopped with lettuce dangling just out of reach of her now gaping mouth. "He did what?"

Stephanie Archer, her best friend since grade school, grinned and nodded. "Yes he did. Can you imagine?"

The fork went down on the plate, all thoughts of food forgotten. "I hope you told him to take his freaky ass hiking."

Stephanie's grin turned wicked. "I'd had a few drinks and a pedicure that morning so I figured, what the hell? I mean he was hot."

Kelly's eyes went wide. "Tell me no."

She nodded, looking incredibly pleased with herself.

"And?" Kelly demanded, shoving her long blond locks behind her ears in earnest.

Her eyes went all pleasure filled. "I never knew feet could be so incredibly erotic. The way he acted, as if he was holding something precious, and then gently kneaded the arches. God, by the time he kissed my foot, I thought I was going to go nuts."

Images of feet, ugly, stinky, gross feet danced across her brain. "I can't believe this. Feet are not erotic. They're gross."

Stephanie made a face. "Not mine, darling. Mine are sexy."

Waving off the comment, because in her book nobody had sexy feet, Kelly moved forward with her questions. "Then what happened? I mean he kissed your foot, and?"

"Feet, as in both of them. Then he took me to his place and gave me the best damn orgasm of my life. I'm seeing him again tonight."

Kelly dropped back against her chair. "God, my life is boring."

Stephanie leaned forward, a challenge in her eye. "What are you going to do about it?"

KELLY GLANCED AT THE clock as she went to check on one of the patients, Mr. Martinez. She'd worked at the clinic for years, and it seemed today was like most. Jose, the bilingual physical therapist, was late coming back from lunch.

Again.

"Hola, Mr. Martinez."

He waved, showing lots of teeth. "Hola." Then he continued to speak a string of Spanish of which she understood not one word.

Kelly blinked. Forcing a smile, she called out across the room. "Hey, Jenn, where the heck is Jose?"

Jennifer Knight, a staff therapist like herself and Jose,

walked into the fitness room and rolled her eyes. "You expected him back on time?"

Kelly made a face. "What am I supposed to do? I don't speak Spanish."

Jennifer grinned, showing her perfect white teeth. She was young, maybe twenty-two, with cute, girl-next-door-type looks. "I can. I've been dating a guy who's teaching me." She walked to stand next to Kelly. "What do you want him to do?"

"I need to test his range of motion."

Jennifer nodded. "Got it." She looked at Mr. Martinez. "Tocame."

"You just told him to touch you." It was Jose.

"What!" Jennifer exclaimed. "No. I said bend your knees."

Jose shook his head. "No. You told him to touch you."

Jennifer covered her gasp with her hand. Jose and Mr. Martinez exchanged words in Spanish and they both laughed. Jose struggled to stop laughing. "Good thing I got here when I did," Jose said.

Kelly shot him a go to hell look. "You should have been on time."

"Yes, Ms. Perfect," he taunted her. "I will try and live up to your standards. Unfortunately, the rest of us here in this world are human."

Jennifer acted as if she heard nothing. "I still can't believe I said that to Mr. Martinez." Hearing his name, he smiled at her, a little too eagerly. "I'm so embarrassed."

"He's not," Jose said. "He was more than willing to follow instructions."

"Grow up, Jose," Kelly said shortly. "We have real patients here, needing real care, on time."

Jose glared at her. "You know what your problem is?"

Kelly knew he was about to tell her. Rather than listen to his rants, she answered for him. "You. You are my problem."

Jose let out a snort and a laugh. "You're so damn school-girl proper, you put everyone else on edge. This place would be completely different if you weren't around."

Fighting the impact of his words, ignoring the emotion spiraling, she focused on the more important thing. "You have a patient and you're talking like a sailor."

Jose sneered. "He doesn't speak English."

Kelly fixed him in a hard look. "He knows we're arguing."

"Mr. Martinez is fine. Let me do my job my way. Go straighten your desk or butt in someone else's affairs."

Kelly opened her mouth and then shut it again. Sparring with Jose wasn't abnormal, but something about his words hit home this time. A dull discomfort settled in her stomach.

Without another word, she turned on her heels and walked toward the kitchen. Thinking a sugar rush might do her good, she opened the refrigerator and pulled out an orange soda, her favorite drink. She always kept a case at work.

Turning to lean on the counter, she found herself facing Jennifer. "Sorry that turned so nasty," she said as she sat down in a chair by the break table.

Kelly sighed and sat down across from her. "Yeah, well, he and I have never gotten along."

Jennifer studied her closely. "When was the last time you went out and had fun?"

Kelly stared at her drink can. The truth was, she couldn't remember. "You know I'm saving for med school." She was twenty-nine. School at night had made her education go slowly. But she had only two classes left and then she could take the MCAT entrance exam. Once she passed she was off to school.

Her savings account was almost big enough, along with student loans, to get her through med school.

"Yes," Jennifer said, "but that doesn't mean you can't relax a little here and there."

Kelly bit her bottom lip. She needed some fun. Actually, a man was feeling necessary. All those damn dreams had her all wanting. The problem was, she was obsessed with not becoming her mother.

Kelly cringed just thinking of the wild way her mother lived. It was all fun and no focus on family or a future. Five stepfathers had come and gone like a lightbulb. In the end, they all burned out.

"It's Friday. I'm going to this really neat club downtown. Why don't you come with me? It'll be fun."

"I don't know," Kelly said, but she wanted to say yes. It had been so long since she had done anything for fun. Surely one night wouldn't turn her into her mother. Still . . . losing focus was bad news.

"Come on," Jennifer said with a plea in her voice. "Come with me. You deserve one night of fun."

What could one night hurt? She needed it. "Yes, all right. What time and where?"

LEANING ACROSS HER BATHROOM sink, Kelly pressed her lips together, smoothing out her pink lipstick. An inspection of her image followed. Dressed in a black skirt she had bought one day on a whim a good two years back, she showed far more leg than usual.

A black silk blouse complemented the skirt. It showed a lot of skin and clung nicely to her full breasts. It had been a birthday gift from Stef. She made a mental note to tell her she finally wore it.

The doorbell rang, and Kelly did a last-minute inspection, patting her long blond hair. It had been a long time since she had felt sexy. Tonight she felt like a woman, and it made her smile.

The doorbell rang again.

Kelly turned off the bathroom light and grabbed her purse. She was going to enjoy herself and not let the future get in the way of the present.

For one night, she wanted to live for the moment.

Tomorrow she would get back to the grind of getting to med school.

Tonight, she was going to be a woman having fun. Nothing more. Nothing less.

2

H<small>E STOOD ACROSS THE</small> bar looking like an invitation into one of her dreams. But his hair was blond and short. In her sleep it was long and dark. This version felt more real. More hands off.

Kelly sipped her Tequila Sunrise, looking over the rim of her glass at his long, muscular body. The man was like the cherry in the bottom of her drink. A single, sweet reward—a bit hard to reach—but oh, so worth the effort.

Only the cherry would come to her once the drink was gone. If only the sexy stranger came so easy. No way could she approach him though she had tried to talk herself into it. He seemed untouchable, a bit elusive. Standing alone, away from the crowd, he seemed out of place.

Several times she had thought she'd felt him watching her, but when she would look up . . . he wasn't. Kelly sighed and glanced around the room. Jennifer had long ago disappeared. Not that Kelly was complaining.

She had danced with her share of men, leaving Jennifer to her own means.

Glancing around the bar, she found the unique structure almost as interesting as most of the men in it. It was named The Aquarium because it sported wall-to-wall fish tanks and had a unique bottle-like structure.

Again feeling watched, her eyes went across the bar, searching. For him. He wasn't there anymore. Disappointment flared. Something about him really drew her attention. All the other men simply filled up space.

With a disappointed sigh, she sat her drink on the bar, deciding it was time to find Jennifer. The night had lost its appeal now that her sexy stranger was gone. Kelly was ready to go home.

She dug out a few dollars from her purse, tossed them on the bar and turned to leave. As she did, she ran smack into the very person she was looking for. "Hey," Jennifer said, steadying herself by grabbing Kelly's arm, clearly a little tipsy. "Would you be terribly upset if I didn't ride home with you?"

"Oh," Kelly said with shock in her tone. "I guess not. Is something wrong?"

Jennifer looked over her shoulder and eyed a young blond man who in turn smiled. "No," she said, looking back at Kelly. "Nothing's wrong."

"Oh," Kelly said again, not seeming to have the ability to say anything more intelligent. "Okay."

"You won't be mad, right?" Jennifer asked, appearing to be genuinely fretful.

Forcing a smile, Kelly squeezed her arm. "No, of course not. Just be careful."

"I'm always careful," Jennifer said with a smile. "See ya Monday."

Jennifer started to turn but Kelly grabbed her arm. "Call me tomorrow and let me know you're okay, will you?"

"Oh," Jennifer said, apparently catching the *oh* disease from Kelly. "Sure."

Then she turned and walked away, stopping to let her male friend put his arm around her. Kelly sighed. Watching the person she came with leave with a guy just seemed to confirm how very boring her own life had become.

She turned toward the door, bumping into a couple with their tongues down each other's throats. A great reminder of just how long it had been since anyone had even put his tongue in her mouth.

"Wonderful," she mumbled, sidestepping the two lovebirds and weaving through the crowd. "Alone and boring."

Silently she added *and horny.*

Once she was out the front door, she only felt hotter. Only this time it was from the heat of the New York night. It was as if it was squeezing her with its strength, reminding her of the cumbersome restrictions of her chosen path in life. She couldn't even manage to go out and just have fun. Tonight she had wanted to let loose and enjoy, and still she hadn't managed to succeed.

Her car was several blocks down from the bar, and though the street was far from deserted, even at one o'clock in the morning it was far from safe. Cautiously she trudged along the pavement, pressing toward her car, holding her key in her hand. The closer she got to her location, the fewer people were near.

Once she was beside her driver's door, she hit her unlock button. She had learned a long time ago that in a city such as this you didn't open a door until you were ready to go through it. No need in giving criminals or dark types a chance to get into your territory.

She was just about to slide inside when a male voice caught her attention. Stiffening, she looked around. Searching for the location of the voice, she scanned, and her eyes caught on a man as he slammed the hood of his car down.

"No way," she whispered. It was him. The man from the bar.

Unmoving, trying to digest the coincidence of the two of them ending up here, on this road, at the same time, she watched him. He paced back and forth and then suddenly stopped dead in his tracks.

His eyes went to hers and held.

Kelly swallowed. She should be afraid. It was the middle of the night, and he was a stranger. But she wasn't. Not at all. Still, what should she do? He obviously needed help. Of course, she knew nothing about cars, and surely he had a cell phone.

Before she could make a decision, he did, stepping toward her, eyes still locked with hers. It was now or never if she planned to flee.

She stood perfectly still.

His walk was etched with an air of confidence, possibly even a bit of arrogance. His eyes were alert, dancing with thoughts she wished she knew.

God, she was attracted to him.

Every line of his body flexed with muscles, lean but de-

fined. He was tall, broad and gorgeous. Her teeth found her
bottom lip as he stopped directly in front of her.

"I saw you in the bar," he said in a voice so deep and sexy
it matched his physical perfection.

His eyes dropped, taking her in from head to toe. It should
have freaked her out, his inspection of her body, but instead, it
only made her feel warm and wanting. He turned her on. She
liked feeling as if she turned him on as well. And she did. It
was in his eyes.

As much as she wanted it to scare her, freak her out, make
her run, it only made her feel lusty. Her nipples tingled, her
thighs ached as wetness dampened her panties.

So he had been watching her at the bar. This little tidbit
felt good. Still, admitting she was looking at him seemed a
risk. Too bold for her. "Which bar?" she asked innocently as if
she hadn't seen him.

He smiled then, a knowing look in his eyes. "You know
which bar."

Damn. She wasn't used to these types of encounters. "Do
I?" she asked nervously.

"Don't you?" he countered.

Okay, games didn't work for her. "Yes," she admitted. "I
suppose I do."

One corner of his mouth tipped upward. "You looked out
of your element."

"So did you," she returned thoughtfully.

He laughed shortly. "I was, and I'm paying the price for
coming. My car's broken down."

She looked over his shoulder toward the fancy sports car.
"Did you call for help?"

He made a frustrated sound and ran his hand through his blond locks. It messed up quite nicely. Sexy and rumpled is how she would describe him. He seemed even more appealing. "I've called three taxi companies but there is a convention in town and I can't seem to get a ride."

Her vocabulary began to shrink again. "Oh."

"Eventually, I'm sure one will show." He studied her for a minute, those compelling green eyes of his making her insides flip-flop. "I'm Mark Majors." His hand extended.

She looked down at it, big and strong, and slowly slipped hers into it. "Kelly Marshall."

The flash of awareness she felt as he touched her was like a lightning bolt in its intensity. This man rocked her to the core. Her eyes flashed with the knowledge, and in his she saw, for the briefest of moments, the same reaction.

Though she wasn't in tune with the dating game, she knew enough to know these types of feelings were so intense because they were shared.

Their hands remained locked. "Nice to meet you, Kelly," he said in a soft, sultry tone that spoke of naked bodies and silk sheets.

The sense of sex floated in the air, and she felt suddenly, overwhelmingly nervous. She tried to inch her hand away. "I, uh, need to go."

His eyes narrowed and then, as if he understood, he released her hand. "I didn't mean to make you uncomfortable."

Fighting the tremble she knew was likely in her voice, she kept her response short. "You didn't."

His eyes dropped to her lips, and she wasn't sure if he saw them trembling. Without warning he took a step backward. "I did. I'm sorry."

She was surprised by his action. She could feel the blood rush under her skin, no doubt making her blush. Tucking a lock of her hair behind her ear, she stumbled through her sentence, not sure what to say. She wanted to stay, but she knew she shouldn't. "I . . . I better go."

Another step backward. "Good night." He turned then and started to walk away.

All common sense fled. Something inside her didn't want him to go. "Wait," she said, taking a step forward.

He turned, looking at her with expectancy in those amazing eyes. His dark brows arched upward. "Yes?"

"How . . . how are you getting home?"

Turning fully again, he surveyed her with curiosity and smiled. "Eventually, I'll get a cab."

"Can't . . . can't you call a friend or something?"

"I just moved here recently," he explained. "I don't know anyone well enough to wake them up in the middle of the night."

Some strange power took over her body. It made her do things she knew were dangerous, wrong and far too risky. Her mouth moved without her being aware of a conscious decision to open it. "I can give you a ride."

A BRIEF INSTANT OF SURPRISE flashed on his face. "Are you sure?"

Laughing nervously, she swiped at her hair. "No, I'm not sure. You're a stranger." She turned toward her car. "Get in before I back out."

Pulling open her car door, she slid inside, not waiting to see if he would follow. It was mere moments later when the passenger door opened and he joined her.

Her hand shook as she shoved the key into the ignition. "I really appreciate this," he said softly, and then lightly, and briefly, brushed her arm with his fingertips. "Don't worry. I'm not some crazy person."

She looked at him then, sensing it was the truth and wanting him all the more for the sensitive way he handled the relaying of the information. Still, her voice trembled as she spoke. "I believe you."

Looking into his eyes, she felt the heat of attraction spike in her blood. "I wouldn't have offered if I was afraid of you."

His eyes narrowed. Slowly, he reached up and touched her cheek with his fingertips, much as he had her arm, only with more tenderness. The impact on her body was like a warm fanning of arousal.

"Thank you for trusting me," he said quietly.

The car felt very intimate, the darkness surrounding them like a silky sheet of seduction. She was alone with this man, a mere stranger, but it made him no less compelling or attractive.

Perhaps it added to his appeal.

"You have beautiful hair," he said, touching a strand and then wrapping it around his finger.

"Thank you," she mouthed, but the words didn't come out in an audible tone. She was too enthralled with the man handing her the compliment.

His mouth drew her attention, full yet strong, inviting yet a bit intimidating. Especially since it was slowly lowering toward her own.

He gave her plenty of time to pull away. Instead, she found herself anticipating the moment his lips would touch hers.

At the last moment, she chickened out, pulling back ever so slightly. Delicately, she cleared her throat. "Where exactly do you live?"

He wasn't deterred, as if he sensed she wanted what he did but needed a bit of encouragement. His hand slid to the side of her cheek.

His eyes searched hers. "Can I kiss you?"

The touch drew her need to the surface, making her want

to reach for him. Her lashes fluttered to her cheeks, battling her urges.

"Kelly?" he asked with a subtle but evident urgency to his voice.

The use of her name in such a familiar way somehow seemed right with this man. Crazy, because she didn't even know him.

Something about him seemed so . . . so what?

So something.

She swallowed, her lashes lifting as she met his gaze. "Yes?"

"I really want to kiss you," he said in a husky voice that told her he was as aroused as she was.

"Yes." This time it wasn't a question.

In the moments before the touch of their lips, time seemed to stand still. Her breath lodged in her throat and her heart pounded in her chest.

She wondered if he could hear it.

The first touch of his lips was soft and ever so slow. Her lashes fluttered as she absorbed the caress, melting inside out.

The distinct feel of arousal, wet and real, dampened her panties. He pulled back, looking down at her, his breath mingling with hers. Then, instead of kissing her again, he surprised her.

He slid his cheek against hers, seeming as if he was soaking in her very essence. It was a tender act, gentle and soothing yet utterly arousing. His lips brushed her ear, nuzzling the sensitive area behind it.

"You smell so damn good," he murmured, his breath warm on her neck.

Her hands settled on his shoulders. "You do too," she said, soaking in his spicy essence of male. "You do too."

He was kissing her neck now, making his way to her jaw and then her chin. Then his mouth slanted over hers, his tongue sliding past her teeth, igniting a passion she barely recognized as her own. Years of suppressing the sensual side of herself had left her charged with needs. And wants. Suddenly, all of these things surfaced. She sunk into the kiss, deepening it to a more sensual level, pressing close to him.

Something inside her just went all hot and needy. Suddenly, not only was her tongue hungrily exploring his mouth, her hands were moving and touching, exploring him with wild urgency. The feel of muscle flexing under her palms only made her hotter. She couldn't get close enough.

He moaned. "Come over here," he said against her mouth, nibbling even as he spoke. His hands lifted her or maybe she did it on her own, but seconds later she was straddling him, her skirt pushed up her legs.

Fervently they kissed and clung. Arms wrapped around his neck, she sunk into him, pressing her chest against his, loving the feel of his hands on her body, touching her and then sliding into her hair.

"I shouldn't be doing this," she said but the words meant nothing. One of his hands had found her breast, kneading gently even as his other hand worked its ways up her thigh.

"Say the word, and we'll stop," he said with a quick brush of his lips across hers before lingering a breath away. "Stop?"

Chest heaving from excitement, she reasoned with herself through the thick fog of lust. There was only the two of them here. No one knew what she was doing. The moment was now, and the need far more than her willpower could stand.

All her good-girl sense had evaporated in the heat of the encounter.

She wanted this man.

Here.

Now.

Tomorrow no one would know, and she wouldn't tell.

She ran her hand around the back of his neck, urging his mouth back to hers. "No," she said urgently. "Don't stop."

Her reward was his mouth, hot and hungry, tasting her, driving her crazy with desire. She felt as if her head was spinning round and round as her body danced with the arousal this man, this stranger, had created and now fed.

Somehow her blouse was unbuttoned, her bra unhooked, and his mouth found her nipple. Suckling lightly, nipping with his teeth, he tormented her with pleasure. Her fingers sunk into the soft strands of his hair as he gently used his teeth to tease one nipple and then the next.

Her back arched as the sensation of his mouth sent the ache between her legs into overdrive. Instinctively, she moved her pelvis to feel the hardness of his arousal more fully.

Responding to the growing need to have him inside her, she reached for his pants. Her hand sought his zipper but instead found his body, hard and ready. Unable to resist, she ran her fingers down the length.

He moaned and reached for his zipper himself, clearly intent on finishing the job she had started. Her hands pressed into the seat giving him room. Only moments later he pulled her back down on him. The thin lace between her thighs, now soaked from her arousal, came into contact with his cock, his hard readiness a tease.

Together they moaned.

He was so hard, and big, and close to being inside her. She hadn't known how much she needed this type of connection until now. Before, it had seemed a shadow of some dream. Her memories of her past sexual experiences had never compared to the intensity she was feeling at this moment.

Was it this man who did this to her? Or was it simply her need for *a* man, *any* man?

Before she could even come close to figuring it out, he made her forget, pushing her thoughts aside for the pure pleasure of the moment.

His mouth found hers, and their tongues touched with new expectations evident in the mating. Each stroke seemed more provocative than the last. Things had changed. The air was charged with the inevitability of the ultimate physical intimacy a man and woman could share.

His hand closed around one of her breasts, applying the sweet, perfect pressure of bliss. "I want you," he murmured against her mouth.

"I want you too," she said and then dipped her tongue into his mouth, stroking it wildly against his. Her hand went between their bodies, finding the tip of his erection.

He moaned again. Against her lips, he said, "I don't have a condom."

She ran her fingers around the ridge of his penis. "I'm safe." Her hand circled his width, and she felt him grow in her palm.

Her boldness was out of character, but it felt good. She wanted to touch him. She wanted to forget tomorrow existed.

Pushing her panties aside, Kelly guided him inside her body. A low growl of pleasure escaped his lips as she slid him inside her. The feel of his hardness inside her body made her cry out.

His hands stabilized her position, allowing her the moment without movement. He kept holding her, balancing her so she could slowly take him inside her.

The instant she had all of him, their eyes locked and held. After long moments, his eyes drifted downward, taking in her breasts and lifting back to her eyes.

He still had on his shirt, and she wanted it off, to touch his chest, to feel his skin.

But it was too late for that. He was buried deep inside her, and she needed to move, to feel his hard length as it stroked her inner core.

The place of her biggest need.

Responding to that feeling, she pressed down on him. It was as if he had been waiting for the green light. His hands moved around her back, touching her with urgency. Their mouths locked in hungry kisses.

And their bodies began a steady rocking, back and forth, up and down.

Kelly clung to him with every ounce of her being, chest to chest, lips to lips, tongue to tongue. Their hands explored, their bodies moved.

It was a slow rhythm that turned quickly to a burning passion of more rapid movement. The pleasure began to swirl around her middle, sending a fog around her brain and moans from her lips.

She'd never, ever, felt this before. Of that she was one hundred percent certain. Everything tingled and cried. She called out. What she said she didn't know.

He stroked her hair, kissed her jaw, moving inside her with growing pressure. With all she was as a woman and a person, she melted into him, trying to turn the building ache into bliss.

A sudden shudder of her body and she dissolved into her own body's release. Ripples rocked her, paralyzed her with their force.

And then they stopped, and she collapsed on him only to feel him tense and hear him moan. Then she felt the wetness of his release, and she buried her face in his neck and smiled.

For long moments they sat there, quiet, holding each other, still oblivious to their public location. A horn honked, distant but it was a wake-up call. They both stiffened.

His hand slowly moved on her back. "We better get dressed before we get caught."

She swallowed and reluctantly pulled back. "I have tissues in the glove box." Reaching behind her, she found the napkins from her fast-food run and handed him several.

In silence and tight quarters, they struggled to clean themselves up and get dressed. Oddly though, Kelly found herself comfortable with him. As much as one could be with a stranger you had just had sex with.

She was about to climb back over the seat when he closed his hands around her waist. "I'll drive if you like."

She found herself smiling because in some odd way she knew he was trying to make her feel less uncomfortable about the situation. "All right."

As he put her car into drive, he turned and simply looked at her. His eyes were unreadable, but within moments she felt the heat of their attraction begin to grow yet again.

The ride was silent. The sexual tension thick. As if they hadn't just both had amazing orgasms. By the time they completed the twenty-minute drive to his high-rise apartment, she was just as hot and ready as she had been when she'd first climbed on top of him.

It was crazy. But it was oh, so real. She wanted him. He wanted her. Did she dare stay with him? As she contemplated her options, he stepped out of the car, handing her keys to a doorman. Making her decision for her. Confident, he walked around the car and pulled her door open, offering her his hand. "Come inside with me?"

She looked into his eyes, noting the heat. The desire. A bit tentatively, she slipped her hand into his. The contact sent a shiver of awareness dancing up her arm. Was this what her mother had felt with all men? It was a brief, scary thought. She didn't want to be like her.

She slid one leg from the car and his eyes followed, tracing the length from toe to skirt hem. All thoughts of her mother were gone. Consumed by what this man did to her with a mere look, she slid her other leg to the ground. He guided her to her feet, pulling her close. Almost thigh-to-thigh, she felt his body heat, scorching her with desire.

"Well? Will you come inside with me?" he asked again, his voice soft and seductive.

"Yes," she said, but they both already knew her answer long before she spoke the words.

His fingers brushed at loose strands of her hair, delicately touching her forehead. "Good," he said softly.

Then with a touch of his lips to hers, he said, "Shall we?"

Mark loved living on the twenty-fifth floor. The ride to the top was spectacular at night. Lights twinkled below, easy to see through the all-glass elevator.

Kelly stepped to the windows, looking out at the city, obviously enthralled at the vision it offered. Sharing his enjoyment of the view made him smile. Something about her simply fit him. Stepping behind her, he slipped his hand around her waist and flattened it on her stomach. The move brought his pelvis to her backside. And just that easy, he was rock hard again.

His nose found her neck and hair. She smelled like flowers. Jasmine perhaps, soft and sweet. Never before had any woman cast such a spell on him. And it wasn't just the great sex in unexpected places. Even before they had gotten intimate in her car, he had planned to take her back to his place.

Something he never, ever, did with women.

His home had always been his castle. He considered it his private escape. No woman was allowed entrance. Yet he hardly knew Kelly and wanted her here with him, in the midst of all he considered sacred.

"It's beautiful," she whispered, melting back against him as if she knew she belonged there. In some far corner of his mind, he wondered if she did.

Pushing the thought aside, knowing it was too outrageous to contemplate, he focused on the moment. "Yes," he said, nuzzling her temple. Moving to New York away from his family had been hard. "I love this view. Actually, I love this city."

He paused, considering. Should he ask where she lived? He wanted to know. Several seconds passed as he contemplated. No. Not yet. He didn't want to scare her off. And something told him she could run with one wrong move. She wanted him, but there was a low vibe of fear in her. Not of him. But it was there. Very alive, ready to make her dart.

He absolutely did not want that to happen.

The elevator stopped, signaling his floor. Silently, he took her hand, leading her toward his apartment. Once they were inside, he flipped on the light.

"Would you like something to drink? Wine perhaps?"

She nodded, her hands twisting together, making her seem a bit nervous. But, he noted, watching her eyes scan the room, it didn't keep her curiosity at bay. She was trying to be discreet, but she couldn't quite pull it off. Her eyes kept catching on things and hanging for long moments.

Finally, she said, "Wine sounds good, but it's late. Maybe coffee?"

He liked her answer. It confirmed what he had already

thought. This was no party girl. She was at the bar, out of her element, just as he had been. As an architect, it had been his first chance to see his creation come to life. He'd sketched the first design for The Aquarium on a restaurant napkin. It had been his vision, but so far away he'd never seen the final product.

He smiled at her. "Coffee it is on one condition."

Her head tilted. "Which is?"

"You come into the kitchen and keep me company while I make it."

She smiled, soft and sweet. "Sure. I'd like that."

This was definitely not some wild party animal woman. No. She was so much more. His experience with her in the car had been a one-time thing. He felt damn lucky.

Once they were in the kitchen, Kelly leaned against the counter and watched as he ran water in the pot. "I drink a lot of coffee," he told her, slanting a quick smile. "Working long hours makes it a necessity."

He thought she would ask what he did for a living so he could ask her as well. But she didn't.

"Any excuse to drink coffee works for me," she said. "It's my one addiction. Where do you keep the cups?"

He wondered why she wanted to stay so impersonal. Was he wrong about the strength of their attraction? "Above you to the right."

She turned, reaching over her head, and he couldn't resist moving in to touch her. He closed the distance and settled behind her as he had on the elevator. Hands on her hips, he felt her sink back to her feet from her toes. Slowly, her head fell back to his shoulder.

"Who are you, Kelly?" he asked softly, his mouth near her ear.

Her reply was a mere whisper but loaded with something raw and pained. "No one special."

His heart raced with her answer. She meant the words. "What if I say differently?"

She turned in his arms, looking at him, searching his face, hands on his shoulders. "Don't," she finally said. "Kiss me instead."

He opened his mouth to tell her she was truly something special. He felt it deep down inside. But she pushed up on her toes and pressed her lips to his, seducing him with the softness of her perfect mouth.

They kissed and the simmer of passion so evident between them began building into a heat wave of desire. Her arms wrapped around him. Her hands trailed his back, his sides and his hips. When they reached his ass, he felt it in his cock like an instant charge of desire.

In one fluid motion, his hands closed around her waist, and he lifted her to the countertop. Without hesitation, he gently nudged her knees apart and stepped between them.

Suddenly they were kissing, but more passionately, tasting each other with a hunger bred of pure, unadulterated lust. He filled his hands with her full breasts, loving how well they fit in his palms, high and firm and exactly the right size.

She reached down and grabbed the hem of her shirt. Their eyes locked and held. What he saw in those beautiful blue eyes took his breath away. She was acting out of her normal character. There was a hint of trepidation in her gaze and perhaps even a bit of nervousness. But he also saw a definitive pleasure.

She liked stepping beyond her normal boundaries and rules.

His hand slid to her cheek. "You're beautiful," he whispered, wondering why he'd talked himself out of approaching her at the bar.

Her lashes fluttered to her cheeks and then lifted. Shyness now in her eyes. "Thank you." She paused and then tugged at his shirt. "Now take this off."

"I'll take mine off if you take yours off," he said with a teasing smile.

She surprised him, her actions not matching the shyness in her eyes. Her response was to reach for her shirt and pull it over her head. His eyes dropped instantly to her breasts, covered in only a lacy pink bra. He looked his fill. In the car, he hadn't been able to fully enjoy the vision of her naked body. Rosy red nipples peeked from the lace—the anticipation of having them in his mouth made his body heat rise. His cock pulsed against his zipper.

Before he could act, she reached behind her, unhooking her bra. He could hardly believe he had a gorgeous blonde sitting, bare breasted and sexy as hell, on his kitchen counter. Filling his hands with the lushness of her breasts, this time without restrictive clothing, he pushed them together and then buried his face between them.

As his tongue traced the inner sides of her bosom, his thumbs pinched and teased her nipples. The sound of her soft little moans, and her hands laced in his hair, made him ache to be inside her. A memory flashed in his mind. That first moment when he had slid inside her and felt the silky heat of her body close around him.

God, how he wanted her again. It was as if he never had her.

Her back arched as his mouth traveled along her skin, tasting and teasing. He pulled away, admiring her aroused nipple, wet from his mouth. He lightly blew warm air on it. She moaned soft and sexy like a mating call. She might as well have said fuck me. Damn, he loved those sounds she made. It was like a fantasy come to life. Hot blonde, topless, legs spread, in his kitchen.

He kissed her, sliding his hands up her legs, thigh highs caressing his palms until he found bare skin. And then lace. His finger slid under the material, testing and judging her wet and ready. "I noticed your legs at the bar," he told her, leaning back to look at them, inching her skirt upward.

She stared down at him, eyes dark with arousal, lips swollen and sexy from his kisses. "You did?" she said breathlessly and then gasped as his finger slid inside her body.

Her hands went to the counter, her neck falling backward. His finger slid along her inner wall. "Feel good?" he asked, but he knew the answer. He just wanted to hear her say it.

"Yes," she whispered.

"Look at me and say so," he demanded, sliding another finger inside her.

Her head tilted downward, her eyes heavy with passion. "Yes. It feels . . . good." She swallowed. "But . . . I want to see *you*."

He slid his fingers slowly from her body, and he could feel her disappointment. His fingers rolled her clit. "Sure you want me to stop?"

"Yes." He spread her wetness around her nub. "No. But I want you naked."

He smiled. "Naked sounds like the best idea yet."

Stepping backward, he undressed, her eyes watching him, hungrily exploring his body. He let her. Even enjoyed it. Within moments he stood before her, his cock erect. When her eyes dropped and her little pink tongue slid across her bottom lip, his restraint snapped. Suddenly, he was between her legs, his tongue pressing past her teeth, his hands exploring.

Barely holding himself in check, yearning to slide his cock inside her body, he filled his hands with her perfect, round ass and lifted her. Her arms went around his neck, her long, sexy legs around his waist. She buried her face in his neck, clinging but not too tight. Just right. She did everything just right.

She was an addictive woman.

One he couldn't get to his bed fast enough.

H E STOOD AT THE END of his massive, king-size bed, staring down at the image Kelly made. Something caveman seemed to rise within. A possessive feeling roared inside him, making him want to claim her. To scream, *mine*. A strange yearning to take her now, hard and fast, burned in his body and beyond.

This woman did things to him no other had. But he held back, wanting to show her all the pleasure a woman should experience.

Her blond hair, long and silky, was spread across his pillow. What a sight she made, eyes dark with passion and nipples puckered with arousal, begging for his mouth. She still wore her skirt and heels. He wanted her naked. "Take off your skirt," he ordered huskily.

HER HESITATION LASTED A mere second before she lifted her hips and reached behind her. He watched in mute fascination as she wiggled her hips and pulled the material down her legs.

A piece of sheer white lace, thigh highs, and heels. She was sexy as hell. Reaching for her ankles, he gently urged her to slide down the bed closer to where he stood. When she was close, he picked one foot up and placed it on his chest and then the next. He stroked her calves with his fingers, inched her knees apart, gently caressing her as he went. His eyes traveled upward, between her legs, seeking the spot he so longed to bury himself in, but he'd settle for tasting her.

"Mark?" she said, a hint of uncertainty in her voice.

He looked at her. Hearing her say his name seemed intimate and right. Leaning over her, he reached for her panties and slid them down her body. "Come closer," he whispered as he tossed the skimpy material aside. His hands were back on her calves and he gently placed her ankles on his shoulders, his hands scooped her ass, lifting her for access.

"What—" she started to ask, but he cut her off with his actions. His mouth closed down over her nub, lightly suckling. "Ohhh," she murmured.

Yes. He loved hearing her sounds of pleasure. His finger found her slick folds, sliding inside with an intimate stroke even as his tongue circled her clit. Damn, she was wet. Turned on and ready for him.

It made him hot. He lapped at her sensitive flesh, licking and tasting, and replacing his finger with his tongue. Mimicking sex, he thrust deep and then stroked a soft lick across the outer sensitive skin. Her hips bucked and he knew what she wanted. He suckled with a steady suction, his finger returning to her body, sliding up and down her inner wall.

"Oh God," she whispered hoarsely.

He could feel her stiffen and knew she was close to orgasm. He moved his tongue in circle after circle around her nub, hungry for her pleasure. Her thighs trembled and then she seemed to suck in her breath. Then the walls of her body spasmed around his finger, her release taking her to completion.

Gently, with light strokes of his tongue, he brought her down, making sure she enjoyed every last possible moment.

When she relaxed completely, all tension out of her body, he carefully moved her legs. He was rock hard and ready to be inside her. Having a woman come in his mouth had always been a big turn-on. Tasting Kelly on his lips, driving her to orgasm, was like an eruption of pure lust taking over every inch of his body.

He needed to feel the warmth of her snug around his cock. Knees on the bed, he started a slow slide up her body, hands on her thighs. Kelly was looking at him with heavy eyelids. "That was . . ." She paused as if struggling for a description and lifted her body to rest on her elbows. "Stunning."

He smiled, his hand palming her breast even as his mouth leaned close to hers. "You're stunning. And I really want you right now."

"What are you waiting for?" Her voice breathless.

He settled between her legs, his lips brushing hers before his hand slid to his cock. Sliding it along her dripping wet center, he teased them both, watching her lashes flutter. "Now," she mouthed, her hips arching. "Now."

But he hesitated, wanting to make this last, slanting his mouth over hers and kissing her long and hot. The soft curves of her body pressed into his, intimate and warm, and his body begged to take the intimate path inside hers. There was an intimacy between them beyond simple sex. Something he didn't quite understand. It was so intense—he felt the tingling reality of awareness and connection. In and out, they breathed as one.

Her hand slid to his face. "I want you." Her voice was a soft whisper that trembled ever so slightly.

No longer able to wait, he slid inside her, forcing himself to make his entry a slow glide. For long moments, they rested there, him buried to the hilt in her warm, tight body. Breathing. Feeling. Then a slow rock and thrust began. He pushed. She pushed. It built into a rhythm, their bodies rubbing together, hands exploring.

And he knew when she was close. She moaned and stiffened just as she had before. It pushed him to a new heat level. He thrust hard. "Come, baby," he said with another deep push. Over and over, he pounded into her, needing. Wanting. Driving for more. The slow ride had become a hard rush.

"I . . . am," she half moaned long moments later.

He felt her body tighten, squeezing his cock like a glove. Ripple after ripple, she took his pleasure. And then he shook, exploding with an intense overtaking of release. He shuddered as he spilled himself inside her. She started kissing his neck, hands running along his back. This time she eased him into the after moment. And she was gentle. Just the way he'd been to her.

KELLY FELT A WARM TICKLING on her neck. Her eyes opened with a sudden awareness. For a minute, she was shocked when she saw a sexy man smiling at her. But reality came quickly. The man from the bar. His mouth brushed hers. "Hey."

She wet her lips. "We fell asleep?"

He nodded. "Yes. It's morning and I'm starved. Want something to eat?"

The truth was she was indeed hungry. Her stomach was uncomfortably empty and already starting to growl. But how her one-night stand had turned into breakfast in bed, she didn't know. "I should go."

He nuzzled her neck again. "Stay. You gave me a ride home. The least I can do is feed you breakfast." Smiling at her, his eyes held a plea.

How could she refuse when she really didn't want her time with him to end? "Well, I guess a little something to eat won't hurt."

He kissed her forehead and then he was gone. Lifting up on her elbows, she looked for him. He stood at the front of a huge dresser, wearing only boxers. She absorbed his nicely defined body, taking in his broad shoulders and tapered waist with a hungry stare.

"You can wear one of my shirts," he said as he turned, one in hand.

Kelly quickly diverted her gaze, pretending she was looking around the room. It was actually her first time to even notice her surroundings. Huge oak furnishings filled a large room with a distinctive male décor. The most unique part of the room was the picture collections, all of buildings. She could feel his eyes on her and wasn't surprised when he answered her unasked question.

"I'm an architect. Those are buildings I was involved in the design of in some way, shape or form."

"Really?" she asked in amazement. There must have been

ten pictures in various places on the walls, all unique structures, all different sizes. She pointed at a triangle-shaped building. "Where is that one located?"

"Dallas, Texas, my home state." He walked toward her and sat down beside her, setting a shirt on the bed. "I love that building. When you're inside it, you can see the elevators go up the angled ceilings."

She looked at him. "Amazing." She pointed to another building. "And that one?"

"San Francisco. It's a museum."

Her eyes lingered on the pictures and then moved to him. "You love your work."

"Yes," he said. "I do. Always have. My father was an architect as well. My mother is a geology teacher. The two things actually mingled together well."

"Where are they now?"

"My father died last year, my mother is retired and living in Georgetown, Texas. It's a small town with a lot of retirees. They keep each other busy."

She didn't dare ask how his father had died because she sensed they had been close. "Must be hard for your mother, you moving here and all."

He sighed heavily. "I struggled with the decision. I worry about her."

Instinctively, she reached out and squeezed his hand. "I'm sure she's fine." The touch sent a wave of sensation up her arm. Their eyes locked. Something passed between them . . . understanding, attraction, something deeper. She wasn't sure. Her eyes dropped to her hand and then lifted. Searching his face to see if he felt it too. But she couldn't be sure. His eyes held interest, but how much she couldn't say. Men were almost foreign to her, she dated so little.

"And you?" he asked after a few moments. "What do you do?"

She swallowed. Should she be talking with him like this if this was a one-night stand? And it was. It had to be. "I . . . I'm a med student."

His eyes lit, not with surprise but interest. And, if she was correct, admiration. "That's big. I'm humbled. You're going to be a doctor one day. That takes a special person."

A wild urge to bolt hit Kelly. His words brought her real focus into play. Her career was bigger than her sex life. She couldn't allow herself to be distracted from her goals. This man could easily do that and more. The last thing she needed was to get off track and become her mother.

"I need to leave." She shoved the covers aside and started scrambling for her clothes, trying not to think about how very naked she was. Unfortunately, everything from the waist up was in the kitchen.

"What?" he asked, sounding shocked. "What about breakfast?"

She shook her head, finding his shirt and pulling it over her head. "I need to go," she said, repeating her words.

He reached for her, shackling her wrist with gentle insistence and pulling her toward him. "I want to get to know you, Kelly."

She wanted to get to know him too, but what if she lost herself and her goals in the process? And rarely was the real thing as good as the fantasy. This, here, now, was a fantasy. "I can't do this. Coming here was a mistake."

He stared at her a long moment and then let his hands drop to the bed. He didn't say another word. Instead, he pushed off the bed and walked toward the closet.

Out of the corner of her eyes, she saw him dressing as she did the same. Before she could pull herself together, he left the room, leaving her alone and wondering why she had gone off the deep end. If only she had handled this differently.

Sinking down on the edge of the bed, she fought back tears. Sleeping with a stranger, no matter how wonderful he might be, wasn't like her. Her biggest fear had always been wrapped around this very behavior. She didn't want to become her mother . . . a woman who fell in love with every man she slept with.

She took a deep breath. But she wasn't her mother. Mark was a nice guy. Another breath. The way Mark impacted her emotionally scared her. Feeling anything but physical attraction during a one-night sex frenzy was crazy.

Her first reaction to the realization Mark was someone she could really like had simply been to run. Now she was stuck with her actions and not as sure of them as she had been only minutes before.

Maybe she could change her mind, tell him she wanted to stay.

MARK HUNG UP THE phone after telling the doorman to bring Kelly's car around. He could hardly believe what a damn ass he'd made of himself. How had he mistaken what he and Kelly had felt for each other as something more than one night of sex?

Obviously, Kelly thought nothing of the sort.

Never, ever, was he the one getting serious on his dates. Not because he was adverse to it. No one ever hit the right buttons. This woman did, and she had all but thrown him aside like trash.

Recently, he'd been thinking about what it would be like to have a family of his own. Maybe he'd been ripe for more. Feeling a bit homesick, and very alone, he could have invented his feelings. But somehow it seemed more than that. There had been times in his life he had wanted more, and no one appeared.

This woman, Kelly, she was unique in the way she made him feel. Which was how? He ran a rough hand through his hair and walked toward the fireplace. Resting his palm on the ledge, he let his head drop between his shoulders.

All he knew at this point was she made him feel things he'd never felt.

A soft sound, Kelly delicately clearing her throat, drew his attention. He turned and faced her. She stood in the hall looking confused and a bit nervous.

And absolutely fucking beautiful. Her long blond hair hung around her face, in disarray from their intimacy. The wild way they'd made love. Correction. Had sex. Her eyes were big and luminous. But he'd never know the secrets behind her surface.

Because she didn't want him to.

The thought hurt. And it made him angry. At himself. At her. "Your car is waiting. I called and had it brought up front for you."

For a flash of a second, her face registered shock. But then it was gone, her voice soft. "Thank you." Then she started to say something else and appeared to change her mind, shutting her mouth. She frowned, seeming to fret, before turning and wordlessly leaving the room.

And his life.

M ARK SAT AT HIS DESK, staring at a piece of paper. It shouldn't be blank . . . but it was.

Once again, he was thinking about Kelly. She knew how to reach him, yet he didn't know how to contact her. But she hadn't contacted him and it was driving him absolutely fucking crazy. Not that she'd indicated she would, but he had hoped.

He'd even tried looking up her phone number. But it was, of course, unlisted. Now he just wanted to forget her. Instead, his memories seemed to get more vivid. Tormenting him.

Kelly.

"You better get going if you're going to make it to your doctor's appointment."

Mark looked up to see Carol, his secretary, staring at him, hands on her hips. Though he hadn't known her long, she'd taken on the role of mother hen as if she had known him a lifetime. In some ways she reminded him of his mother, being around the same age and just as fussy.

Dropping his pencil on the desk, he blew out a breath. "I don't see what a physical therapist is going to do for me." Even now his hand felt stiff. It was irritating as hell and a major problem when he needed to draft. He flexed it several times.

"The doctor is going to keep you from having surgery, mister," Carol said quickly, as she had many times since she'd made his appointment. "Carpal tunnel is nothing to mess with. It can ruin your career. You know what your doctor said. You need this treatment. Physical therapy or the knife? You decide."

He let out a breath. "Maybe I need another opinion. I don't have time for physical therapy."

"Maybe you need to take a little time now so it won't cost you a lot later." Her face was stern, as was her voice. "Don't make me get tough with you. Get up and go. I made this appointment late on a Friday so it wouldn't interfere with any of your work. You have no excuses."

Mark had learned a few things since moving to New York. Not a lot but a few. The important things like where to get great pizza. Another critical one . . . never try to win a battle with Carol.

He pushed to his feet, limbs heavy as he gave in to her prodding. "Fine. I'll go."

"Good." She gave a little nod of satisfaction. "That girl from down the hall keeps stopping by to flirt with you. She's on my last nerve. Please tell me you're not interested so I can get rid of her for good."

Mark laughed despite his foul mood. "Yes, please. I wish I

would have had such a service back in Texas." And he wished he could find the cute brunette from down the hall interesting. The problem was no one had interested him since Kelly.

Damn, he wished she would get out of his head.

"Well?"

Carol's voice once again snapped him back to reality. "Well what?"

"Get rid of her? I want a clear confirmation."

"Yes, please," he said, but while Carol was talking about the girl from down the hall, he was thinking of Kelly.

Would someone please get her off his mind?

IT HAD BEEN A MONTH since her encounter with the sexy stranger from the bar.

It felt like a lifetime.

She'd regretted how she departed since the moment she had stepped out his front door. But it had been for the best. That she didn't doubt. Yet she felt an odd sense of loss. Dissatisfaction with her life seemed to grow by the day, thoughts of that night, by the hour. Would she ever find a way to balance a personal life and her goals?

Mark had made her feel things she had never felt before. Now, in the aftermath, she wondered if anyone would ever make her feel that way again. So many times she had been tempted to go see him. But each time she talked herself out of it. The fear of rejection held her tightly. Instead, she wallowed in self-pity and "what ifs." But the more time that passed, the less appropriate it seemed to visit him.

Sitting at her desk, Kelly said a silent thank-you. It was, at least, Friday. Even though this particular one hadn't gone as planned. She'd come into work early to finish her paperwork, intent on hitting the door the minute her last patient left. Usually that meant no later than lunchtime.

But not today, a day she needed to be alone and get lost in her schoolwork. A day she needed to remember exactly why she had isolated herself from the world. A day when working toward her dream would do her good.

But nooo. Somehow she had gotten booked with a two o'clock new patient appointment when they were supposed to close at noon on Fridays.

The sound of a moan broke her out of her self-pity reverie. Kelly's brows dipped. She heard a male voice. It sounded like Jose. "Higher. Ohhh, yeah."

What the heck?

Kelly pushed to her feet, moving toward the sound. It seemed to come from the other side of the exercise room. Her frown deepened. That meant the exam rooms, but she was quite certain there were no patients in the building.

"Push harder, oh, yeah, that's it. Now up and down."

Kelly was now close enough to the voice to know, without a doubt, she was hearing Jose's rather distinct accent.

The door was cracked open to one of the exam rooms, and she could see flashes of movement. Inching her way to the edge of the doorway, she tried to confirm her suspicions . . . that sex was happening right here, right now, in the office.

It was almost too much to comprehend . . . except in her dreams. The thought made her feel a bit sick to the stomach. Perhaps she was just a prude. Maybe other people did those things when they were awake. . . .

After all, she did it with a stranger. In her car. No telling what someone less conservative would do. She pushed the thought aside.

No.

She refused to believe Jose was having sex in the exam room. Surely not. Jose was a lot of things, but stupid wasn't one of them. Lazy, arrogant and a pain in the butt, but not stupid.

If the doctor caught him having sex in the office he'd be fired.

A breathless female voice danced through the air. "I can't keep going."

Kelly went completely, utterly still.

Oh my god. No. It couldn't be.

"I need this, Jennifer," Jose said urgently.

Not Jennifer.

Footsteps echoed in the hallway. Kelly knew the distinctive walk of the doctor's tyrant wife. Heavy footed, she sounded like a drill sergeant, and she was always on the lookout for trouble. Kelly knew she had to act. Not giving herself time to chicken out, she pushed open the exam room door, darted through it and then shut it again. "Get dressed. We have company." Back against the wall, chest heaving, she stared at the sight before her.

"What the heck?" Jose blurted. He was on his stomach, shirtless, but pants still intact. He pushed up on his palms and stared at her, confusion and irritation in his eyes.

Jennifer stood beside him, fully dressed, elbow in his back. She dropped her arms to her sides. "That's it. I'm done. No more free massages for you."

"Hey," Jose said, sitting up. "You owe me. I jumped your car last week when you left your lights on, remember?"

Kelly blinked. "What's going on in here?"

Jennifer rolled her eyes and then rubbed her elbow with the palm of her other hand. "He's impossible to please."

"Are you two . . . um . . ." She couldn't ask if they were sleeping together. The words came out in a forced tone. "Seeing each other?"

Jennifer laughed and then shot Jose a mean look, her expression changing the instant her eyes settled on him. "Not a chance in hell."

Kelly looked from one to the other. "You mean this isn't . . ."

Jose laughed. "Foreplay?"

Kelly didn't know what to say. "I, uh, thought—"

Jennifer made a disgusted sound. "I am so out of here. I have a date with a real man tonight."

She stomped forward, stopping in front of the door as Kelly stepped to the side to allow her exit. Jennifer looked Kelly in the eyes. "Give me some credit, will you?"

Diverting her eyes, Kelly mumbled an apology. When Jennifer continued her heavy stomp toward the exit, Kelly looked at Jose. He smiled. Pointing to his back, he said, "Don't suppose you would—"

Jose was always making sexual remarks. He was a pervert of perverts. "No." Kelly's response was adamant and a bit rude. She shoved her hair over her shoulder and walked out of the room feeling more than a little foolish.

She was almost back to her desk when Jennifer came walking toward her, eyes sparkling with some newfound something. "Your appointment is here. Oh, my God, he is gorgeous. I almost want to say I'll cover for you." She sighed. "But I can't." She bit her bottom lip. "Too bad." Winking at Kelly, she said, "Have fun. I'm leaving. Tell me all about it Monday. I put him in exam room two and hung the doc's notes on the door. He's all ready for his therapy."

Jennifer waggled her fingers and turned to leave, giggling like a schoolgirl. Kelly didn't care how good-looking the guy was, she just wanted out of here for the weekend.

Walking briskly to her desk, she reached for her notes on the new patient. Just as her cell phone rang. Digging it out of her purse, she checked the call ID and answered.

"Hi, Stef."

"Hey, sweetie. You up for lunch?"

"I'm starving but I have a patient."

"It's two o'clock." Stephanie said the words as if it was a crime for Kelly to work past lunch. "You always get off early on Fridays."

Kelly sighed heavily. "I know."

"I waited to eat thinking I could catch you. You must be starved. Want me to bring over a nice big pizza and we can share?"

The very thought of a slice of cheese pizza made her stomach rumble. "Yes," she said wistfully. "That would be wonderful."

"Be there in a jiff, sweetie. Don't keel over before I get there."

The line went dead.

Jose cleared his throat from a few feet away. "Your patient is getting anxious. Says he has to be somewhere at four."

Kelly gritted her teeth. "And you couldn't see him—why?"

He glared at her. "I don't specialize in carpal tunnel. You do." A smart-ass fake smile followed. "Remember?"

Kelly looked down at her notes. Damn. No hope of getting out of this. If only she had eaten before this appointment. Her nerves were on edge and hunger wasn't helping.

Letting out a defeated sigh, Kelly grabbed her file. "I'm going to see him now."

Jose kept glaring. "I'll be up front until you leave. The doctor thinks you shouldn't be here alone."

Kelly snorted. "Like you're any form of help. I need someone to protect me from perverts like you."

"You might be a hottie, but you're too damn cold for me. Latin men like our lovers hot-blooded so consider yourself safe. There's plenty of women around who don't need thawing."

"Whatever," she mumbled as she held her chin high and started walking toward the exam rooms, outwardly ignoring his comments. Unfortunately, she felt every word like a knife in her gut.

Ever since Mark had shown her passion, she had questioned her life decisions or at least her approach to the present, future and in between. Though she had no aspirations to be like Jose, she wasn't sure she wanted to remain as prudish, and without a life, as she had been.

When she arrived at the exam room, Kelly knocked but immediately opened the door, pasting on a fake smile. She wanted out of this office. Her own apartment would allow her the space to think through her current emotional state. Kelly rounded the door and shut it. She turned and then froze.

There, on the table, sat Mark. Her stranger. Her one-night

stand. The man she couldn't forget and had wished a hundred times for another chance to get to know. Now, here he was, in *her* exam room. What was she supposed to do with him?

"Kelly?" he said with as much shock in his voice as she felt. Pushing to his feet, his eyes seemed to trace every inch of her body from head to toes before settling back on her face. "Is that really you?"

M ARK WAS FLOORED. What were the odds of running into Kelly, in a city as big as Manhattan, in such an odd type of circumstance?

She took a step backward. "What are you doing here?"

He countered quickly, not liking the accusation in her voice. "What are *you* doing here?"

"I work here," she declared with a tiny little lift to her chin.

Of course she did. "Doing what?"

"I'm a . . ." She stopped herself mid-sentence. "What business is it of yours?"

"Plenty considering you just walked into my room," he told her, loving the glint of defiance in her eyes. It showed spunk and strength of character. They were bluer than he remembered. Amazing considering how vividly colored they had been in his many fantasies. She was guarded though.

He decided to egg her on. She was taking a defensive stand, so he'd feed it. Maybe a bit of anger would make her talk. People said things when they were mad that they might not otherwise say. "Are you following me?"

"What?" she gasped. "Following you." Her voice inched up a notch. "Following you?" Her finger pointed at him. "You're in *my* exam room and you're asking me if *I'm* following *you?*"

Biting back a small smile, he crossed his arms in front of his body. "Yes, and I want an explanation." Cautiously, he took a small step toward her.

Anger bubbled in her throat, easy to hear in her words. "You want an explanation?" Her voice held utter disbelief. She took a step backward and hit the door.

"Yes," he said, stepping even closer. He was mere inches from touching her. The smell, her smell, had lingered on and on in his mind and danced along his senses in each dream. Now that very smell rushed into his nostrils, flaring an array of sensual memories. "And I intend to have one. What exactly are you doing in my room?"

"Look," she said, her finger poking into his chest. "I'm a physical therapist. I work here. What's your excuse?"

The touch of her finger, even in anger, did crazy things to his insides. She had his attention, rock hard, and standing ready. His eyes went to her finger, and hers did the same. Instantly, her face lost the anger, and a blush rushed into her cheeks.

She started to pull her hand away. "I'm sorry."

He grabbed it. "Don't be." They stared at each other. "I can't believe you're here, now, with me. I had hoped to see you again."

Her eyes searched his with anxiety evident in her expression. "You did?"

"Yes," he said. "I have wished many times you would come by. To run into you like this is almost impossible to believe." He paused, his voice softening. "You're even prettier than I remember."

She swallowed and fidgeted a bit. "Right. I'm wearing blue scrubs."

She would look great in a paper bag. "And the blue brings out your eyes. You look beautiful."

Her eyes fluttered shut, lashes resting against her creamy white skin. He reached up and ran his knuckles along her cheek, gently, a mere caress. "Tell me you're glad to see me too."

Her eyes abruptly opened. "We had sex together. Nothing more."

Suddenly, he realized she did indeed feel what he did but she was fighting it. That unique attraction, so rare and special, was just as real to her. Kelly was afraid for some reason.

He pressed her. "It was more than sex and we both know it." He still held her hand, and he brought her knuckles to his lips and kissed them.

"No," she whispered.

"So it was just sex to you?" he asked, trying not to get angry, fighting the hurt her words caused.

"Yes," she said and then immediately added, "No. I mean—"

His brows inched up. "Yes or no?"

She tugged at her hand. "I don't know. I don't do one-night stands."

"It didn't have to be that. You made it what it was when you left the way you did."

"You called for my car."

"Because you all but ran for the door."

She made a frustrated sound. "I didn't have a choice."

"You did."

"I didn't."

"Why?"

She opened her mouth and then shut it again. He gave her a minute, not pressing, sensing she needed to gain composure. Finally, he gently prodded. "Why, Kelly?"

Her hands moved to his chest, flattening. "Stop crowding me. Step away and leave me alone."

His hands moved, lightly shackling her wrists. "I want to kiss you. Just once."

"No," she whispered.

"Don't you want to know if what we felt that night still exists? Was it a combination of all the right things or was it more? Tell the truth. Haven't you wondered?"

Her eyes fluttered shut and then back open. Her sweet little pink tongue darted across those full lips, and he knew her answer before she spoke.

"Yes," she said softly, her eyes locking with his, her elbows easing so that he could lean toward her. "I've wondered."

JUST ONE KISS.

Kelly needed to know what it felt like to kiss Mark just one more time. It was crazy, stupid, wild, but still somehow a necessity. Maybe the strange coincidence would yield answers. This was her opportunity to find out he wasn't all she remembered him to be.

Finally, she could forget him.

Of course, it was terrible logic, given the fact he already had her skin dancing with warmth. Her thighs aching with desire. Even her nipples tingled. Images of his mouth suckling them, her hands in his hair, made her bite her bottom lip.

Still, a kiss would prove what was fantasy and what was real.

She needed to know.

Her fingers spread on his chest, feeling the flex of muscle under her hand. He wore dress pants and a dress shirt, well pressed and fitted to his muscular form. His attire, all black from head to toe, was a striking contrast to his light hair. He took her hand and pulled her away from the door, his fingers sliding into her hair, cradling the side of her face.

"I can't believe I'm going to kiss you again." His voice was rough and sexy, laced with desire he did nothing to hide. "I thought I'd never see you again."

Looking into his eyes, she felt as if he could see clear through to her very core. And she had no ability to shield her feelings from him because she was too lost . . . falling it felt like.

Staring into his eyes, she saw things that took her breath away. Tenderness, and perhaps true emotional attachment. The heat of passion did nothing to shadow the possibility of more. It was there. Waiting to be discovered.

"I can't believe it either," she whispered truthfully. Even as she said the words she forced herself to discard her prior thought, knowing it was mere wishful thinking. They had shared a night of sex, albeit great sex, but still just sex. To think he felt more for her was pure foolishness.

So why did she want to believe it so badly?

His breath, warm and with a faint scent of peppermint, enticed as he lowered his mouth to hers. The first brush of his lips was like an electric shock in its intensity but no less delicate and sensual.

Gently his tongue stroked hers, erotic in the way it moved. She felt herself sink against him, unable to stop the reaction of her body to his nearness. She wanted to be close.

To this man.

To Mark.

From one stroke of his tongue to the next, something changed. Desire spiked. Their kiss became hungrier, hotter . . . ravishing. Her arms wrapped his neck, her toes lifting to reach him more fully.

His free hand moved along her back, his pelvis pressing into her stomach. He was hard, and she knew she was already wet. A single kiss had proven they wanted each other every bit as much as that first night.

If not more.

There was something so thrilling in the way he tasted her, almost possessively, with a force almost overpowering, yet it remained gentle. She felt herself sink into his spell, a whirlwind of lust and needs that had built over a month, and in some ways a lifetime, took over.

A knock on the door pulled them out of their trance, making Kelly jump with guilt. "Your friend is here," Jose called through the door.

His voice was like a splash of cold water in her face. Her

job, her life and her dreams could all be lost with a single bad decision. She took a step backward. "This can't happen."

"It already did. What are you running from, Kelly?" he demanded in a frustrated tone.

She turned for the door and yanked on the handle but Mark's hand held it shut. "What, Kelly? What are you running from?"

Turning to face him, anger in her voice, she glared. "Let me out of here."

He stared at her for an intense moment. "Fine. Run if you have to."

Kelly flung her hair over her shoulder and tried to tune out his words. She didn't want them to get to her but they did. She knew she'd have to deal with their impact later. Just not now.

Stepping into the hallway, Kelly wasn't prepared for what he did next.

Mark came after her.

Turning on him, hands on her hips, she made an angry sound. "Stop following me. You can't just walk the halls."

"If you can, I can. We need to talk."

"I work here. I can walk wherever, whenever I want to. You can't just follow me because you want to talk to me."

"I don't see why not," he countered almost nonchalantly. "I'm a patient here."

"No. You're. Not." Each word was spoken through clenched teeth. "I refuse to treat you. Besides, even if you were you couldn't just walk around."

His eyes danced with challenge. His voice held exaggerated astonishment. "You'd refuse to treat me because we slept together?"

Her face flamed bloodred as she made a quiet noise. "Keep your voice down."

"No one could hear," he said with a hint of amusement in his voice. "You can't refuse to treat me."

She turned and mumbled under her breath. "Watch me." Her back now firmly in place, she walked away from him, hoping he wouldn't follow.

He did.

As Kelly approached her desk, she found Stef standing there, waiting on her, looking the perfect image of high fashion. She was dressed in a tan designer pantsuit and high-heeled sleek leather boots. As usual her hair and makeup were perfection. Kelly felt like a bag lady in her scrubs.

Stef waved Kelly forward. "Hurry. The food is getting cold. One more second and I wasn't waiting anymore. I'm starving."

Kelly knew the minute Stef saw Mark because her eyes went wide. She had a flash of what her friend must see. Sexy blond Adonis, well-defined body, dressed in a pressed black shirt and pants. He looked like male sex appeal personified.

Damn the man.

She had to get away from him. He was trouble. Whirling on him, she stomped her foot. It was childish, she knew, but it somehow just happened. "Stop following me."

"Stop running," he said with a lazy drawl, "and I won't have to."

"Hello," Stef said to Mark, stepping toward him, smiling flirtatiously. Kelly rolled her eyes. "I'm Stephanie. Who might you be?"

Mark gave her an engaging smile and held out his hand. Stephanie eagerly accepted it. "I'm a friend of Kelly's."

"You're not my friend," Kelly said indignantly. "You're a patient here." She looked at Stef. "He's a patient."

Mark's brows lifted, and a slight twinkle crept into his eyes. "You just told me I wasn't a patient. Which is it?" He paused, clearly letting his words play with her temper a bit. "Am I or aren't I?"

Balling her fists by her side, Kelly all but growled at him. "You are impossible and irritating." She couldn't think of anything else. "And . . . that is what you are."

Stef, gossip queen extraordinaire, had eyes alight. She waved a finger between the two of them. "How do you two know each other?"

Mark looked at her and opened his mouth. Kelly pointed at him. "Don't you dare," she warned angrily.

Stephanie nodded. "Do dare. Please."

Kelly fixed her in an angry stare. "Stop it."

Stephanie was still staring at Mark with curiosity. "Are you Mark?"

Kelly was appalled. Why had she ever told Stef about him? Now her soon to be ex-friend's big mouth made it sound like she had been going on and on about him. She hadn't. At least not out loud. And not to Stef.

She had simply given in to the need to tell her best friend about her one night of bliss.

Mark looked interested now. His eyes went to Kelly, brows raised, and then back to Stephanie. "Well, yes, I am. I take it Kelly has talked about me?"

Kelly's eyes went to his. "Once. I talked about you once. Don't go thinking I've been obsessed or something."

"So you're the guy who finally made Kelly loosen up a

bit?" She looked him up and down, not bothering to be discreet. It wasn't her style. "I see why she was tempted."

"Oh my God," Kelly said, plastering her hand over her face. Mark laughed.

Stephanie ignored Kelly as she pinched her arm. "Stay and have pizza with us, Mark."

"No!" Kelly blurted.

"I *am* hungry," Mark said with amusement in his voice.

"You can't stay," Kelly said.

"Why not?" Stephanie asked.

"Shut up," Kelly bit out angrily.

"I'm hungry," Mark said nonchalantly.

"Go home."

He countered quickly. "Come with me."

Just as quickly, she said, "Not happening."

"Then I'm staying for pizza."

She let out a low growl. "Then I'm going home. Enjoy the pizza." She started toward the door.

"Don't go," Stephanie said, a pout in her voice.

Kelly turned and walked back toward her desk, realizing she had forgotten her purse. She stopped in front of Stephanie. "Move." Stephanie's eyes went wide. "I need my purse." Stephanie didn't move. "Move or I'll move you," Kelly warned, feeling angry and embarrassed enough to do it.

"You wouldn't." Stephanie didn't sound sure.

"Try me," Kelly challenged.

"What's going on in here?" Jose asked from the doorway.

"Move," Kelly said to Stephanie, ignoring Jose.

Stef stared at her a minute, as if trying to decide how serious she was. Abruptly, she stepped aside. "I can't believe you're doing this."

"Believe it," Kelly said, grabbing her purse in a quick move and starting toward the door.

"What's going on?" Jose repeated with frustration in his voice.

Kelly stopped beside him and motioned toward Mark. "Check him out, will you?"

"Why can't you?" Jose complained.

Mark's voice reached out to her. "Kelly."

"What?" she said in a clipped tone.

"I know where you work now. This time you can run, but you can't hide."

His words were a promise. This thing between them wasn't over. And deep down she was happy about it. But just as quickly as she had the thought, she shoved it away. No way. Couldn't happen.

She turned to Jose. "Check him out. Don't give him another appointment." She didn't wait for an answer, walking past him and toward the front door as quickly as her feet would take her. She needed out of here and fast.

Mark watched Kelly leave, knowing he had to let her have some space. What he really wanted to do was go after her, grab her, kiss her and then make wild, passionate love to her.

And he would.

Soon.

"You're good for her."

Stephanie's voice broke him out of his self-absorbed thoughts. His eyes settled on her face. She was a pretty woman but a bit too aggressive for his taste. He liked the way Kelly handled herself. Tough but reserved.

"She doesn't think so."

Stef waved off his words. "She doesn't know what's good for her."

His brow inched up. "But you do, I suppose?"

She nodded and smiled. "You bet. Why don't we eat pizza and talk?"

This could be informative. How could he pass? "All right. Let's eat pizza."

A smile of satisfaction filled her face. "Have a seat." She sat down at Kelly's desk and motioned towards another chair. She grabbed a piece of pizza before he even sat down. Holding it—halfway to her mouth—she said thoughtfully, "Now, I can't give you her address or she'll kill me." She took a bite of pizza.

Mark sat down across from her and watched as her mind worked. He could almost hear the wheels spinning in that pretty head of hers.

She sat the piece of pizza down. "I have an idea."

THE OFFICE WAS DIMLY lit by the open windows.

Kelly didn't turn on any lights. She liked it like it was, sensual and intimate.

He would be here soon, and she was ready for him. She could hardly wait to feel the touch of his hands. The way he so perfectly knew just the right spots to give the ultimate pleasure.

She moaned as they hardened, thinking of his mouth, warm and hot, suckling. Oh, how she wanted him.

Her eyes shut, fluttering lightly, images moving through her mind like a seductive dance. Her hand went to her waist as she imagined his there, sliding up . . . up and then pressed to her breasts. Kelly palmed them, tracing her nipples with her fingers, feeling his hands in the place of hers.

Thinking of his lips, hot and perfect, suckling her hardened nipples, she moaned. Oh, how she wanted, no needed—

A light knock sounded on the door. Her eyes opened, her lips parted. Sliding her hands back down her sides, she knew she was ready. "Come in," she called. Even her most vivid fantasies didn't come close to matching the absolute depth of masculinity he radiated. He stood in the shadows. She couldn't see his eyes, but she felt them like a fine mist all over her body. She wore a black dress, slim fitted and easy to remove.

Stepping backward, she bent a finger and motioned him to move inside. When he did her bidding, letting the door swing closed behind him, she rewarded him.

With several steps still separating them, she unzipped the front of her dress. It ran top to bottom. She slowly moved aside the material that now did little more than decorate her shoulders. She displayed her pink and black lace garter, bra and tiny panties. Sheer, with little coverage offered, she had chosen it to entice. His eyes, now visible, were hot and hungry. He took a step forward, and she could almost feel the hunger in him.

"I want you."

"Show me," she said.

He came another step closer. Just knowing he was about to touch and taste had her sizzling. Anticipation danced along her nerve endings while dampness formed between her thighs.

He came another step closer. She could smell the male spicy scent of his arousal.

His next step brought him within reach. He took one finger and touched her nipple through the silk. So light, the touch teased. Then he moved to her other breast. She sucked in a breath.

He flattened his other hand on her stomach and slowly

slid it downward. His fingers touched silk, and in a quick move he yanked her panties away. He walked them backward, was all the way kissing her while his hand stayed where her panties once were. When her back hit the wall, he lifted her. She grabbed on to him, her hands exploring, finally pushing under his shirt.

But he was too impatient for her exploration and grabbed her hands, pressing them over her head.

"Keep them there."

She blinked, surprised but incredibly turned on. Before she could fully digest how hot she really was, he took her even higher. Her skimpy, barely there bra came off with little more than a moment's effort on her part. His eyes dropped, devouring her. She reached, needing to touch him.

He grabbed her wrists and pushed them back over her head. "No touching," he said, and then his mouth closed over hers. Tongue thrusting into hers, even as he let go of her wrists. She left them over her head. He was unzipping and she wasn't about to do anything to distract him.

And then he was there, his hand lifting her leg high. His cock sliding deep in her body. She cried out in pleasure, ready for more. Needing more. But the pleasure threatened to escape as a loud ringing noise filled the air. Mark plunged deep inside her and started moving, making the intrusive noise start to fade. But only for an instant. The blaring sound got louder and she couldn't think, let alone feel.

Suddenly everything went dark and Mark was gone. No matter how hard she tried she couldn't touch him. See him. Nothing. He no longer held her leg. She stepped forward but he wasn't there.

She wanted him back. No. She needed him. Where was he? Emptiness formed and told her she was alone. "No!" she screamed. "Come back."

But there was no answer. Just darkness.

KELLY SAT UP, HANDS on her burning cheeks. The noise, make it stop. What was it?

Looking around, she realized she was on her couch, not in her office. How? What was going on?

The noise stopped. Her head seemed to clear.

Oh, God, another dream. Of Mark. It was so real, so . . . her eyes went wide. An intensely erotic dream. This was so unlike her. Having sex dreams. Wasn't it?

No matter how hard she pushed him away during the waking hours, her mind and body found him in her sleep.

What did it mean?

The phone started ringing.

Needing an escape from her own thoughts, she reached and grabbed the receiver. "Hello?"

"Why do you sound asleep? I can tell from your voice."

It was Stef. "Do you know how to say hello?"

"Hello. Why do you sound asleep?"

"Because I was," she said with irritation.

"I need company. Come eat with me. I have a great bottle of wine we can split."

"I don't think so," Kelly said, sitting up, brushing hair out of her eyes. "I'm not hungry."

"Red wine and extra cheese. You know you can't resist."

"Extra cheese?" she said weakly. Pizza always made her feel

better, which of course Stephanie knew after years of being her best friend.

"That's right," Stef said. "From your favorite pizza parlor, sweetie. Your favorite. You didn't get any at lunch the other day so I thought—"

Damn, the woman knew how to get to her. "Fine. But I want black olives too."

"You know I hate those things."

"Put them on half."

"They always get them on both sides."

"No olives, I'm staying home."

"Fine. I'll get olives."

Seconds later, they hung up. Kelly sighed and tucked her knees under her chin, the dreams already back on her mind. Was she just like her mother? Was her destiny not to be a doctor but a husband hopper?

She bit her bottom lip. A real relationship was something she didn't really have experience with. The ones her mother had been in made lonely look good. But sometimes lonely felt pretty bad.

So where did that leave her?

Several seconds later, she put her feet to the floor and made an angry sound. Those old feelings of being alone in the world with no one she could really count on had started to surface.

They were familiar feelings but ones she had tucked away in some far corner of her mind quite securely. She needed to get to Stef's place ASAP so she would be too busy in conversation to think.

"Damn it!" she yelled to the empty room because her

stomach had butterflies and her emotions seemed to have wings. She was having a bad case of motheritis, and it was threatening to take hold.

She couldn't let that happen.

SITTING WITH HER LEGS crossed on the living-room floor of Stef's apartment, back against her huge tan sofa, Kelly sipped her wine. A cozy fire burned in the brick fireplace directly in front of her, giving off just the right amount of heat.

Stef was the closest thing to family she claimed, and she felt welcomed and wanted. Two things she had an immense need for as of late.

Having finished off a large slice of pizza, she was ready to dig into another. True to past history, her appetite miraculously returned the minute she got a whiff of the food.

But what she hadn't managed to escape were her thoughts of Mark. They lingered. And they were as potent as if he was in the room with her. Even in her dreams, he came to her. He was like a ghost, haunting her, teasing and taunting. Yet he was worse. A ghost had limitations. Not Mark. He was very much alive and quite impossible to dismiss as a product of her imagination.

"I'm seeing him again tomorrow," Stef said.

Suddenly, Kelly realized Stef had been talking and she hadn't heard a word of what was said. She blinked, and lightly shook her head. "What?" she asked. "Who?"

Stef raised her voice a bit. "The foot guy."

"Oh," Kelly said. "The foot guy." Damn, what had she missed? Oh well. "What about him?"

"You weren't listening." Stef said it with a flat tone.

"Ah," Kelly said, cringing ever so slightly. "I guess not."

Stef rolled her eyes. "Listen, woman. I'm making a major confession here."

Kelly made a face, not knowing what to expect. However, strange as this conversation might get, she was glad for the diversion from her thoughts. "About the foot guy?"

"Jim," she said testily. "His name is Jim."

"Jim," Kelly said, surprised at her friend's irritation.

"I think I love him."

Kelly was shocked. Was a foot massage that good? "What? In love with the foot guy?"

"Jim," she said through clenched teeth. "His name is Jim."

"You barely know him," Kelly said with concern. Stef was an attorney, levelheaded, and though sometimes a bit wild at heart, always rational in thought.

A hint of wistfulness slipped into her tone. "The heart knows."

"Is this about the foot thing?" Kelly asked, needing a logical explanation, no matter how weird it might be. "I mean, do you two share some weird foot fetish that's clogging your brain with lust?"

Stef's eyes flashed. "I can't believe you just said that. I tell you, my best friend, I'm falling in love, and I get treated like some sex freak?"

Kelly felt an instant prick of defensiveness. "I just want to make sure you see things clearly."

"I do," Stef insisted, turning her body slightly to be eye to eye with Kelly. "Maybe you're the one who needs to reassess your thought process."

"Me? What's that supposed to mean?" Kelly demanded, feeling more on edge with every word. "I'm not the one falling in love with someone I barely know."

Stef's cheeks had turned red with anger. "Because you're too damn afraid of getting hurt to take a chance."

The words dropped and lingered in the air with heaviness. Neither spoke for long moments.

"I'm sorry. I didn't mean to blurt that out that way." Stef reached for Kelly's hand but Kelly pulled it back.

"But you meant what you said, right?"

Stef let out a long breath. "I planned to talk to you tonight about this very subject. Just not like this."

"Don't turn this around and make it about me."

"Kelly," Stef said. "I'm not turning this around. You are afraid."

"Am not!"

"You avoid relationships like they are the plague."

"I have a career to think about."

"You hide behind that."

"Whatever."

"Don't whatever me. You pushed Mark away because he got to you."

Kelly moved to her knees, barely fighting the urge to get up and leave. "This is crazy. You think you're in love with the foot guy, and suddenly I have some problem with men?"

"Jim," Stef bit out. "His name is Jim, and I *am* in love with him. The foot thing has nothing to do with it."

Whatever. "This conversation is over or I'm leaving."

"Your mother is her own person, as are you. Just because you like a man, maybe even have sex with him, does not make you a husband hopper in the making."

Kelly didn't like where this was going. "How did my mother become a part of this?"

"You made it that way, not me."

"I don't have to listen to this." Kelly's voice trembled with the impact of the accusation. She started to get up.

Stef's hand came out and lightly shackled her arm. "No," she said. "You don't." Their eyes locked. Her voice dropped an octave. "I really wish you'd hear me out."

Saying no was impossible. After hearing the tone of Stef's voice, so laced with concern, she knew she had to listen. She nodded, not able to find words.

An odd need to cry was already building. Kelly started to sit down, but Stef grabbed her and hugged her. Not understanding why or how it happened, Kelly started to cry. She clung to Stef, and with each tear came another.

Stef ran her hand down the back of Kelly's hair, softly soothing her with her hand and voice. Kelly felt as if some corner of her mind had been opened and her own personal hurricane unleashed.

For long minutes, she cried. She cried over a mother who had never been there for her, a career she might not ever have and a life that had become lonely rather than fulfilled.

She had become an empty shell.

When finally the tears began to calm, she leaned back and swiped at her cheeks. Sniffling, she accepted a tissue from her friend.

"Feel better?" Stef asked with concern.

Kelly nodded. "Yes. Thanks for that. I'm not sure what happened."

"I think I struck a nerve."

Pulling her knees to her chest and wrapping her arms around them, Kelly let out a quivering breath. "I think you might be right."

"You really liked Mark, didn't you?" Stef lightly touched her arm, encouraging her to respond.

"I did," Kelly admitted softly, regretting how hard she had avoided admitting the truth up to this point.

"A good man doesn't take away your identity. He supports your growth as an individual. He gives you support and encouragement."

Dabbing at her eyes, Kelly said, "Sounds too good to be true."

"How would you know?" The words were confrontational, but the tone wasn't. "You haven't given anyone a chance."

"Avoidance mode has been my life with men. I'm not sure if I know how to open up to one."

"Step one is to try. Are you willing?"

She let out a breath. "I know I'm not happy now. I need to make changes."

"Start with Mark. You already admitted you like him. Why not give him a chance?"

"Mark and I had sex. That is all there was or is to our relationship."

Stef gave her a knowing look. "That's not true and you know it. You both really want to know if there is more to your attraction than sex."

"How do you know?"

"I talked to him, and I know you. So make me a promise."

"What?" she asked skeptically.

"If he contacts you again, you'll give him a chance."

The doorbell rang. Stef smiled. "That might be Jim. He was going to stop and say hi." She leaned forward and kissed Kelly's cheek. "Promise me you'll give him a chance."

Kelly nodded. "I'll give him a chance."

"Good." The doorbell rang again. "Better get that."

Kelly watched Stef leave, and reached for her wine. It was going to take some self-assessment, and some courage, but she did want to give Mark a chance.

She felt something for him beyond attraction, and she wanted to know what it was.

"Kelly."

The deep, sexy voice, potent in its impact, seemed out of one of her dreams. She looked up to find Mark standing there.

10

KELLY COULD HARDLY BELIEVE Mark was there.

Turning toward his voice, she blinked several times to make sure he wasn't a figment of her imagination. Had she fallen asleep, and had one of her dreams?

"What are you doing here?" she asked, stunned by the realization that he was real, and this was no dream.

He smiled, taking several steps toward her. "I came to see you."

"Here?"

"I didn't want to wait until Monday," he said as he stopped walking, looking down at her. "We need to talk. Your friend didn't think you would be pleased if she gave out your address or phone number."

Understanding came instantly. "So she brought you here."

He knelt down to be eye level with her. "Yes. She's been quite helpful."

"And nosey."

"I pressed her," he insisted. "Don't be too hard on her. I really wanted to see you."

His eyes always got to her. Looking into them now, she felt her stomach flip-flop. He was here, now, for her. His eyes said so, as did his actions.

"You seem to show up at the most unexpected times," she whispered.

"Yes." Mark reached out and touched her cheek with the tips of his fingers. Her body's reaction was instant. Every inch of her skin felt as if it was now on fire. Seduction had begun with a mere brush of his fingers.

Yearning to touch him in return, she gave in to the desire. Her fingers touched his face, as his had hers, a light caress, but she didn't stop there. Instead, she trailed her fingers along his square, strong jaw. Slowly, she explored his face with her hands.

He didn't say a word, letting her take her time, touching him with a leisurely hand. "I'm sorry about the thing at my office."

His hand came up and covered hers. He brought her palm to his mouth, pressing his lips there, and lingering, even as his eyes grabbed her gaze.

As he stared at her, his tongue dipped against the sensitive skin of her hand, making her suck in a slight breath. After a long moment, her hand in his, he lowered them both to his lap. "Why did you push me away?"

"It's complicated," she said, not knowing how to explain.

He studied her a long moment. Eyes probing her expression, he seemed to be looking for something specific. The room was quiet, their breathing the only sound for several seconds. "After that kiss in your office, I am more certain about getting to know you than ever."

"Why?" she asked suspiciously. Having a man interested because the sexual chemistry was good wasn't enough. At least not with Mark. She knew she had deeper feelings growing inside. Yes, they were new and she might be confused, but that didn't make the feelings any less devastating in their impact.

She didn't want to get hurt.

If she was going to change her method of living, starting out with a major heartbreak wasn't a good approach.

His voice was low and compellingly tender. "There is something between us, Kelly. Not just sex. I know you feel it, just as I do."

She wet her lips, watching as his eyes followed. Her body thrummed with the need to feel his against hers. Yet she was scared. "I don't know how to deal with you," she said, fear not keeping her from the truth.

She had made a promise to Stephanie that she would give Mark a chance, and deep inside she knew that meant being honest with not only him but also herself.

"Just be yourself."

Her heart beat faster. "I don't know how with you."

"Why?" He watched her with probing eyes. "Just relax. Come have a drink with me, or lunch tomorrow if you're more comfortable. I'll pick you up, and we'll go eat and talk." He paused and then gave her a sexy smile. "Or both."

Laughing a bit nervously, she tried to hide her anxiety. "Don't you think it's a little late for formality?"

"No," he said firmly, pulling her into his arms. "I want

you," he said hoarsely. "Make no mistake about it. Making love to you was completely amazing. But I want to know you fully, inside and out."

His breath trickled across her mouth, so close she could almost taste him. "I want to get to know you too."

"But?" he asked obviously sensing her hesitation.

"I don't do the relationship thing well. It's a family trait."

"All you have to do is be yourself, and we'll be great together." His voice dropped a notch and then his lips brushed hers. Fire rocketed through her body as he whispered, "I know it."

"How can you be so sure?" she asked just before she pressed her lips to his. "How?"

"I love a challenge," he said, smiling and then lightly nipping at her bottom lip. "I'll help you overcome the family traits."

"You don't even know what they are," she said, leaning back to look into his eyes, searching for some hesitation in him but finding none.

His hand slid to her cheek. "Don't you see?" he asked. "It doesn't matter. What matters is you and I, and what we share between us. I believe we can be great. But do you believe? That's the real question."

She wanted to believe. "What if it's not as good as you say it will be?"

"It will be. You know it. I know it. Can you take the risk and reach beyond the physical?"

She thought a long moment. Kelly knew she wanted this. She wanted him. For once, she wanted to believe in something other than her family patterns. She wanted to believe in Mark.

She also wanted to feel him next to her, touching her, making her feel cared about. He had said he had made love to her, and maybe he had. Maybe, just maybe it hadn't been just sex.

Her arms slid around his neck, and she decided to use a little Stephanie skill and negotiate. "I'll make you a deal."

His eyes twinkled. "Let's hear it."

"Make love to me tonight, and then get to know me intellectually tomorrow."

He laughed low and sexy. "We do have the place to ourselves. Stephanie went to Jim's."

She smiled. "I'm ready to get to know you, Mark."

His hand slid around her back, pulling her body snug against his. "Good," he said in a low, seductive tone. "Because I have a feeling it is going to take all night just to re-introduce myself."

Kelly laughed. "Promise?"

Sizzle

SAHARA KELLY

Prologue

Senior Prom night, eleven years ago . . .

Dylan Sinclair was naked.

Totally, gorgeously naked.

Well, as naked as a senior could be with his pants round his ankles, a beer can in one hand and the Winters twins all over him.

His body was a work of art. Finely sculpted muscles were starting to ripple across his chest and abdomen and there was not a doubt in Susanna Chalmers' scientifically oriented mind that the cock standing proudly away from its nest of curling dark hair was one splendid example of masculinity.

Not that she'd had much chance to run a comparison study. But oh my, what a baseline sample he'd make.

He was unquestionably the most beautiful thing she'd ever seen, even with his pants hobbling him.

And she bloody well *shouldn't* be seeing him now.

Dylan Sinclair. Dynamite Dylan, Dylan the Doll, Darling Dylan, Mr. Sin, all those silly names girls bestowed on boys they thought were gods. And here she was, as silly as the rest of them, mouth gaping at him as if he were a dream come true.

He'd come to this secluded corner of the stadium where she was hiding. Of course he didn't know she was there, trying to find someplace where she didn't stick out like a sore thumb. A spot where she didn't have to see pitying glances from her classmates. A little hidey-hole for the girl who got straight A's but didn't have a boyfriend, just a "friend" who had left her alone as soon as they'd arrived.

Yes, Dylan Sinclair had come to this spot, but not alone, and not with Dixie Carmichael, the busty blonde he'd brought to the prom. Susanna pressed farther back into the darkness of her hiding place, praying they wouldn't look too closely into the shadows behind the bleachers.

Katy and Kiki Winters had already hit the spiked punch by the looks of things, because their dresses were dangling from their fingertips, and their lingerie was almost nonexistent.

They giggled as they dropped what was left of their clothes and turned to attack Dylan. He laughed and raised the beer to his lips as they stripped him of his pants and freed him from the tangle around his feet.

Tumbling onto the piles of clothing, Dylan pulled them down with him, his mouth suckling eager breasts, hands seeking, stroking, tugging and caressing.

The giggles turned to moans under her fascinated gaze.

Dylan paid attention to Kiki's nipples and apparently Kiki liked it. Her face contorted and she gasped.

His hand slid down Katy's stomach into her fluffy mound of springy curls. Susanna was close enough to see his fingers pressing right into Katy's body and hear the sounds of pleasure they both made.

She watched, unable to look away, as his cock grew to astonishing proportions, the low light catching on a tiny bead of moisture bubbling from its tip.

"C'mon girls, don't make me do all the work," he growled softly, tugging on one breast with one hand and rubbing a soaking cunt with the other.

"Oh Dylan . . ."

"Mmm, Dylan . . ."

The voices flowed across the space between her and the writhing threesome and touched something deep inside her. Her own nipples were hard and aching and she could feel her panties getting wet and cool against her heated flesh.

She tried to suppress a squirm as one of the twins moved down and took Dylan's cock between her hands, running her tongue up and down as he continued to play with the nearest breast.

She gasped as she found she'd lifted her skirt and slid one hand down inside her underwear and her cold fingers were even now mimicking his as she stroked herself in silence.

A slurping sound came from one twin who was now energetically sucking Dylan's cock and making his hips thrust upward. She was straddling his thigh and rubbing her body against his muscles as she moved.

The other moaned and writhed as his hand continued its ceaseless rhythm against a sensitive clit.

Susanna echoed the rhythm and for one precious moment

felt herself a part of the group, one of the naked, writhing, heaving bodies, experiencing the thrilling touch of flesh on flesh.

The air turned hot around them, the moans becoming grunts and gasps as they sought their goal.

One twin rolled onto her stomach, trapping Dylan's hand beneath her. Her hips rotated as she ground herself onto his fingers. The other was lowering her head from his gleaming cock to his balls, where she extended her very long tongue and swept them with long strokes.

Susanna remained hidden, but a car suddenly turned in the distant parking lot, sweeping her with its headlights.

At that second, Dylan opened his eyes and stared into hers.

Her world faded down to a pair of gold-flecked hazel irises almost filled by the inky black pupils that were dilating as his climax approached.

His gaze never wavered as her hand continued to stimulate herself, and the girls writhed around him.

The moment became surreal as she felt her orgasm break, jerking her body into waves of silent pleasure.

She held his gaze as she withdrew her hand.

He gave a deep sigh that was half a groan as he came, spurting over one of the twins and thrusting his cock high into her hands.

Incredibly, he still held her gaze.

He winked.

She stumbled to her feet and ran, heedless of the noise she made, the fact that she'd left one shoe somewhere on the football field, or that her neglected date might wonder what had become of her. She just ran.

Ran from the image of Dylan, naked and writhing with two women all over him.

Ran from his groans as he came in spurts over soft skin.

Ran from the knowledge that she wanted it to be her hand stroking his cock, her body naked all over him.

Ran from the absolute conviction that it would never happen, and ran from the pain that the thought inflicted on her heart.

Eleven years later, she was still running.

The present . . .

"So, in conclusion, I'd like you all to think about how important it is to communicate fully with your chosen partner. Only by sharing your feelings with *and* about each other can you explore the true potential that lies in such a wonderful meeting of the minds."

Dr. Susan Chalmers glanced over the fifteen to twenty people in the small lecture hall with a polite smile as she wrapped up her lecture.

"How about sex?"

The deep male voice slid through the room like honey, but Dr. Chalmers was well used to interruptions of such a nature. Two years in an advanced program on Public Speaking had taught her well.

"Not tonight, I have a headache."

The snappy retort earned her a big laugh, a polite round of applause and the general murmur of the crowd as they gathered their belongings and moved on.

"I have an aspirin."

Susan looked up from her papers as the voice came again.

She narrowed her eyes against the glare of the fluorescent lights, trying to see who was speaking. She pushed her tortoiseshell reading glasses more firmly up against the bridge of her nose.

"The lecture for this evening is over. Perhaps you'd care to sign up for one of our other available dates."

"No."

He neared the low podium, a tall figure, and familiar somehow.

"No?"

"No. When we date it will be without the benefit of an audience or a sign-up sheet."

Dr. Chalmers' mouth fell open and she got her first good look at the man staring at her.

"I . . . I . . ." she floundered, completely off balance as she glimpsed his eyes.

Hazel, with flecks of gold, they were familiar eyes. But the rest of him was a stranger. At least she thought he was. There was something about him that was setting off alarms in her gut. And a few other places.

"Dr. Chalmers, isn't it? Dr. Susanna Chalmers?"

He closed the distance between them, bringing an inexplicable wave of heat with him.

"Susan Chalmers, actually," she answered without thinking.

"Oh no, that's wrong . . ." His gaze stroked her face and she was horrified to feel a blush creeping beneath the surface of her skin.

"I beg your pardon, that is my name . . ."

"No it's not. You're not a Susan, all buttoned up in your neat suit with your little brooch guarding your secrets . . ."

He flicked the collar of her crisp white blouse, fastened at the neck with a tasteful cameo. It was paired with her tidiest gray pinstripe pantsuit. The entire ensemble screamed elegant and informed academia.

But not, apparently, to him.

"It would appear that you are suffering a misconception. I am Dr. Susan Chalmers. Now, you'll have to excuse me, as I must finish my notes and make sure the room is cleared. The lecture is over."

This acerbic little speech was designed to end the conversation, and was emphasized by Susanna turning her back and rustling her papers.

Suddenly she felt a heat down her spine.

Two strong arms slid down either side of her to the table, trapping her between him and her laptop.

"You're Susanna. Susanna Chalmers. You may hide it, button it down, lash it into tight little knots . . ." His nose brushed the neat coil of hair at the nape of her neck. " . . . and talk knowledgeably about the value of interpersonal communication and sharing . . ."

His breath fluttered the air around her neck and she felt a shiver begin somewhere near her knees and travel upward to her breasts. Unbelievably, her nipples were hardening beneath their practical covering of white cotton.

"But you and I know better, don't we, Susanna?"

She tried to straighten, to put a little steel back into the spine that was threatening to turn into a Mobius strip just from the nearness of this man.

"You and I know that men and women need more from a relationship than a few good chats. You and I know that fucking is one of the best methods of communication there is . . ."

The heat was spreading to her loins and she knew she was starting to dampen her matching white cotton panties.

"Getting hot and sweaty . . . getting naked and rubbing against each other. Learning little places that scream to be licked and other places that want to be nibbled on. Having fun, Susanna . . ."

This was awful. This was dreadful.

"Being able to share something with someone who doesn't require conversation. Sometimes it doesn't even require contact. Not physical contact anyway . . ."

This was against every precept she'd embraced during her education and career. He was invading her personal space and reducing her lectures to irrelevancy.

And if he stopped, she'd kill him.

She closed her eyes.

"I'll be outside in the parking lot waiting, Susanna. We're going to have a drink together, and you're going to tell me the story of how you ended up giving lectures on unreal topics to uninterested people, and looking like the president of the virgin-of-the-month club."

She drew in a deep breath to rebut all of his statements, but in the next second his arms were gone.

"And I'm going to see if the girl *I* remember is still around someplace . . ."

She turned, frowning.

"So, what do you think? Is she still there? Will she come out for a drink with me?"

Susanna gaped as a wickedly smiling pair of eyes ran up and down her body.

"So, whaddya say? Want to come with me, *Sizzle?*"

The color drained away from Susanna's face as she heard that dreaded school nickname for the first time in over ten years.

Before she could refuse, before she could shout any of the twenty-nine things that were jostling in her brain, he'd turned to leave.

"It's the black Jeep. I'll park near the steps . . ."

He pushed the steel door open and glanced back at the dumbstruck woman leaning against the desk.

Dylan Sinclair winked.

THE BAR WAS SUBDUED, reflecting the fact that it was a Tuesday night. There were plenty of empty tables near the dance floor, but that wasn't what Dylan wanted.

He wanted a booth.

Somewhere where he could sit close to Sizzle Chalmers and feel the heat of her thigh next to his.

He was still in shock that she was actually here, allowing him to steer her between the tables toward the quieter section of the large room.

It had been a gamble, coming on strong to her like that, but he'd had no choice. From the moment he'd walked into that lecture hall and seen her standing there discussing who-knew-what, all rational thought had fled from his brain and graciously allowed his cock to step into the vacant space.

She'd given him a couple of nasty moments when she'd formally introduced herself to him at the door of the Jeep, but he'd teased her out of the pretense.

"Yes, I'm Dylan Sinclair, and you're Sizzle Chalmers. As if either of us could forget."

She clenched her jaw and gave him a tight smile, saying nothing in response. She didn't realize that the little squirm of her hips spoke volumes to him.

He wanted this woman so badly he could taste it. He wanted to taste *her*.

He wanted her naked and sprawled beneath him, on top of him, beside him, upside down on her head if need be, anything to get inside her. With his cock. And his fingers. And definitely his tongue. And perhaps his toothbrush.

He shook his head a little, trying to clear away some of the sexual fog that had settled between his ears.

She was sliding across the leather bench and smiling politely at the waitress.

"We'll take a couple of drafts," he said, automatically.

"Um . . . sorry. I don't drink. Could you make that a diet soda?"

"Sure," said the waitress, losing interest in Susanna as she got a good look at Dylan.

"Anything else, honey?" She smiled widely, leaving Susanna in no doubt of the kind of service she could expect with Dylan as an escort.

"That'll do it for now, thanks."

He slid into the booth beside her. Close beside her.

She inched away.

He inched toward her.

"Will you stop?"

"Stop what, Sizzle?"

"*Don't* call me that." She all but spat the words at him. "I hated it then and I still hate it now."

"But why?"

"Why? Why did I hate being called that stupid name?"

"Yes. Why."

"Well, I'll tell you why," she hissed.

"Good. I want to know. That's why I asked."

Befuddled, she blinked. "Stop it. You're confusing me."

"Good again."

Susanna closed her eyes as if in pain.

Dylan grinned to himself and decided to give her a little slack. Enough to let her think she was back in control.

He leaned away from her against the back of the booth and accepted his glass from the waitress.

"You want to take care of that now or start a tab, honey?"

"Run us a tab, would you . . . Babs?" He couldn't help but notice her name tag tipping drunkenly over one large breast.

He heard Susanna's indrawn breath and bit the inside of his cheek to keep himself from grinning. She was aware of him. No matter what her mind was telling her, her body knew what it wanted and didn't like the thought of sharing it.

"You got it, babe." Babs left with a nod.

Susanna tapped her foot on the floor and carefully unwrapped her straw, rolling the paper into a neat coil.

"How's your soda, Sizzle?"

China blue eyes clashed with hazel ones. "You know, high

school has been over and done with for many years. Some of us have actually grown up during the intervening period."

"No, really?" God, he loved yanking her chain and watching her eyes spit fire. Soon, very soon, he was going to coax those eyes into blazing with an orgasm to end all orgasms.

He hardened underneath the table and cursed his own lack of control.

"Yes, really. I understand the adolescent need to categorize and make familiar those with whom they interact. To assign titles to those about whom they are uncertain. People like myself who didn't necessarily run with the right crowd. People like myself who also had red hair, which just cried out for some kind of nickname—"

"People like yourself who almost blew up the Chem Lab and left Mr. Simmons with no eyebrows for a year?"

A sputter of laughter chased away her anger. "Oh lord, I did, didn't I?"

"You did. Best chem class I ever had."

"You were in my chem class?"

"We actually shared a couple of classes early on in that semester. Then my schedule changed as the sports schedule got moved around a bit."

"Ah yes, Dylan 'The Jock' Sinclair." She grinned at him, earlier anger forgotten.

"Right. You want to talk about nicknames, I had enough of them to last a lifetime." His rueful laugh echoed around the booth.

"Yes, but they were all complimentary. I mean, 'Jock' is okay, and 'Dynamite' is downright generous. You take something like 'Sizzle,' and what kind of an image does that present?"

Did she really want an answer to that question?

Apparently yes. Her bluer than blue eyes were innocently meeting his.

"Someone hot. Someone who can burn and heat a man's mind as well as his flesh. Someone who makes his lips tingle and his gut ache. Someone who has hair like an open flame and who would probably turn his bed to toast if she ever let it loose . . ."

Susanna's mouth hung open.

"Someone whose blue eyes have haunted me for years. Someone who knows how to get herself off as she watches me fuck . . ."

H OLY *SHIT*, HE KNEW it was her.

Every ounce of self-control Susanna had developed over her college and professional career came to the fore and allowed her to remain calm while sitting next to Dylan after his outrageous statement.

"I haven't a clue what you're talking about."

She spoke what had to be the biggest lie of her life without batting an eyelash. Of course, the fact that her conscience was hyperventilating and had its hand clapped over its mouth in horror was quite incidental.

"No?" The word stroked up her spine like cold fingers, bringing a shiver to her body and incidentally hardening her nipples beneath their serviceable cotton covering.

Then Dylan smiled.

A wickedly enchanting and arousing twist to the lips that took his mouth up more on one side than the other and made him look like a cross between a repentant little boy and some-one who could go from zero to orgasm in less than six seconds.

She was lost. She did not, however, reveal it by so much as a twitch. She daintily sipped her soda, ignoring her sweaty palms, her aching breasts and the fact that her underwear was now approaching the "soak" cycle.

In her clinical opinion, she would certainly qualify as aroused.

In her personal opinion she was horny as hell and it wouldn't have taken much encouragement to rip Dylan's clothes off right here, right now. With her teeth.

In her conscious mind, she was horrified.

"I'm sorry, Dylan, you lost me there. Another school refer-ence, I presume?"

She was extraordinarily proud of the level tones she had produced to answer his question. She also thought she might have just ruptured a portion of her diaphragm.

"Sizz . . . sorry, Susanna, that was the hottest night of my life. Ever."

Dr. Susan Chalmers raised one eloquent eyebrow in a gracefully controlled move.

Susanna Chalmers, a.k.a Sizzle Chalmers, wanted to squirm under the table and hide there for a millennium or so.

"Prom night? In the stadium, over by the bleachers?"

Susanna shook her head, managing not to go for overkill by batting her eyelashes innocently.

"Me and the twins, whatever their names were, and you with your wide blue eyes . . ."

Susanna allowed herself a little chuckle.

"Oh Dylan, time will play tricks with one's memory, won't

it? You'd never have asked me to go anywhere with you, especially not if the twins were involved."

There. That was neat, truthful, and got her off the hook.

"I didn't *ask* you, Sizzle, you were there. Watching, playing, sharing with us but doing it by yourself."

Susanna maintained her "I can't imagine what you're talking about" expression, while sipping her soda. It tasted like plasterboard and went down just about as easily. She restrained the urge to cough.

"It was a warm night . . ." Dylan apparently felt the need to reminisce in detail. Oh *shit*.

"Dylan, these old school stories, I—"

"Bear with me. This one affected my life."

She snapped her mouth closed, staring at him in amazement.

"I'd certainly been into the beer, that much I remember. And the twins . . . what were their names? The ones with the big—um—well, you know them, Kooky and Kitty Summers or something . . ."

"Katy and Kiki Winters."

"See? You do remember." Dylan grinned as he obviously felt he'd scored a point. "We were getting naked, as I recall, which those two were known to enjoy doing at the drop of a football, I might add. It was kinda fun, you know? Two of them, one of me?"

Susanna nodded sagely. "Very common male fantasy. Especially at the height of male adolescent hormonal levels. Late teens, early twenties. Lots of enthusiasm, lots of testosterone. The ability to fantasize about experiences which have yet to become linked to any emotional involvement." She grasped at her repertoire of professional techniques and hoped for a lightning bolt to hit the bar. Very soon.

Dylan pursed his lips. "Thank you, Doctor."

"Well, it's quite true. No getting around it. The male fantasy of one man being serviced by two women is so common that it forms the basis for a good number of pornographic movies, not to mention erotic literature."

"And what, pray tell, do you know about pornographic movies and erotic literature?"

"My dear Dylan," she laughed, allowing a slight note of condescension to creep into her voice, "I am a relationship counselor. A therapist for involved couples. It has been necessary for me to research many areas of interpersonal communication, and occasionally, pornographic movies can help. I don't recommend them too often, however."

"Did you enjoy them?"

Damn, he could fluster her. "I watched a few with the intent of seeing if they could encourage couples to be more at ease with each other on a variety of personal levels. I did not watch them to critique the plot, production value or performance. Enjoyment didn't come into it." She closed her mouth with a snap.

"So you didn't feel the need to slip your hand inside your panties, like you did on prom night?"

Susanna slanted an incredulous gaze at him. Her heart was doing leaps all over her rib cage and her gut was churning. If he didn't get off this subject soon, she was going to get up and go. Or stay seated and come. It was a toss-up which would happen first.

"You didn't get all hot and bothered by those movies, like you did when you spied on me and the twins?"

"I wasn't *spying!*" She couldn't help it. She spat out the denial before she realized what she was admitting.

Dylan leaned back with a look of satisfaction on his face. "Now we're getting somewhere."

Susanna bit her lip and sipped her soda, mentally flaying herself for her stupidity.

"I have to share something here, Sizzle." Dylan's expression wasn't the triumphant grin Susanna had expected, but more an intense and penetrating gaze that bore down to her toes and did nice things to her hot spots on its way. "That experience, you watching me and taking your pleasure as the twins brought me mine, was the most erotic moment I've ever had. Ever. In the past eleven years, nothing I've done has come close."

Susanna snorted. Fortunately she'd swallowed her soda so she didn't disgrace herself with a stream of reprocessed liquid. She had improved a little since high school. But not much.

"You, Dylan Sinclair, are—if you'll pardon my rather nonprofessional opinion—full of shit."

HE HAD HER. In his sights, under his crosshairs, right where he wanted her. Almost.

There were a few minor details, like she was still wearing clothes, they were in a public place and not his bed, and he hadn't got his mouth on her breasts yet, but they were little incidentals that could be taken care of in moments.

Oh, he had to get her to let that hair down, too. He wanted that *really* badly.

From the hair on her head to the hair between her legs

was a very minor leap of logic and he wondered if it was as red as the fire shining under the bar lights or a darker shade. Did it curl tight or was it loose and soft? Or, horror of horrors, did she shave? He liked a nice bald pussy as much as the next guy, but it would be a complete denial of all he held sacred if she lopped off a brilliant thatch of hair that would frame her soft pink cunt so perfectly.

It was his turn to shift uncomfortably in his seat. If he got any harder, she'd think they were being visited by spirits or something, because he was rigid enough to lift the table in front of him. Without using his hands.

"I may be full of shit, but you were there. I watched you and you watched me. I saw your eyes widen and your mouth open on a silent moan as you touched yourself. I knew what you were doing. Damn it, Sizzle, I could practically smell you."

She snorted again. He was rather coming to like that endearing little sound. He wondered if she'd make it when he pulled her buttocks up against him and took her from behind.

He closed his eyes momentarily in case they were rolling back in his head. With his luck she'd think he was having a seizure, and have him in an ambulance before he knew it.

"You are, as I said before, full of it, Dylan. You and the Winters twins were obviously having a fun time, and couldn't possibly have known I was there. I couldn't move, or say anything; it would have been too embarrassing for words. As soon as I could, I left. End of story."

Neat and tidy. And the biggest crock he could remember hearing since his cable company had promised him one hundred and forty-six exciting channels for his viewing pleasure.

"Sizzle, I watched you. Not the twins, not their boobs, nor

anything else they did. It was you. Your eyes, sparkling blue lights . . . getting wider as I got harder, and I got harder as they got wider. Was it because I was being watched?"

Susanna refused to answer such a provocative question.

"Well, I thought it might be. So I tried it again. But no go."

"You tried . . . you mean you made lo . . . with people . . . what . . . ?"

"For a professional, you stutter a lot, don't you?"

"I have to say I was not expecting quite such a personal confession, Dylan," said Susanna, admirably recovering her poise.

It was a facade, of course. Dylan knew that. He really could smell her body next to his. She was getting so turned on it was fun to watch her fight it. He hid his grin.

"I tried a lot of things, Sizzle. It was college, and hey, what's college for, right?"

"How about getting an education?" she snapped.

"Oh I did, honey, I can assure you I did." This time the grin was quite open. Susanna closed her eyes in disgust. "I got my Master's in Engineering and my Doctorate in fucking."

"I'll bet," she sniffed, unimpressed.

"And I may have qualified for a Minor in Unusual Sexual Practices."

Susanna's eyebrow quirked up and Dylan quelled a smirk of satisfaction. Gotcha!

"Define 'unusual' . . . "

She'd always been curious, that much he could remember. An overriding fascination with the need to know. It was why she'd been an Honor Roll student while he'd been a student on a roll, and why their paths had never really crossed in high school. But she'd always been there, in the back of his consciousness, like an ember just waiting its time to burst into flame. Damn, it must be her tightly pulled back red hair—he was thinking in fire metaphors. Not good.

"Well, a little to the left of 'run of the mill' but a far cry from de Sade," he answered, watching her eyes.

They widened slightly as she considered his words.

"So, will you have dinner with me?" Dinner wasn't what he wanted, of course, but saying "would you have lusty, unbridled sex with me that will probably last at least three days and might well put us both in traction" might not go over too well. At least, not yet.

"No."

"No?"

"That's correct. No. Thank you for the invitation, but no, I won't have dinner with you." Susanna closed her lips firmly, ending the conversation. She thought.

"Why?"

"Why?"

"That's correct, why won't you have dinner with me?"

"Probably because you do things like that."

"Like what?" Dylan gave her his best innocent blink.

"Start very annoying conversations like this."

"I didn't start it, you did. By saying no when I invited you to dinner."

"*I* didn't start it, *you* did, by asking me to dinner in the first place."

"But if you'd said yes, then we could have moved on to when and where and if you needed panties or not . . ."

Susanna gave up and burst into laughter, the first real laugh Dylan had heard from her. He was charmed.

She laughed from her gut, letting her joy spill out into the room and inviting others to share.

"I give up."

"Now those words are music to my ears." Dylan leered wickedly at her. "Saturday?"

"Can't."

"Can't or won't?" *Please don't let her say she has a date already.*

"Can't. Unless . . ." She tapped a fingernail on her lips sending a very nice warm flood of arousal through Dylan and straight to his cock, which was throbbing quietly against the fabric of his pants. He ignored it.

She straightened against the back of the booth, sipped her soda, put it down with a plunk and looked him in the eye.

"I'm not sure if seeing each other is a good idea, Dylan. However . . ."

Thank god, there's a "however" to this, he thought, itching to feel that fingernail tapping *his* lips. Or other places.

"On Saturday night I will be attending a seminar given by Dr. Jonas Allen, the noted therapist and couples intervention specialist. His lectures are sold out months in advance, his books are becoming hot sellers, and I was very lucky to get a ticket because he limits the numbers of his audience. The ticket says couples only, but I was going to ignore that, of course, being a professional in the same field."

"Of course," Dylan answered dryly. He had an awful feeling about what might be coming next.

"Well, how about we attend together?"

Damn. He'd known it. Two hours of sitting listening to some new-age wiener ramble on about some idiotic psycho-babbling theories on relationships, when all he wanted to do was cement this one with a hearty helping of his cum and her juices. Mixed. Together. Several times.

He sighed.

"Sounds like a plan to me." *If it'll get me closer to you, Sizzle, I'll go for it.*

"Excellent. I'll pick you up at six forty-five if you give me an address."

She was gathering her things. She was going to leave. This was not acceptable.

"How about I pick you up? This may be a brave new millennium but I still kind of like the old-fashioned way. You remember, the bit where the guy picks up his date at her door? Chocolates, corsage, stuff like that?" Dylan raised his eyebrows at her.

"Well, I don't know if we should, strictly speaking, call this a date." She had her bag clutched under one arm and was already sliding out of the booth.

Stifling a curse, Dylan tossed some money onto the table and followed her as she almost ran for the door.

"Hey, it's going to be Saturday night and we are going out someplace together. Dinner or a seminar, I still think it's a date."

"Well, that's just semantics."

Dylan opened the door of the Jeep for her before she pulled the handle off in her haste, and hurried around to the driver's side, anxious not to lose the thread of the conversation.

"Semantics is not the best argument. A date is a date, Susanna. Two people, usually one male and one female, spend time together as a result of choice. That's a date."

"Well, it could also be viewed as two people enjoying an evening together regardless of gender. Sharing a similar experience, so to speak."

"Hmm. So by saying 'date' you regard that as putting a sexual connotation on the evening?"

"Well, it's certainly not the same as saying 'let's go to the mall together' or something, is it?"

"You think going anywhere with me on a date would be sexual, but going to the mall with me wouldn't?"

"I . . . well . . . I didn't . . ." she stuttered slightly as she struggled for words.

Taking pity on her, he pulled up next to her car.

"We're here, Susanna. I'll wait and make sure you get into your car okay. Want me to follow you home?"

"Good lord, no. I'm not far from here and it's all main roads. But thanks for the offer, and the soda."

He reached out his hand and stopped her as she turned to open the door. He felt the warm skin of her neck beneath his palm.

"Oh—one more thing, Susanna . . ."

She turned to him, eyes wide, shining a clear blue in the dashboard lights.

"*Any* time you spend with me will be sexual . . ."

He pulled her toward him as he moved to the center of the car.

Their lips met in a heated rush, she on an intake of air, he on a surge of need so great it nearly blew his shoes off.

Their moans were nearly identical.

He slanted his mouth firmly over hers and urged her lips apart with his tongue. For a few seconds he was terrified that she wouldn't respond, but suddenly she melted in his arms, opened her lips and welcomed him.

He slid into a totally new kind of heaven.

Angels were singing, bells were ringing, and the sweetest mouth he'd ever tasted was sucking his tongue inside.

He could feel shivers running through the woman he was devouring, and knew she was struggling with the need to get into closer contact with him. He cursed the shift gear.

He wanted her bare breasts against him in the worst way and couldn't stop his hand from sliding inside her jacket to feel her warmth.

Her nipple was marble hard beneath his fingers, standing proud beneath the soft shirt and bra. She was damn near clad in armor, and impossible to undress, even for his skilled fingers. The portion of his brain that dealt with such things gave up, sat down and sobbed.

She sighed into his mouth, letting her hands stroke his neck and sift his hair through her fingers.

Her breast swelled into his hand and she arched her back even more as if to give him greater access.

A little sound struggled through their kiss as he fondled her, gently sliding his thumb across the tiny peak.

Suddenly, she wrenched herself away.

"Oh my God, what am I doing?" A look of absolute horror passed across her face.

"Having a very nice time kissing me?" asked Dylan mildly, ignoring the overwhelming urge to tip the seat back, rip her clothes off and fuck her on the spot. Repeatedly.

"Yes, but . . . I mean I don't ever . . . I never . . ." A blush was starting to turn her creamy skin bright pink, and Dylan sighed.

"Well you should. You're a very good kisser. But I have a feeling that *that* particular portion of this evening's entertainment is concluded. Am I right?"

Seeing as Susanna was now plastered against the passenger door and as far away from him as she could get without actually hanging out of the window, that wasn't an unwarranted assumption.

"I . . . um . . . thank you for the soda and . . . everything."

"You're welcome. More for the everything than the soda, though." Dylan grinned unrepentantly. "So—six forty-five on Saturday?"

"I . . . well, yeah. Sure."

Internally, Dylan heaved a sigh of relief. He hadn't scared her off.

"I'll be there. And hey . . . Sizzle?"

She turned as she slid out of the car.

"Bring your lips. We *have* to do this some more."

Susanna gave him a quick uncomfortable smile and shook her head. She practically ran to her car.

Dylan Sinclair grinned. Life, as he knew it, was about to change for the better thanks to one fiery redhead and one dull seminar. He'd have to think of a few ways to liven it up.

Humming to himself, Dylan watched as Susanna's car pulled out of the lot. He'd follow her home anyway, but give her a couple of car lengths for privacy. It was going to be a long few days until their Saturday "date," but he figured he'd make it. Knowing that he'd be seeing her again would be incentive enough.

Thinking about a way to seduce her out of her frosty little cocoon would just be icing on the cake, even if it did mean spending a little extra time in the shower. He glanced down at the hard bulge distorting the front of his pants.

Okay, maybe quite a bit of extra time in the shower.

S USANNA CHALMERS WAS IN the shower. Again.

   She was starting to wonder if she'd scrub herself raw by the time Saturday night rolled around, but she couldn't help it.

   Clinically, she guessed she might be trying to wash away what she viewed as her fall from grace in the front seat of a car.

   Personally, it might also have something to do with the erotically stimulating massaging showerhead she'd bought recently.

   She had to smile as she remembered her assistant's recommendation.

   "Sweetie, you'll love it. The Tubmate II is guaranteed . . ." and she'd said it with a real southern drawl, " . . . guar-on-teeeeed to make you shiver. No therapist should be without one. I mean, what a recommendation for exploring a relationship. Three in the water, a guy, a gal and a Tubmate II. Whew. It boggles the mind."

Sylvia had fanned herself with a sheaf of papers.

Susanna had laughed and agreed she'd look into it.

She was now looking into it. Or, to be accurate, looking *at* it.

Setting it on "low pulse," her personal favorite, Susanna leaned back against the wall and raised her leg, putting her foot gently on the ledge surrounding her bath.

The showerhead went to work and Susanna's mind went happily off on some fantasies, most of which involved one handsome-as-sin guy, and his tongue. And his hands.

Oh, and mustn't forget those glittery hazel eyes.

Would he be as good in bed as she'd remembered everyone saying? The girls had "oohed" and "aahed" over him before they knew anything about sexual expertise.

He might just be a well-hung stud, out for a good time. Some women thought that size, good looks and stamina were all it took to make a sexual superhero.

She, Dr. Susanna Chalmers, knew better.

A true sexual superhero required finesse, skill, caring, and technique, along with size, good looks, stamina and hazel eyes.

Well, the hazel eyes bit was a personal preference, of course.

She groaned as the pulsing spray caressed her clit.

A true sexual superhero would know that she liked her nipples tugged a tiny bit, not to the point of pain, but just enough to send that wonderful shot of electricity to her cunt.

Her free hand slid up her torso to a waiting breast. There—just like that.

She felt her juices begin to mingle with the warm water cascading down her inner thighs and moved slightly to open herself even more to the delicate pounding.

He'd need to have a good and talented mouth, too.

She drifted on her own sensual haze, imagining a dark head between her thighs and those hazel eyes gazing at her from over her mound as he learned her secrets.

The pounding on her clit became a teasing, tantalizing, not-quite-enough urge.

She quickly upped the speed and closed her eyes again, moving the showerhead nearer now.

God, she was actually considering sex with Dylan Sinclair. It would, at least, lay a few old ghosts to rest. And it seemed that he wanted her, if that kiss they'd shared was anything to go by.

She'd noticed his erection, of course. She was a trained professional and paying attention to the sexual signals people gave off was her job.

But knowing this one was for her and her alone had been a new kind of thrill.

She imagined how it would feel, caressing her clit.

The water was working, and her breath was starting to come in harsh gasps. She had one last vision of a strong body pressed against hers and a hard cock sliding deep into her warmth as the showerhead lived up to its "guar-on-teeeee" and shoved her over the edge.

She came with a loud gasp, dropping her leg and pressing her thighs together to ride out the spasms.

A few moments later she sighed and reached for the shampoo.

Saturday couldn't come fast enough.

"So, what are you going to wear tonight?" Sylvia poked her head in around the door.

The question came out of left field for Susanna, who was trying to get caught up on her patient files and lecture notes before finishing up her Saturday morning office hours.

"What do you mean?"

"You know, clothes? Those things that keep you warm and dry? The things that hang in your closet, or in my case, sleep on the floor? The things you have to take to the cleaners now and again because they don't like coffee spilled on them?"

Susanna blinked.

"I hadn't thought about it."

Sylvia sighed.

"You have a date with Mr. Hottie, the same Mr. Hottie you've lusted after since high school, and you haven't thought about what to wear? Susanna, you are *not* a normal woman."

"This is *not* a date. I told you he was simply accompanying me to the seminar. And I probably shouldn't have told you that much. Now you'll be wanting to know every single detail." She sighed. "I have *not* lusted after him since high school either. It was a simple crush. Perfectly explainable given our circumstances."

For some reason, Susanna blushed.

"Riiiiight. The circumstances being you female, him male?"

"No. The circumstances being me dork, him jock. Me—president of the chess club, him—martial arts all the way. Me—ungainly glasses and no breasts. Him—gorgeous eyes, good muscle tone and a cute butt. Am I getting the point across here? It was a normal, healthy crush."

"So dress nice, go have normal, healthy sex and get it out of your system."

Susanna giggled, then slapped her hand over her mouth. Respected and serious minded therapists did not *giggle*.

"On a first date?" She tried to sound shocked.

"You're not a virgin, you've had the hots for him for—what—eleven years now? What's to consider? Sure, on the first date."

"Well, tsk tsk, Sylvia. You know that's a really bad idea." Susanna tried to look stern as she reminded her assistant of the ground rules for interpersonal relationships. "No sex until both parties are ready for a commitment. You know that as well as I do."

Why did that stick in her throat this morning?

"Yeah, yeah. Sure, sure. Now, *real* life is different, honey. Real life is where you look at the right guy and can't wait till he rips your knickers off and fills you so full you don't know where he ends and you begin. And you don't care. . . ."

Susanna looked appalled. "You've been reading those spicy romances again, haven't you?"

Sylvia shook her head. "Look, I've been married more years than I care to remember. I love my husband and I've been faithful to him. But time marches on, and so does a physical relationship. What is good for us now, might not be the same as what was good for us when we were newlyweds. Doesn't mean I don't enjoy reading about it, just that I can't always do it anymore." She grinned at her ample thighs. "Besides, if I did the splits now, I'd probably damage something vital."

"Sylvia. We are getting into *way* too much information here." She stopped her friend with a raised hand.

Sylvia was not to be put off, however. "Look, I'm just saying that good sex is not always easy to find. You've been wandering around here reeking of unfulfilled lust since you met Mr. I-want-your-hands-on-me President of the Martial Arts Club again last week. For once, dress cute, let your hair down and go boink him. It'll do you a world of good."

"Excuse me, did you just say 'boink'?"

"Yup."

"That's what I thought."

"And spare me the lecture about therapy-talk. This is you and me, woman to woman. No elegant and mature professional therapist-speak. Just the facts. Go fuck him, honey. You know you want to."

Sylvia stood with her hands on her hips, grinning at Susanna.

Susanna dropped her head to the desk and moaned. "Oh God, do I ever want to . . ."

"Well, there you go. So. What *are* you going to wear? You got a thong?"

SHE LOOKED LIKE EVERY wet dream he'd ever had, and then some. Dylan tried to keep those thoughts to himself as he picked Susanna up for Saturday night's exciting seminar.

Her sweater was the green of lime sherbet and its soft fuzzy surface invited the touch of his hand. Her long skirt was some Scottish plaid. He didn't care whether it was the authentic Chalmers tartan—it could have been Scrooge McDuck's for all he knew. All he was interested in was how it came off.

Aha. Back zip. Note taken and filed.

Long black suede boots finished her outfit, and Dylan was trying to decide if he should leave those on her or not when he realized she was staring at him.

Oh God, she'd been talking while he was off in his sensual fantasies. Worse yet, he'd been driving like that. What the hell was the matter with him?

"Are you sure you're all right?" Susanna's voice finally registered in his mind.

"Um, yeah. I'm fine. Just looking forward to the seminar." And if a bolt of lightning struck him dead as they walked through the parking lot to the hotel, it would be no more than he deserved for a lie the size of *that* one.

The small crowd gathered around the registration desk in the lobby of the hotel murmured politely, as only small crowds of would-be professionals can.

"Yes, excellent speaker."

". . . recommended by Dr. Franks . . ."

The conversation was restrained and scholarly, and set Dylan's teeth on edge.

"Are you sure about this?" He leaned closer to Susanna, seizing the opportunity to inhale her scent. It was something light and floral with a dash of woman. He liked it.

"But of course. This lecture is titled 'Research into the Influence of External Technology on a Non-Tactile Interpersonal Interaction Leading to Fulfillment.' So you see how interesting it's going to be."

"Does it come with an English translation or will there be subtitles?"

Susanna looked a tad superior. "Well, for the layman, that would mean something along the lines of a discussion on how external things, technological things—probably like computers and the internet—influence relationships between two people in their everyday life. Situations where they are together but not touching, if you know what I mean. Like a couple on a date, for example."

"Together but not touching, huh?"

"Exactly."

A movement at the head of the line snagged Dylan's attention. "Is there a chance that you and I will be watching this lecture from different sides of the hall?"

"What? No, don't be silly."

"Well, then perhaps you can explain why the female guests are going that way and the male guests are going that way . . ." He nodded to indicate two doors behind the registration table.

Sure enough, the female guests were exiting the foyer on one side, the men on the other.

Susanna's brows came together on a frown. "I can't understand why that would be necessary. But I'm sure Dr. Allen has a valid reason. Like I told you, he's extraordinarily well respected in the field. He has a very high success rate when it comes to counseling. And his books are top sellers."

"Ever read one?"

"Well, I . . . ah, now that you mention it, not actually the entire thing . . ."

"Hmm. How much *did* you read?"

Susanna blushed as they neared the table. "The jacket?"

Dylan sighed. The books were neatly presented on the far end of the table, and all featured a picture of a remarkably handsome man smiling from a variety of non-threatening poses.

He noticed several women casting yearning glances toward the photos. He supposed he could understand why. Helpful information was probably better dispensed by someone who looked like a cover model, than someone who looked like an auto mechanic.

"Dr. Chalmers. How lovely you could come—I know Dr. Allen will be very pleased to have a colleague in his group this evening. And Mr . . . ?"

The attractive receptionist smiled at Dylan and Susanna. Especially Dylan.

"Sinclair, Dylan Sinclair."

"Lovely," murmured the woman, clearly losing her train of thought for a few moments. "Oh—here is your program, reading list, evaluation survey and a special coupon for a discount on Dr. Allen's books."

The receptionist wrenched her eyes away from Dylan.

"So if *you*, Dr. Chalmers, will go through the ladies' area, you will be able to meet Mr. Sinclair on the floor of the auditorium. Mr. Sinclair, we ask that *you* go that way, please?"

The woman motioned them to the separate doors.

Raising one eyebrow Dylan sauntered off, leaving Susanna staring at the other door with a rather puzzled look on her face.

SUSANNA CAREFULLY MADE HER way onto the auditorium floor. She was about as mad as she'd ever been, mad to the point that one more drop of anger would have smoke coming out of her ears.

This was not what she'd envisioned.

This was not in her leather-bound appointment planner.

This was not supposed to happen on an evening where Dylan Sinclair was going to be sitting next to her.

This was the fact that she was practically naked.

She'd gone through the doors from the lobby and found herself in a small locker room where several women were chatting as they stripped.

Sensing her shock, another assistant had come up to her.

"You must be Dr. Chalmers. Would you come with me?" She'd been polite and smiling, welcoming Susanna and making her feel more comfortable. She'd led her to a small cubicle.

"In you go, Dr. Chalmers. Please remove all your clothing, and put on the robe you'll find inside the locker. Also the other garment—there are three sizes there, but you look like about a medium. I'd suggest trying that one first. You'll find a key in the locker door, just give it a turn and then you can bring it back to me. I'll be keeping all the keys with me this evening, so your belongings will be quite secure." She reached down and jingled her belt where a key ring held about a dozen keys already.

"I don't understand . . ."

"Didn't you read the program? This evening's lecture requires audience participation. Dr. Allen believes that to be able to relate to couples therapy, it is good to pretend to be a couple in need of therapy. The robes level the playing field, so to speak, and the lack of personal baggage removes any external distracting stimuli. No cell phones." She smiled conspiratorially. "Dr. Allen *hates* cell phones."

"Ah." Susanna chewed over that piece of information.

"When you're done just bring me the key and I'll send you on through."

Susanna had reluctantly followed directions, noticing several women passing through another door all wearing the same kind of toweling robe. Well, maybe this *would* level the playing field.

Sighing she hung her clothes neatly in the locker and slipped her boots in underneath.

She nearly choked when she saw the "garment" hanging on the back of the door.

Bright red, it was a thong. A lacy thong. With black bows. It was the kind of underwear that Dr. Susan Chalmers would abhor, and the kind of underwear that Sizzle Chalmers always wanted to try but never had the nerve.

Well, it looked like tonight was going to be her chance. Slipping her cotton briefs off and folding them into a discreet little bundle, she pulled the thong up over her hips. It felt strange. Her buttocks were uncovered to the air and distracted her from the heavier weight that kept the crotch in place. She'd thought the whole thing would weigh nothing, but this seemed to be a solid garment.

Quickly, she snuggled into the terry robe, rather annoyed to find that it wasn't quite as long as she preferred. This one just brushed the middle of her thighs. She was going to have to be extraordinarily careful of how she sat down. Especially with Dylan around.

Oh God. Dylan. He was going to see her like this. And she'd know she had a thong on underneath.

A ping of sexual awareness shot through her body. She stifled it.

The thong rubbed her buttocks as she bent to close the locker and remove the key.

Another ping made her fidget as she wondered if the men had been made to change too.

She started to get mad. Surely there should have been some mention of this in the literature. What if she hadn't shaved her legs? Oh yeah, like she was going to spend the evening with Dylan Sinclair and *not* shave her legs.

But supposing she hadn't?

Her anger grew until it was a very tight little smile that crossed her lips as she handed over the key to the assistant.

"Right through here, Dr. Chalmers. You're in booth number seventeen."

"Booth?"

"You'll see when you get in there."

And here she was.

Teeth gritted, stride determined, Susanna Chalmers was marching past a number of booths.

And they were booths, too. They looked like trade-show leftovers, little curtained boxes facing a dais, a podium and a projection screen. Only these booths contained two recliners, upon which couples were reclining. One couple to a booth.

Privacy, yet within a communal environment.

The professional part of Susanna's mind applauded the setup and the concept. Personally, she was cringing and furious at herself for not checking this whole situation out more thoroughly.

Then she found booth number seventeen.

Dylan was waiting for her.

She stopped, stunned, at the picture he presented.

Also wearing a white robe, he was relaxed and leaning comfortably back against the recliner. He'd raised the footrest and one leg was resting on top of the other. His bare feet wiggled at her.

"Hello. Welcome to our little slice of 'interpersonal, interactive space.'" He gestured to the paperwork on his lap. Obviously he'd been reading.

"Um. I probably don't need to tell you that I had no idea what was involved here." Susanna had decided that honesty was probably going to be the best way to handle this awkward situation.

"What? You mean you didn't intend for us to strip to our skivvies and spend time in a private booth listening to someone tell us how to handle our relationship?" He grinned. "I'd never have guessed. And here I was, thinking you'd hit upon the perfect way to get me naked." He wriggled. "Well, almost naked."

"Oh, did you get underwear too?" It popped out of her mouth before she could stop it. She covered her confusion by settling down carefully onto her recliner, making sure her robe met neatly and completely in front of her.

"*Too?*"

She sighed. "Never mind. Care to share the paperwork, so that I can have a shot at figuring out what the heck else is in store for us this evening? I might not be able to stand any more surprises."

The lights dimmed as Dylan slid a few papers across the short distance between their chairs.

"Damn. Too late."

She leaned back, trying to ignore the thong, which was subtly pressing against her cleft.

Her gaze rested on Dylan's legs, casually crossed at the ankle. His feet were strong and manly, toes slightly crooked, and with a smattering of hair. His legs were solid, and very masculine, but nicely shaped.

Her eyes traveled up, noticing that a little thigh was showing through the gap in his robe. Also firm, also hairy and also *very* masculine.

"I'll show you mine if you show me yours . . ." His whisper penetrated her consciousness and brought a blush to her cheeks.

"I don't think so."

"Sure?" His hand parted his robe even more, and Susanna couldn't have turned her eyes away if a gun had been held to her head. She got a quick glimpse of black silk.

She closed her eyes before her retinas could burn out.

"Good evening, friends."

The lecture had begun and Susanna offered a small prayer of thanks. The thought of Dylan in black silk underwear was stoking some inner furnaces. She struggled to find the damper and shut down the flue.

Dr. Jonas Allen claimed her attention.

An impressive figure of a man, also wearing a white robe, he was obviously at home in his surroundings, introducing his assistant with a smile and a joke about her husband.

His ideas were fascinating, touching as they did on the nature of relationships in the new age of technology, chat rooms for example, computer introductions and the changes in dynamics that such interactions permitted and in some cases encouraged.

Susanna was completely engrossed, forgetting for a little while that a hot bodied man was relaxing next to her in black silk skivvies.

"Now we come to the interactive portion of our lecture." Dr. Allen's soothing voice echoed throughout the small auditorium. "If you look to the side of your chairs, you will all see a small remote device? Ladies, please use the pink one, and gentlemen the blue. Sorry about the gender stereotyping, but you'll see in a moment why it is so important."

Susanna and Dylan located their small devices.

About the size of a box of matches, there were two buttons on the front, a large one and a small one.

Susanna looked over and, as promised, Dylan was holding the same sort of thing, only in blue.

He quirked an eyebrow at her, and she shrugged.

"Now, folks. It's time to play 'let's pretend.'"

A sudden squawk came from a booth a little distance away.

"Oh oh, not too soon, please." Dr. Allen laughed. "First let's get into our mind-set. You are a couple who are experiencing some sexual difficulties. The relationship started off hot, but has slipped into routine encounters. The thrill, as they say, is gone. There is even the possibility that one partner may be silently considering looking elsewhere."

Dr. Allen's voice reflected his deep concern at this situation.

"How do we, as professionals, help this couple? Should we instruct them to withhold sexual relations for a while? Tell them to try other people on for size? Or is it possible to allow them to explore each other's sexuality in a different way? To introduce the issue of control into the equation?"

Susanna frowned slightly as she considered the possibilities. She wasn't too sure about the control thing.

"Gentlemen, may I ask you to press the small button for the count of three?"

Susanna strangled a scream in her throat.

Her panties had just come alive.

For three seconds something had vibrated around her most sensitive flesh and sent a shiver up her spine.

The hubbub from the floor suggested she wasn't the only one who had been caught by surprise.

"My, my." A sly grin crept over Dylan's face as he realized what he held in the palm of his hand.

She turned her head to see him raise the remote. Before she could say a word, he pressed the button again.

She froze, unable to move as silent electronic fingers massaged her clit. It was incredible, it was embarrassing and it was arousing her rapidly.

He released the button and she sighed, torn between begging him to do it again and horror that he'd been staring at her.

"Ladies." Dr. Allen's voice cut through her haze. "It's your turn. Three seconds on the small button, please."

Fumbling, Susanna found her remote and pressed the small button. She raised her eyes to watch and see what would happen.

Dylan's mouth fell open and his robe fluttered as an erection grew steadily beneath the fabric.

She removed her finger from the button.

Well, wasn't that interesting?

She couldn't help it, she giggled.

"Oh fuck." Dylan wasn't sure if he'd said the words out loud or not. All he knew was that his underwear had suddenly shot some kind of lubricant over his dick and started massaging it. No wonder it had felt rather uncomfortable getting dressed. Now that his cock was getting a major hard-on, the fabric was tightening and swelling into a facsimile of a real snug cunt. God, it was even warming itself.

His engineering mind wondered where the hell the batteries were and what kind of safety precautions the designers had taken.

The rest of him wanted to howl.

He groaned as Susanna took her thumb off the button and he raised his eyes to see her giggle. Damn her.

He gave her two seconds of the small button.

She gasped.

He smirked and she hit the button.

Oh God.

"Ladies and gentlemen . . . I see you're all getting the idea behind our little devices." Dr. Allen's voice rang out over the murmurs and squeaks and groans from his audience.

"Let's discuss this further." Dr. Allen activated his own remote and his assistant squirmed. "May I suggest that you both open your robes? There is to be no touching, of course, but the sensations can be heightened with visual stimuli."

He spread his own robe apart, and Dylan saw Susanna's jaw drop open. Even Dylan had to admit that Dr. Allen was one fine-looking man. And his small dark green silk g-string did nothing to hide his awesome erection.

Dylan got a little pissed. Button time.

Five seconds of the small button drew Susanna's attention back where it belonged. On him.

He spread his own robe defiantly, showing off his black silk g-string and the erection that rivaled Dr. Allen's for size.

Susanna snorted. That got her five more seconds and a glazed look in her eyes.

A movement from the dais attracted their attention and they both watched as Dr. Allen's assistant spread her robe. Magnificently naked breasts emerged, topped by hard nipples visibly reddening as her panties stimulated her.

Dylan couldn't help but turn to Susanna with a question in his eyes.

The flush in her cheeks told him all he needed to know. He quirked an eyebrow.

She slid her hands to her tie and shamelessly spread her robe apart.

Oh God. He didn't need another five seconds of the small button. She had perfect breasts, full and white, topped by dusky brown nipples. Just as a polite thank-you, he decided to give her a healthy ten seconds on the small button.

Her nipples hardened even more as she bit her bottom lip.

She zapped him back and he couldn't hold back a groan as his cock was rubbed and held tight by the incredible massaging action of the fabric.

"You see now, I hope, that allowing your partner to control your physical arousal can lead to many delightful possibilities."

Dr. Allen seemed to have no trouble lecturing while sporting a major hard-on and making his very good-looking assistant writhe with sexual pleasure. Dylan envied the man his focus, because he was really afraid that he was completely losing his.

Between the shudders his underwear was giving him, the sight of Susanna's breasts trembling next to him and the scent of her arousal, he was having a very hard time concentrating.

The only problem was that his cock was enjoying all this from a rather clinical perspective. What he actually wanted was the warmth of Susanna's body under his, the soft silkiness of her cunt around his cock, not a toy, and her breaths feeding his need for air.

But, hey, this was a close second.

Susanna was dying. She was completely and absolutely convinced she'd never survive this experience.

It was like every fantasy come true and yet also like every

nightmare. She was almost naked, exposed in front of the man who'd haunted her dreams for years, and he was controlling her sexual arousal. And not *nearly* enough.

Sure, she was returning the favor—there, take that, ten seconds of the small button—but it was different for a guy. Wasn't it?

He moaned and she stared, fascinated, at his chest. His nipples were tight little buds. She hadn't realized that men could have such a reaction.

Oh God, she wanted to lick them and nibble on them. *Real* bad.

Something in her expression must have clued Dylan in because he slid the robe completely off his shoulders and hit the small button.

She fought against the urge to throw herself onto his recliner. And his body. Maybe she could just say she fell. Yeah right. *Sorry—I slipped and my vagina accidentally fell onto your penis.*

The magic fingers in her thong were sending shivers all through her body now, her juices were flowing, and she knew that she was not far from an orgasm. The words from the title of the lecture flew back into her mind . . . something about "Fulfillment." Oh my God. She was supposed to climax.

Nooooo. It couldn't happen. She couldn't possibly let it. This was Dylan, Dylan Sinclair, the god of high school. She could not allow herself to orgasm in front of him. He probably wouldn't care, but she would. She'd look ugly, or scream, or cry, or do something *really* embarrassing and turn him off forever.

"Now try the large button, folks. And then we'll wrap up the session."

Dr. Allen suited words to action and pressed the large button on his controller. His assistant appeared to levitate several inches off her chair.

Dylan did the same thing to Susanna.

"Ohmigod!" The squawk was surprised out of her as her underwear felt like a thousand tongues delved into her clit and her throbbing cunt.

She managed to hit her own large button, and was vaguely aware of Dylan next to her thrusting his hips off the chair and shouting something at her.

She fought desperately to stop her own climax. Dammit, this was not something she wanted to share at a seminar.

She struggled to her feet, but Dylan's thumb was firmly glued to the large button.

She tripped and stumbled, reaching out to the wall of the booth to catch herself. The insubstantial wall wasn't built to withstand the impact of a tumbling, half-naked, pre-orgasmic woman.

It collapsed.

It took the next one with it.

Like a row of dominoes, booths number sixteen through four collapsed, one after another, smothering the climactic screams of the couples within who were just attaining their own personal nirvanas.

Unable to fight it anymore, Susanna came. Shuddering and gasping, her body spasmed and she felt strong arms go around her as she struggled to survive the experience.

Screams and groans were emerging from the chaos of cluttered screens and tubular steel supports. She closed her eyes and leaned back against Dylan as she finished her orgasm and the disaster before her assumed its true magnitude.

"Look out . . ."

The shout took her by surprise and turning, she stared right at a large piece of steel piping that was falling.

Falling onto her.

A blessed darkness swam across her vision and she knew no more.

W ARMTH SEEPED INTO SUSANNA'S consciousness as she
struggled to wake up. She was warm all over, and
snuggled into something soft.

She was lying on her stomach, her head resting on a pillow
that smelled—good. Kind of like sandalwood, herbs and Dylan.
Oh God, she was even fantasizing about him in her linens.

Then she felt a hand rubbing gentle circles on her back. It
was soothing, comforting and oh-so-wonderful.

"Mmm . . ." She couldn't stop the groan of pleasure.

"D'you like that?"

"Oh yeah," she sighed.

"Good." The hand continued its movements, being joined
by another hand. They both stroked the length of her spine
and moved from shoulders to buttocks with rhythmic pressure.
The warmth penetrated the thin cotton something she seemed
to be wearing.

"Oh God, Dylan, that is sooooo good." She spent a minute or so enjoying the feeling until the words she'd spoken actually contacted some kind of awareness center in her brain. The rest of which was obviously out to lunch.

Dylan.

Dylan Sinclair was rubbing her back. "Just relax . . . I can feel your muscles tensing. You're fine."

His words unexpectedly soothed her. She wondered why. "Where am I?"

"Aha. Glad to see you read the right books. That's the classic first question after returning to the world of the living."

"Yes. Where am I?"

Dylan sighed. "You're at my house. We went to a seminar and during the third period a fight broke out, you came out of the penalty box and got hit with an iron strut of some kind."

"Hockey fan, are you?"

"Go, Bruins."

"Hmm. Okay—I remember the booth falling. What happened next?"

Dylan's hands kneaded her shoulders making her groan with pleasure.

"Well, you got yourself knocked out and all hell broke loose. Luckily Dr. Allen—who is a real medical doctor too, by the way—took a look at you. Your pupils were, and I quote, 'normal and responsive' so he figured it would probably be okay for me to bring you home, provided I kept an eye on you for a while. I have to make sure you don't throw up or pass out or get dizzy. Are you planning on doing any of the above?"

"I don't think so. I feel too lazy right now."

"Good. That's what I was hoping."

"Umm, Dylan?"

"Uh huh?"

"My underwear seems to have disappeared . . . along with my clothes. Offhand, I'd say I seem to be in bed with you. Did we . . . I mean did I . . . er . . . when we got home . . ."

A snicker from behind her stopped her embarrassed questions.

"Susanna Chalmers. I'm horrified you'd think such a thing of me. How dare you insinuate I'd take advantage of you."

"I didn't, I mean, I couldn't help wondering, you know—"

"For your peace of mind," he pushed her shoulders back down since she'd started to rise slightly, "all your belongings are here. I had the assistant get all your stuff before we came home. And yes, I did put you in one of my old shirts before I put you to bed, and yes I did remove that damnable underwear. But did I take advantage of you? Certainly not. I am not into necrophilia, even if it's with a woman who is only unconscious. I much prefer my women moving underneath me. Moving quite a bit, as a matter of fact." She could hear the grin in his voice.

"Oh." She didn't quite know whether to be glad or sorry. All Susanna knew at that moment was that Dylan's hands were working magic on her back. He couldn't know, of course, that back rubs were—in her opinion—the world's best foreplay.

She decided that for once she'd let all her inhibitions go. This was the culmination of many years of fantasizing about this man. She was in bed with Dylan Sinclair. And he was giving her a back rub. It didn't get much better.

His next move showed her that maybe it did.

"I wouldn't dream of taking advantage of a woman who couldn't feel it when I did *this* . . ."

Dylan moved slightly and nipped her buttock through the soft fabric of his T-shirt.

"Oh," she muttered, twitching a little.

"Or this . . ." His hands slid to her naked thighs and kneaded their way up the outside of her legs to her hips. Under the T-shirt.

"Um, Dylan?"

"Yeah?"

"What are you doing?"

"Giving you a back rub."

"Yes, but you're doing other things as well."

"Mmm hmm. Like them?"

"Oh yeaahhh," she sighed, unable to be anything but truthful at that moment as his warm hands were now rubbing up toward her shoulder blades and around the sides of her body to where her breasts were squished flat.

She felt him straddle her hips and lift the shirt away from her skin, bringing goose pimples as the cool air hit her flesh.

She also felt a very healthy erection press against her buttocks. She fought against the urge to thrust upward. It wouldn't be the right thing to do, her mind argued. Her body was screaming obscenities at her mind. She closed her eyes and ignored the debate, concentrating on Dylan's marvelous hands.

"Dylan?"

"I'm here."

"Why didn't you take me home?"

"Are you nuts? I get an almost unconscious woman in a thong, and not much else, to collapse into my arms. And you wonder why she's here in my bed? Susanna . . . tsk tsk. And here you are, so smart and all."

She could hear the grin in his voice.

"Yeah, but you never liked me in high school." Dear God, had she said that? That steel bar must have knocked her mind clean out of her head.

"Honey, that's soooo not true."

"Really?" Sizzle Chalmers, the uncomfortable and shy senior, raised her head and asked the question. Her head swam a little and she eased it back down.

"You were a walking wet dream, sweetheart. All the guys were wondering if you'd be as hot in the sack as you were striding across the quad with an armful of books."

"You're joking, right?" Susanna's mouth had dropped open onto the pillow.

"Nope. Thing was, you were so damned smart, none of us were brave enough to try and find out. You had that particular 'look' over the top of your glasses that gave us amazing and frequent hard-ons, but then you also had the one that turned us into dirt and shriveled our boners to winkies."

Susanna sputtered into the pillow.

Dylan's hands slid down and brushed the sides of her breasts. She shuddered slightly.

"I never knew . . . I never meant . . ."

"Ssshhh . . . relax. That was part of your charm, I think. You never knew what that red hair and those blue eyes did to us. Not to mention these legs, which, I might add, still go on forever and make a man wonder what it would be like to have them tight around him or over his shoulders, or . . ."

Susanna gave a muffled squawk as her hips responded to

his words. She knew she was getting really hot for this man. The back rub had started the process and his conversation was taking the whole thing to another level. She forgot about the headache that was beginning to plague her.

"Susanna," he breathed, leaning his whole body close to her. Fingers pulled and tugged at her hair and before she knew it her pins were gone and he was spreading out the fiery mass over his pillow.

"God yes . . ." His fingers went to the hem of the T-shirt and he pulled it up and away, leaving her naked underneath him.

She felt his heat. "Dylan," she mumbled, unsure of what she was saying. Did she want this? Did she want him?

Did she need oxygen to breathe? What headache?

Okay, so wanting this *and* him was really high on her list of "things-to-do-in-this-lifetime." In fact, "fuck Dylan Sinclair" was number one on that list. She realized, in a sudden intuitive flash, that it had been number one for eleven years or so.

She grinned.

Then she moved her buttocks.

She could feel Dylan jump and his cock thrust even harder into her cleft.

"If you keep *that* up, Sizzle . . ." His hands came down on her shoulders and he lifted himself as he turned her over to face him.

"If you keep *that* up . . ." she quipped, raising her hips and nudging the fine erection now tenting his sweatpants.

She rolled completely onto her back and raised herself onto her elbows to look at him.

Big mistake.

Pain rolled through her head and she raised her hand to find a sizeable lump on her hairline.

"Ow." She winced and closed her eyes.

The bed bounced as Dylan's weight shifted. "Don't move."

Moving, at this point, was not an option.

"Here . . ." A nudge to her arm encouraged her to open her eyes a slit. Dylan was holding out his palm with two pills on it and had a glass of water in his other hand.

"What are they?" she asked, looking suspiciously at the pills.

"Aspirin. Seriously. They'll just take the edge off that ache. You got a nasty bump there. It's bound to hurt for a while."

"But I . . . we . . ." Tears filled her eyes as she realized she'd lost her shot at finally making it with Dylan Sinclair.

"Yeah. We. I. You and me. It'll happen, honey. But just not right now. Even I'm not that much of a sex fiend."

Susanna struggled to swallow the pills and gratefully accepted the water. "So how much of a sex fiend are you?"

Dylan grinned. "You'll just have to wait and see. Now lie down and rest. It's almost Sunday and there's nothing for you to do but get rid of that headache. Okay?"

"Okay."

She lay back with a sigh and allowed Dylan to tuck the covers around her.

"Dylan?"

"Yeah, babe?"

"Why are you being so nice to me?"

"Gosh. Maybe because I like you? I don't know. I'll have to

think about it. When I decide, can I have Jimmy Thompson pass you a note in gym?"

His smile caressed her face and made her sigh with contentment. She closed her eyes against its brilliance.

"You really are the most devastating man . . ."

She drifted off to sleep, unaware of the lips that dropped a light kiss upon hers.

DYLAN SAT IN THE kitchen area of his town house and tried to read the newspaper. It was the third time he'd read that page, and for the third time he couldn't remember a single word of the editorial article in front of him.

His feet were up on his counter, his favorite tea steamed in the mug beside him, and all was as it should be. Except for one thing.

She was upstairs.

Sizzle Chalmers. The girl who'd featured in most of his masturbation fantasies from the time he'd gotten creative enough to have his own fantasies. The red hair, blue eyes and curvaceous body of the incredibly hot Sizzle Chalmers was in his bedroom.

He turned his head as he heard a sound. Okay, amend that. Sizzle Chalmers was now in his bathroom. And probably taking a shower.

There was an image guaranteed to raise his body temperature and his cock. Sure enough, the thought of Sizzle covered in lather, naked and slithery was enough to send his poor cock back onto high alert. Especially when his mind flipped to the visual of her naked body as he'd undressed her last night.

The fiery thatch between her legs had tempted him beyond belief, and burned itself into his subconscious. He'd seen it every time he closed his eyes. All he could think of was sinking his hands, his lips, his tongue and his cock deep into it and her. He reckoned it was some kind of permanent brain damage, which had resulted in a hard-on that would have done a teenager proud.

It had only taken him the last two hours to get it to settle down.

Oh, he'd dealt with it in the shower. While Susanna slept, he'd stood under the cool water, hoping the beating of the water droplets would diminish the ache. It hadn't.

He'd been forced to take matters into his own hands, so to speak, and with the image of Susanna's pussy in his mind, he'd brought himself to a savage orgasm, which had left him breathless for whole minutes.

His body, however, was dead set on betraying him, because shortly after dressing and coming downstairs to his kitchen he'd found her white cotton panties.

It was all over but the screaming. His cock was hard, his mind boiled and his palms began to sweat.

He drank some tea with a trembling hand. But even Earl Grey couldn't help this time.

He raised the white cotton to his face, and slowly inhaled. Catching sight of his reflection in his toaster, he blushed.

He looked like an idiot teenager, mooning over a crush. But the scent of Susanna had imprinted itself on his mind, and instead of throwing her serviceably ugly underwear in the trash where he considered it belonged, he folded it and tucked

it away in a closet. And made a mental note to himself to re-
place it with black silk at the earliest opportunity. Or maybe
dark green or midnight blue perhaps.

Lord, he wanted this woman. And he was going to get her
too.

Whatever it took.

He folded his newspaper regretfully and rose to pour himself more tea. Hearing the shower turn off, he pulled out another mug and set it on the counter.

Before too long a cautious step sounded and Susanna
walked into the kitchen.

"Hey."

"Hey yourself. How do you feel?" Susanna's eyes lowered in
embarrassment.

"Like a bit of an idiot. But a clean one and my headache's
just about gone. I hope you didn't mind." She gestured vaguely
back up the stairs.

"Not at all. I'm glad you found your clothes." Now *that* was
a huge lie.

"Well, I did find most of them. But there was . . ." she
cleared her throat, " . . . there was one thing missing."

Dylan raised his eyebrows and nodded at the table. "If you
mean those, then yeah. You won't be wearing those again, I'm
afraid."

Spread over the surface of the table was an assortment of
small mechanical parts, some jeweler's tools and a flashlight on
a stand. Draped to one side was her thong, comfortably next to
his. They looked happy.

Dylan wished he was.

"Good lord. You took them apart?"

"Yep. I've also made tea." He held up a mug and looked at her questioningly.

"Oh, yes please. Milk, no sugar. Thanks very much." Susanna moved to the table, poking at the assorted gadgetry. "I can't believe you took them apart."

"Well, I wanted to see how they were assembled. I was nosy. What can I say? It's the engineer in me."

He brought her the mug of tea and stood beside her, surveying the chaos.

"Yes, you said you were an engineer . . . did you figure them out?"

He pulled out a chair and seated her, then took the one next to her and moved a couple of pieces closer to her hand.

"Well, not much to figure out. Yours was a pretty straightforward vibrating unit, but micro-wired so that it was almost undetectable. Until I did *this* . . ."

A portion of the unit bulged and rippled, and Susanna blushed.

"Small but effective, yes?" His grin was lighting up the room.

"Um." Susanna poked at the other unit. "So how about yours?"

"Well, this was the most technologically fascinating, I must admit." He reached over and pulled a small tube toward them.

"This was inserted into the lining of my . . . my thong thing . . ." He lisped over the tiny electronics.

"Oh yeth?"

Dylan frowned at her quip and continued with his lecture. "Yes. Now putting it on was a bit uncomfortable, as you can imagine . . ." Dylan demonstrated with his finger.

Susanna found *herself* getting a bit uncomfortable, forget about the underwear. She squirmed in her chair.

"But once I got aroused, fantastic things started happening."

"So I've heard."

Dylan sighed. "Susanna, knock it off. I'm trying to respect the fact that you hit your head last night. So don't tease, or I'm going to drop my pants and you can watch as I deal with it myself. Are we clear on that?"

The evil and wicked Sizzle, who had completely possessed the right-minded sober Dr. Chalmers, grinned. "Whatever you say, Dylan."

Dylan closed his eyes and took deep breaths for a few moments.

"So when you pressed the button, here's what happened." He showed Susanna how a small stream of lubricant oozed from tiny openings along the tube, and how the jelly-like tube expanded to fit his growing size.

She stared, openmouthed, as he demonstrated the rippling effect that had followed the moisture and jumped as he put her finger inside and let her feel the gentle warmth that was also being generated.

She turned to him, wide-eyed. "Good lord."

"It's quite technically innovative, isn't it? I asked your Dr. Allen about it and he said it's a prototype. But the engineering is amazing. And the micro-circuitry . . . well, it's years ahead of itself."

"Is that what I . . . what a woman . . . is that what it feels like?" A flush spread over her face, but she couldn't stop herself from asking the question. Her curiosity, as always, ran ahead of her tongue.

Dylan smiled and pulled his chair closer.

"Oh no, honey. It's not like that at all. You're feeling something nice, something that's fun, but it's not real. Anymore than this"—he held up her vibrator pak—"feels like the real thing."

"Well, I don't . . . I mean, that is to say, I couldn't really . . ." Her cheeks were approaching combustion.

"Susanna Chalmers. You shock me. You've never enjoyed a man's mouth on you?"

"Dylan, please." Susanna's eyes dropped to the table and she jerked her hand out of the vibrating unit.

"Oh, Sizzle. What a lot you have to learn."

"I beg your pardon. I am well versed in matters of human relationships, Dylan. It is my profession, after all." Susanna had grabbed for her career-woman shield and was bravely struggling to hide behind it.

A quirk to his eyebrow betrayed his knowledge of her attempts at control.

"Yes. And a very interesting career choice it is too, if last night is anything to go by."

"Dylan, I have to apologize about last night . . ."

"It was quite an eventful night, wasn't it?"

"I really had no idea . . ." Susanna was stammering again, and obviously worried about his reaction.

He quietly celebrated. Now he had her just where he wanted her. The game was about to be played. "Well, I suppose it would be wrong of me to hold you responsible."

"I would never have suggested it if I'd known . . ." Her eyes begged his for understanding.

Fifteen-love.

"And I really am so sorry if I put you in an embarrassing position . . ."

Thirty-love.

Dylan managed to pull up a thoughtful expression. "Well, I suppose I could be persuaded to forgive you. Of course, you'd have to make it up to me."

"Just tell me how . . ."

Forty-love.

"Spend next weekend with me? I have been invited to the grand opening of the new Aurora Club and I'd love to take you along. It'll give us a chance to spend some time together without benefit of mechanical appliances." He waved at the table.

"I'd love to."

Game, set and match, Dylan Sinclair.

"But . . ."

Oh shit. Here it comes. She's lodging a protest with the umpire.

"Isn't that some kind of . . . of . . . *domination* club?" She whispered the words, wide-eyed, as if just by saying them she was committing a cardinal sin.

"It does have a few bondage rooms, I understand. Are you afraid of the thought of being tied up, Susanna?"

"Well, I haven't really considered it all that much."

Dylan pulled his chair even closer. "How about the thought of being tied up with soft silk scarves, in a warm room with candles scenting the air. Being turned so that your bare back is facing the room, and knowing that behind you is a man who wants to worship your body . . ."

A bead of sweat appeared on Susanna's upper lip and she closed her eyes, as if swept by his words into his fantasy.

"But also knowing that you've been a naughty girl. He's going to have to remind you about the rules of good behavior. He's going to run his hand over your deliciously bare bottom, and give you a little tap . . . then a sharper one, making your skin tingle and your breasts ache . . ."

Dylan's voice fell even further as his breath brushed her ears.

"Your body gets soft and moist and your pussy swells full of juices. Another harder slap and you breathe in quickly, smelling your own arousal and the heat of the man behind you . . ."

Susanna breathed in.

"You are burning now, waiting for the next touch. Will he slap your bottom again or caress you? Perhaps he might run his tongue over your rosy cheeks . . ."

Susanna's tongue passed over her bottom lip.

Dylan's cock was approaching meltdown.

"Or perhaps he might press his hardness against you, letting you feel his heat all the way down from the back of your beautiful neck to the back of those long . . . long . . . legs."

Dylan drew nearer and nearer until his lips touched hers.

Willing and wanting, they opened, allowing him inside to play.

She was sweet and soft and tasted of his toothpaste mixed with her tea. The little sound she made in the back of her throat turned him on even more and with one swift tug he had her out of her chair and on his lap.

"Are you okay?" He breathed the words into her ear as he ran his tongue around the edge.

She shivered in his grasp. "Yes, thanks."

He wanted to laugh. Polite to the last. But his need to

touch her was greater. His hand slid beneath her sweater and caressed her breast. She arched her back a little, making the contact easier for them both.

It was all the encouragement he needed. This was his chance to make sure of her. To make her want him enough to be with him, to not stand him up Saturday night after her sharp little brain had decided that seeing him would be a bad idea.

He slipped her bra catch and cupped the soft heaviness of her naked breast. The nipple was hard and getting harder beneath his fingers as he rolled it, first roughly then as gently as a delicate flower.

She moaned and her hips ground against his arousal.

He wished for at least four more hands, knowing that he was going to have to leave her perfect breasts and visit other places that were begging for his attention.

With a mental wave goodbye he pulled his hand away from under her sweater, only to hear her groan in distress.

"Don't worry, there's more."

He showed her.

His hand easily moved up her thigh under her skirt. And without underwear, her warmth was ready for him, soft, moist and hungry.

Her mouth devoured his as his fingers found her core.

She was wet for him, hot and wet, and she spread her legs wider as he pulled her hard against him.

He answered her call with his fingers, pressing, circling, flicking, driving her into a wriggling mass of need.

"Dylan, please Dylan, ohmigod," she gasped, struggling for breath.

His cock was screaming, but he knew it would have to just shut up. This one was for her. It was a case of thinking long term. An investment now would pay off handsomely later.

He proceeded to ensure the safety of future dividends.

"Lift your sweater for me," he growled, wondering if she was gone far enough to do as he asked.

She was.

Bending her over his arm, he lowered his head, seeking her nipple with his lips.

She sobbed as he latched on, one leg sliding to the floor and opening her secrets to his hand. He felt her muscles begin to tighten, and suckled harder, rolling her nipple between his teeth and allowing himself tiny nips that he softened with strokes of his tongue.

"Dylan—" The word was torn from her throat as her hips pressed up against his hand. She was soaking wet, hotter than fire and he could feel her pulse pounding in her clit.

He slid two fingers inside her and his thumb up under her clit.

He pressed.

She screamed and came around his fingers; strong muscle spasms grabbing him like a satin vise grip. He raised his head and watched as her eyes rolled back, her mouth fell open and she sobbed, lungs desperate for air.

One more wriggle and he'd come in his pants just from looking at her. His hand went to his zipper, but then he remembered her injury.

She wriggled her hips as her spasms died away.

He did something he hadn't done in fifteen years. He came in his pants.

"Oh lord." His eyes fell to his lap as a stain spread over the front of his jeans.

"I . . ." Susanna was recovering. "Oh my. Is that for me?" She eased back and slid off his knees, gazing at the moisture on his fly.

"It should have been."

She raised her blue eyes to his face and looked at him uncertainly.

Well, at least he'd done that much today. Managed to get Sizzle Chalmers completely off balance. Time to tip the scales a bit more.

"Of course it might have been for the other three women who were writhing and screaming on my lap as they came."

"I didn't writhe. Did I?"

"Yes. You writhed. Or wrothe. Or whatever the past tense of writhe is. You did it. And very well too, I might add." He crossed to the counter and grabbed a towel. Rubbing at the front of his jeans, he sighed. "I haven't had this happen in years."

Susanna took the towel away from his hands, and put her palm flat against his zipper, surprising both of them.

"Thank you, Dylan. For this. For what you just did."

His gaze fell to her lips, reddened and puffy from his kisses. He leaned forward.

"You're welcome." He kissed her again, softly this time, but as soon as she slipped her tongue into his mouth he felt a chill run up his spine and his cock move beneath her hand.

He wrenched himself away, knowing that one second more and he'd have her naked on his kitchen floor.

That was soooo not how he wanted it to finally happen between them.

"I . . . I . . . have to go . . ." she stuttered, looking as shaken as he felt.

"So it's a date for next Saturday," he insisted, trying to keep a predatory growl out of his voice.

"Yes. Okay. All right. I mean, sure. Whatever. Dylan, I really have to get out of here. I can't breathe."

Dylan grinned, slipped on his sneakers, and pulled a long sweatshirt over his ruined pants.

He grabbed his car keys and opened the kitchen door. If she thought she was breathless now . . .

O H. MY. GOD.

Susanna stared at herself in her mirror, wondering who the hell she was looking at.

The note in the box had been short and to the point . . . *Sorry, I didn't realize until the last minute it was a Black-and-White Ball. This should cover it.*

"This" had turned out to be the most magnificent full-length black silk gown. Halter style, it locked at the back of the neck and at the wrap waist with small magnetic clasps concealed as jeweled medallions.

It was elegant, sexy, and like nothing she'd ever worn. Especially when paired with the black silk thong and thigh-high pantyhose. Susanna couldn't decide if she looked like a society queen or a hooker. No, make that a call girl. She'd certainly have to charge a lot for a night when she looked like this.

She giggled at herself. As if *that* would happen.

She ran her hands through her hair and decided on the spur of the moment to experiment. Instead of her usual sleek updo, she pulled the red locks into a soft tumble and secured it on top of her head, allowing wispy curls to drift willy-nilly down across her bare back.

She loved the feel of her hair just brushing her skin. Braless, her nipples poked through the silk as she responded to the sensual touch of her own hair.

The phone jangled and roused her from her reverie.

"So how's the dress? Does it fit? What does it look like? Are you going with the thong, too?" Sylvia's voice came over the line, full of questions and curiosity.

"I should never have let you look inside the box, should I?" laughed Susanna.

They'd both been struck dumb when the box had arrived at Susanna's office the day before, but it hadn't taken Sylvia long to find her tongue.

"Holy shit, woman. This guy wants you baaaaad. . . ."

"Oh really? And on what evidence do you base that supposition?" Susanna had raised a clinical eyebrow at her friend.

"This kind of gives the whole thing away." Sylvia was holding the little piece of fabric that pretended to be underwear. "Butt floss. Of course you can get away with it, not having much of a butt for it to floss. However, when a man buys that for a woman it says only one thing . . ."

"And what would that be, *Dr.* Sylvia?" laughed Susanna.

"'*I want to take it off you. Slowly.*' Or maybe he wants to work around it . . ."

Susanna had ended the conversation right there, the image of Dylan removing her panties being far too unsettling to be enjoyed in her office. That was a fantasy better shared with her Tubmate II.

"So, c'mon . . . tell me . . ." Sylvia's voice all but shrieked into Susanna's ear as she held her phone between her neck and her chin and struggled with her thigh-high hosiery.

"It looks fine, Syl, just fine. If I could just manage these damn . . . hang on . . ." She put the phone down and adjusted the hose, amazed at how well they fit. Dylan had certainly paid attention to her clothing sizes when he'd had the chance. Everything had slid onto her body like it had been made for her.

"Okay. Got them. I've never worn thigh-highs before. Did you know there were shoes in here too?"

"Really? Damn, you should have let me dig some more. Are they slutty shoes? You know, CFM's?"

"CFM's?"

"Yeah, those high-heeled, strappy little numbers that scream Come-Fuck-Me?"

"Yep. Those are the ones." Susanna dangled one high-heeled, strappy little number from her hand and watched as it definitely screamed "Come-Fuck-Me."

"Oh boy. Just once, I'd give anything to be in your CFM's. You're going to have one hell of a weekend, Sus. Make sure you enjoy every second, okay?"

Susanna grinned at the shoe. "I'm planning on it."

"Well, good for you, girl. It's time the real Susanna Chalmers came out to play. And your Dylan is the perfect playmate, too, I'd guess . . ."

"I don't know about perfect, but he's certainly a playmate."

"Do I sense some caution there?"

"Look Sylvia, I'm going along this weekend for several reasons. Firstly, I'm extremely curious about the Aurora Club—who wouldn't be? Secondly, I owe Dylan for the fiasco of last weekend's seminar, and thirdly, I'd like to get him out of my system once and for all. This is going to be the prom night experience I wanted but never had. When it's over, I'll be able to get back to normal."

"Hmm."

"Hmm? That's all you have to say, hmm?"

"Susanna. If those are your goals for this weekend, then fine. I think you are forgetting something, however."

"Oh? And what's that?"

"You're nuts about Dylan Sinclair."

"*What?*" Susanna's screech could have melted steel at twenty yards. "I am not *nuts* about Dylan. I'm probably a little obsessed with what he represents . . ."

"Honey," said Sylvia patiently. "You've done nothing but think about him since that first night, and let's face it, you probably are what and where you are today because of your need to explore your relationship with him. Or lack thereof. Okay . . ." she continued, sensing Susanna's indrawn breath. "He's been out of your life since high school. But what he represented stayed with you and drove you into your career. Examining relationships. Figuring them out. Fixing them."

Susanna stared blankly at the shoe, not seeing it, but thinking about Sylvia's words.

"All I'm saying is, be careful. Sure, go ahead and screw each other's brains out, play Indiana Jones with his leather whip at this fancy club. Have some really wonderful adult sexy together. But don't think you're going to be able to toss it aside when you're done. You can't. You're not that type of person."

"Well, you may be wrong there, Syl. In this dress I might well be that kind of person." Susanna gave her image one more glance, smoothing her hand over the soft silk.

"Honey, have a wonderful time. Enjoy every second. But don't go pretending or hiding. Not with this guy. He'll call you on it. Oops . . . pizza's here. Gotta go. I want *all* the details on Monday, remember . . . and don't forget condoms."

A click signaled the end of the conversation, and Susanna thoughtfully put the phone back on the table.

The doorbell rang.

She debated whether to answer the door or go to the bathroom and throw up.

Deciding it would be a shame to waste such a cool dress, she swallowed her stomach back down, told it to stay put, and went to open the door.

"HELLO."

Her voice slid down his spine, offering all kinds of delights and asking if he would like to share in a few.

"Yes, please . . ."

"Sorry?"

"Umm . . . I mean hi. I'm here . . . it's . . . er . . ." Good God, he was stuttering like a lovesick idiot. Pulling his thoughts out of his cock with an enormous effort, Dylan smiled at Susanna who was staring at him as if he'd lost his mind. "It's that dress. It took my breath away, wiped my brain of all rational thought and also did some rather nice things to my libido."

"Yes. I see. Um . . . thank you for the dress, by the way. It's . . . it's a perfect fit. It was very nice of you to think of it." She turned to pick up her coat and bag, and blew away a few more of his brain cells with a flash of perfect creamy back.

She had one small mole just above her waist where her back curved.

Dylan found, to his surprise, that he wanted to cover it with his hand. That was *his* mole. He didn't want anyone else seeing it. He was busily making plans for that mole.

She turned again, removing the mole from his sight as she slipped her coat over her shoulders.

He shook off his possessive instincts and helped her.

"You look very nice too," she said, a rather husky note in her voice.

He shrugged. They were his favorite leather pants and he'd grabbed the most comfortable white silk turtleneck he had. He was in black and white, that was all he cared about. If she liked his clothes, so much the better. She'd like what was in them more.

He settled her in the Jeep.

"I'm glad you decided to come with me, Sizzle." He started the engine to cover the noise of her protest. "Don't bother. Tonight you are Sizzle. I don't want to take Dr. Chalmers with me, for all that she's an intelligent charming woman. I want Sizzle as my date. The Sizzle with all that soft red hair falling onto creamy white shoulders. The Sizzle who burns when I touch her. The Sizzle who's going to play with me and learn new things about herself and her limits. The Sizzle who's wearing the thong I sent her, even though I wish she was wearing nothing at all under that fabulous dress . . ."

Susanna wriggled on the seat and Dylan grinned. "We're going to have fun, Sizzle. Trust me."

"Humpf." Dylan couldn't tell from that sound if she was agreeing or not, but her body language was speaking volumes. The whisper of silk as she crossed her legs was matched by her indrawn breath and he smiled as he caught her hands brushing against each other.

God knew *his* palms were sweating already, it was only fair *hers* should be too.

"How did you get this invitation, Dylan? To the Aurora Club? I've read about it, of course, what with all the zoning hubbub . . ."

She was referring to the purchase of the old Mathers estate by a rather wealthy corporation, headed by none other than Aurora Swann, heiress to the Swann brewery gazillions.

"I know Aurora."

"You do?" Susanna's voice nearly rose to a squeak and she turned her head to stare at him. "You actually know Aurora Swann? Filthy rich heiress? Woman who is reported to have a collection of every antique piece of bondage equipment from 1814 through the Edwardian era?"

"Yep."

"How . . . does she . . . I mean . . . has she . . . did you . . ."

"There you go again, Sizzle. Spit it out before you choke, will you?" Dylan grinned at her confusion.

He heard her take a deep breath. "How did you cross paths with Aurora?"

"We were in college together. She was a year ahead, but we ended up in a couple of the same engineering courses."

"Oh, I see . . ." Susanna digested that information for a

moment. "Engineering? Aurora Swann was an engineer?"

"No. I didn't say that. We both ended up taking a couple of extra credit engineering study courses. Not really on the books. More like project courses. And make no mistake, Sizzle . . ."—he flashed her a quick glance. . . —"behind all the razzmatazz, Aurora Swann has an exceptionally sharp mind. One of the best engineers I've run into. And she was majoring in biology too, along with social studies."

"Ah."

"She had a double major, and, if I remember correctly, a minor in history, which helped when it came time to assemble her toy box. That's what she calls her antiques collection . . . her toy box."

"Really."

"Victorian bondage items were the ones that really did it for her. As soon as eBay became a reality, she was buying up every paddle, flogger and spanking machine she could get her hands on."

"Oh my."

"We kept in touch off and on, and she's always wanted to invest in my company, but I like to keep friendship and business separate. Nice to know that the Swann millions are there, though."

"I'm sure."

There was no mistaking the gritted teeth tone coming from the woman sitting stiffly next to him. Dylan restrained his snigger. She was sooooo his.

"And no, we never slept together."

"I didn't ask. Nor would I. It is no business at all of mine who you do or don't sleep with."

"Tsk, tsk, Sizzle. Ending a sentence with a preposition. What would Mrs. Farber say?"

Susanna refused to rise to the mention of her old English teacher and Dylan judged, rightly, that she was still steaming over his praise of Aurora Swann. Perhaps it was time to find out.

"Mad at me?" he asked the question softly.

"Mad? No, of course not. Why would I be mad? I asked a question and you gave me a fair answer. Along with a paean of praise about our hostess, to be sure, but certainly nothing to get mad about. And I couldn't care less whether you two slept together or not."

"That's pretty liberal of you. Of course, I don't want to know who you've slept with either. However, I don't want to know because I'd get real mad. I don't even want to consider that anyone else might have stroked those soft shoulders of yours. Or perhaps touched their lips to that little spot inside your elbows."

He watched, delightedly, as she wriggled again on his front seat. They were nearing their destination and he wanted her hot by the time they got there.

"I'd go crazy if I spent any time at all thinking about some-one else running their tongue up your back and nipping at that spot where your muscles meet your neck."

She sighed.

"And you'd probably have to lock me up if you told me that anyone had buried his face in that sweet spot beneath your breasts. I want to nibble you there, Sizzle. I want to feel the weight of your breasts on my face. I want to bury myself in your warmth and your scent. I want my hands all over you, finding erogenous zones in places where you never even knew you had *places*, let alone erogenous zones. Last weekend in my kitchen was an appetizer. This weekend I want the entree. And dessert. And possibly even a sherbet interlude."

Her breath was coming in ragged gasps now and he could smell the heat coming from her skin beneath her clothes.

He smiled as he steered the vehicle into a convenient space next to the huge circular driveway.

"I want to be the one to fuck you, Sizzle. Fuck you until you forget who you are, who I am, what day it is and where we are. Fuck you until the only thing that exists for either of us is my cock deep inside your cunt, driving us both along the path that leads to madness . . . or heaven."

He'd turned the engine off and leaned toward her, letting his eyes reinforce his hot little speech. Her china blue gaze reflected the dashboard lights and he saw her pupils dilate with desire.

"But for the moment, shall we go play?"

NUMBLY, SUSANNA LET DYLAN lead her from the car to the house.

His words were clanging in her brain and ringing all her sex bells in harmony. Her nipples felt like raw nerves, abraded by even the slightest touch of her silk gown, and she knew her thong was soaked. She was close to leaping on Dylan right this second, dragging him behind a very large azalea and finding out exactly where that pathway to heaven he'd talked about led to.

Damn, another preposition. Her mental processes were definitely fried this evening.

Of course, the fact that he looked like the living embodiment of every fantasy she'd ever had wasn't helping calm her state of heightened arousal.

Those dratted leather pants fit just *right*, and the slight sound they made as he moved simply added to the overall impression of super studliness. His white silk turtleneck slid over his strong shoulders rather like she thought her tongue might. She kept remembering the feel of his cock swelling beneath her palm and his wet jeans. She stifled a moan.

He handed his coat to the maid in the little French outfit and waited as she removed hers.

Once again, his eyes traveled over her body, detailing her dress, probably counting the number of goose pimples in her cleavage and bringing another rush of moisture to her pussy. If he didn't cut it out she was going to drown before the night was half over.

Self-consciously she turned away, only to feel the warmth of his palm as he placed it low on her spine.

"Get used to it, Sizzle. My hand is going to be right there tonight. You have this little mole . . ." His fingers flicked at a little sensitive spot on her spine and she shivered. "Yeah, right there. I want to sink my teeth into it, so bad . . ."

The color flushed through her cheeks as they passed into what had to be the main ballroom.

She'd been too distracted to pay much attention to her surroundings, but now Susanna could only gasp.

Everything was in black and white.

The decor, the candles, the flowers, even the food. There were small touches of green where live plants insisted on their own natural colors, but other than that, the entire room was an exercise in chiaroscuro.

The guests, other than flesh and hair, were also in black and white. It was like stepping into an old-time movie.

"Ah, here's Aurora. Let me introduce you."

Dylan's warm hand urged her across the floor to where a strikingly tall woman was holding court amidst a small crowd of smiling men.

She saw Dylan's approach and waved off her admirers, turning her whiskey-brown eyes on him and Susanna.

Her full lips curved in a welcoming grin. "Dylan, sweetie. So glad you could make it."

She slid one arm around his neck and brought his face close. "Now I know it's party time." Shamelessly, her tongue flickered out and licked his lips. She pulled his head to hers and kissed him thoroughly, ignoring the seething redhead at his side.

"Ahem."

Pulling back, Dylan quirked his eyebrow at Susanna. "Ah, Aurora. Let me introduce Dr. Susanna Chalmers. Sizzle, this is Aurora."

"Sizzle. How quaint. The hair, I suppose. Poor dear, you must have hated it."

Susanna opened her mouth to respond politely, but was prevented from doing so as her hostess rambled on.

"Dylan, I took a look at those plans you sent over last month. I like them, but I think you could definitely upgrade the circuitry. I'll fax over the name of a developer I found recently. He's got some great ideas." She wriggled her hips against him. "And some great moves, too."

"Aurora, cut it out. You'll give Sizzle the wrong idea."

Susanna snorted. Too late. She'd already gotten them. Quite a few of them, too.

Aurora grinned and pinched Dylan's butt. "God I love a man's backside in leather, don't you?"

Susanna gaped.

"Don't worry, honey. Dylan's always been off-limits. I guess this was one time when having a friend seemed more important than having sex. Although looking at him tonight . . . weeeellll . . ." She drawled the word out and licked her lips lasciviously.

Susanna had to laugh. This was quite a woman, and one she could probably like. Now that she knew there was nothing going on between her and Dylan, of course. It wouldn't have bothered Dr. Chalmers, but Sizzle definitely felt better.

"Yes. A man's backside in leather is a splendid thing. No arguments from me there." She grinned up at Aurora.

Close on six feet, Aurora Swann was one powerful woman. Her dark hair tumbled every which way, and her gown couldn't decide whether to be a designer original or a very badly fitting leftover from the seventies. All things considered, Susanna would be glad to call her a friend. She'd be even gladder if Aurora would go away and let her explore Dylan's backside on her own. In a dark place. Without interruption. And maybe with some whipped cream and ice cubes.

God, where had *that* thought come from?

Shaking her head, she was recalled from her erotic fantasy when a stir at the door heralded another guest.

Susanna's heart sank as she saw Dr. Jonas Allen stride into the room.

He was wearing a bright red sweater.

Aurora drew in a breath. "Have that one bathed and sent to my quarters."

Susanna turned to see Aurora staring at Dr. Allen, her mouth slightly agape.

Ignoring both Dylan and Susanna, she moved forward to meet the newcomer.

"You'll have to take that sweater off. It's a Black and White ball."

Susanna could hear Aurora's voice clearly.

"I will if you will. We'll have our own pink and rosebud ball."

Dr. Allen had glanced down at Aurora's exceedingly low cut gown. The two of them towered over everyone else in the room.

"You're on."

Before Susanna's amazed eyes, Aurora grabbed Dr. Jonas Allen by the hand and whisked him out of the room.

"Well, I never . . ." she muttered, turning to find Dylan grinning from ear to ear.

"Aurora knows what she wants. I think she's going to get more than she bargained for with Jonas, though."

"Jonas? Now he's a friend of yours?"

"We had a chat last week—I was impressed with his product and called to tell him so. Sharp guy."

"Ah." Susanna was beginning to feel that her life had somehow unraveled and been knitted up again into someone else's.

"But that's neither here nor there." Dylan's hand went back to "his" spot on her spine.

"Now I think it's time for us to either eat, dance, or go find a place to fuck ourselves blind. What do you say?"

O<small>KAY. S</small>O <small>ASKING HER</small> what she wanted to do had been a
tactical error. Memo to self—never ask a woman you
want to fuck if she'd like to eat or dance first. You'd end up
with a belly full of tasteless hors d'oeuvres, ears ringing with
dance music and a hard-on that could double as a towel rack
after wasting an entire hour on social idiocies.

And to exacerbate his frustration, she was probably perfectly happy.

In fact, Susanna was humming along with the band as she
snuggled into Dylan's arms. He couldn't believe she was unaware of the large lump in his leathers that was threatening to
drill its way into her soft flesh. He swallowed.

Enough was enough.

He guided their steps toward a darkened hallway that led
from the main ballroom.

"Where are we going?"

"I thought a little guided tour might be in order."

"Oh. Okay. I admit I'm nosy about this place."

Dylan smiled as he led her down the softly carpeted hall. "This is one of the smaller corridors," he said, chattily. "In case you're wondering, my firm consulted on some of the engineering modifications Aurora wanted. That's how I know about it. I haven't actually been here before, so it's all new to me too. Ah . . . here we are . . ."

They reached a stairwell and Dylan pulled her up behind him.

"We're now crossing into the upper wing, which is basically reserved for club members only."

Susanna hesitated. "Should we be here?"

"Oh yes. We're members. Didn't you realize that?"

She shook her head, wide-eyed. "Dylan, I don't have that kind of money . . . it's thousands of dollars to become a member."

"Perks of knowing me, babe. We got comp memberships along with the invitation. We're in, whether we like it or not."

"What's not to like?" she murmured as the stairs opened out onto a darkened space. Doors were spaced at regular intervals, and low, flickering sconces illuminated heavy wrought iron hardware.

"Why do I feel like I've stepped back in time?"

"Aurora wanted this to look Victorian. But there are some differences. Come see . . ."

He led her to a large portrait of a woman reclining on a riverbank. Touching a panel at the side of the painting, the image disappeared, to be replaced by a clear view of the occupants of the room behind.

Susanna gasped. "My God. They're . . ."

And yes they were. Naked and writhing, a man and a woman were engaging in one of humanity's basic activities. They were fucking. Energetically too. Her legs were wrapped tightly around his waist and his hands were clenched on her buttocks as he lifted her body off the bed and drove into her.

His cock shone with moisture as he pulled himself from her body, then his face contorted as he plunged back again.

Susanna was unnaturally still. Dylan glanced down. She was glued to the scene before her, teeth gnawing at her bottom lip. He could see her pulse throbbing in her neck. He ached.

Touching the panel again, the couple disappeared, replaced by the electronic Old Master.

"Incredible . . ." she muttered.

"Yes, interesting technology, isn't it?"

"No, not that. Well, yes, that too, but I mean . . . did they know that we could see them? This seems almost voyeuristic. We shouldn't—"

"Oh, they knew." Dylan raised one eyebrow at her. "You of all people should be well aware that the possibility of being watched while having sex is a turn-on for some folks."

"Well, yes, but I never—"

"Oh, really? What about prom night?"

Susanna shut her mouth with a snap.

Moving down the hall and dragging Susanna behind him, Dylan stopped in front of another painting. This one had a man in a suit of armor looking very uncomfortable.

But not as uncomfortable as the man inside the room. He was revealed in all his naked glory as Dylan hit the switch.

The light gleamed off the firm back of a man whose arms

were tied to posts secured to the wall. He was spread-eagled and hooded, and behind him stood a woman flexing her hand as she snaked a long length of leather along the floor.

It was Aurora.

Clad in little more than a lace bustier, her mile long legs and tumbled hair gave her away.

That meant that the man in the hood was Jonas Allen.

Dylan heard Susanna gulp as Aurora raised the whip.

He closed the image before the thong landed, cutting off the scene before them and catching Susanna as she nearly toppled into the window.

"Liked that, did you?"

"I . . . I . . . did you see? She . . . he . . ."

Judging by the stuttering that Susanna was more than interested, Dylan moved her along the corridor to a second stairway.

"I think it's time to find *our* suite."

"*Our* suite? We have a suite?"

"Yes. Up here. On the next floor. Where there are no windows. Either real or electronic. What we do will be for our eyes alone. Is that okay with you, Susanna?"

AT THIS POINT, SUSANNA didn't dare answer Dylan's question. Her voice would have been a grunt, or a squeak or some strange mix of the two. Either way, it would have certainly betrayed the fact that she was more turned on than she'd ever been in her entire life.

It was probably wiser not to let Dylan know. At least not yet.

He led her to a darkened doorway and turned the huge key.

"Keys? Seems a little archaic . . ." She watched as he withdrew the ornate metal contraption.

Two rivets blinked green.

Dylan smiled. "Never underestimate technology, sweetheart." He ushered her into their room and allowed the door to swing shut behind them. The key went back into the lock and more rivets changed color. There was even an accompanying "clang."

"Very impressive," muttered Susanna.

Her mind still swirling with the images of the couples she'd seen on the lower floor, she moved to put a little space between her and the hot body of Dylan Sinclair.

The room was large. Darkly paneled walls soared above her and one end of the room was dominated by a huge fourposter bed that looked like it could have slept ten in a pinch.

Dylan was busily lighting the candles that were placed in sconces around the room and turning off the electric lights.

The more candles he lit the more authentic the room seemed, and when he fiddled with the controls next to the fireplace and a leaping flame shot flickers of light into the room, Susanna could almost see Queen Victoria toasting her royal toes.

He adjusted the flame.

She sighed.

He caught her eye and shrugged. "Hey, at least I don't have to go chop wood. The effect is the same."

"So much for complete authenticity . . ." She let her mouth droop downward. He grinned at her, and caught by the playfulness of his smile she allowed herself to return his look.

Prowling the soft carpet, her attention was caught by a chain hanging from one of the posts at the foot of the bed. On either end was a leather cuff, lined with soft fur and ending in a solid metal buckle.

"Are these . . . ?"

"Yes. They're handcuffs."

"Well, duh. I figured that out all by myself." Susanna glanced scornfully at Dylan who was now standing in front of the fire and watching her. She couldn't see his eyes, just his silhouette against the glow of the flames.

"Try them on. See how they feel . . ."

Cautiously, she picked them up.

They weighed less than she'd expected, and she turned them over in her hands, admiring the craftsmanship. Unable to resist, she slipped one around her wrist, tightening the buckle.

It was not an unpleasant feeling, other than the slight tickle from the fur on the sensitive skin inside her arm.

"Oh you have to use both, Susanna. If you really want to know how it felt to be a slave, bound in your master's quarters . . . awaiting his pleasure."

His voice had dropped to a whisper and sent a thrill through her stomach, coming to rest in a hot coil low in her pussy.

She was a victim of her own curiosity. Reaching up, she pulled the chain down and awkwardly fastened the other cuff. She had to raise her hands because the entire chain didn't allow her the room to drop her arms by her sides.

The buckle clicked shut loudly in the almost silent room.

"Well. There we are . . ." She jokingly smiled over her shoulder at Dylan. "Now I'm the upstairs maid. Let me see, you can be Lord Witherspoon, and I'll be Daisy. Now, what are you going to punish me for?"

"Oh, I'll think of something." Dylan's smile was pure, one hundred percent organic wickedness.

His hands dropped to his waist and he pulled his shirt up over his head.

Susanna's eyes widened.

Suddenly, with tousled hair and a naked chest gleaming in the candlelight, he seemed much more masculine and raw. The leather pants hugged his body and outlined his erection and he made no attempt to hide it.

Susanna caught her breath, swamped by a sudden flood of need.

"Oh yeah. That's better. Too many clothes."

She swallowed at his words, and tugged on her chain. "Well, I'm afraid that's out of my hands." She laughed, trying to joke her way through a screaming need to plaster her body all over his.

"Not a problem."

Dylan reached onto the mantel and removed a small, rather familiar looking, little box. There were two buttons on it.

"Oh no . . . Dylan, noooo . . . ." Susanna almost shrieked the words. "Please, not the damned underwear."

Dylan choked back a laugh. "No, it's all right. Don't worry. No mechanical toys this time. Well . . . almost none."

He pressed the button and Susanna closed her eyes and held her breath.

There was a slight click behind her and the neck of her dress unfastened, dropping to her waist.

She gasped and looked at Dylan.

He grinned and pushed the other button.

The waist of her dress unfastened and the whole thing tumbled to the floor in a black pool of silk.

She was chained to the four-poster in nothing but a thong, her thigh-high hosiery and her CFM's.

"Dear heavens . . ." she murmured, stunned.

"Well, hot damn. It worked. *Okay*." A huge grin pasted itself across Dylan's face.

"*Now* we can have some fun."

If his cock didn't self-destruct first.

Seeing Susanna chained to the bed, practically naked, and his for the taking, was doing terribly wonderful things to his erection.

He flipped the hook open at the waist of his pants and breathed a little easier.

Susanna's eyes followed his hands.

His cock swelled even more. She was all but licking her lips. Her nipples were budding points casting shadows down over her soft breasts, and he could see the faint glimmer of moisture on her thighs.

She wanted him. Almost as badly as he wanted her.

He crossed the room. It was time for him to take over as "Master" for a little while. After all, he had gone to great lengths to set the whole scene up. Damned if he was going to waste it by just laying her down and thrusting into her blindly until he was sated. Which would take until a week from Thursday, give or take a month or two.

Silently, he unclipped her chains and reattached her cuffs together behind her back.

Gently he pressed on her shoulders, urging her down onto her knees. He ran his hand through her hair, spreading it over her shoulders.

He wanted to caress her breasts, but didn't dare. He should get some sort of a medal for restraint, he told himself, but he'd promised her some fun and games and that, by God, was what they were going to have. Or die trying.

Her blue eyes looked questioningly up at him.

"Take my pants off for me."

"How? I'm cuffed here, in case you hadn't noticed." She raised a quizzical eyebrow.

"Improvise. You're a smart woman." He thrust his hips forward slightly, wondering how long it would take for her to figure something out. Wondering how long he'd survive when she did.

The answer to the first question was not long, and, as she leaned forward and delicately grabbed his zipper with her teeth, he had a gnawing suspicion that it would be the same answer for the second question too.

Her head slid down, drawing the zipper with it, and he heaved a sigh of relief as his cock forced its way between the leathers.

Susanna's breath fanned his balls. "Dylan . . ." She sounded almost shocked. "No underwear."

"After last time, did you think I'd risk it?" He gave her a wry smile.

She turned her head to look up at him and brushed his cock with her hair. He couldn't help the gasp.

A gleam entered her eye and she went back to removing his pants and demonstrating her considerable dental dexterity.

She managed to lick her way down one side of his buttock as she pulled the fabric away from his hips, and her breasts "accidentally" rubbed over his knees as she dragged the waistband down as far as she could.

No doubt about it, Sizzle Chalmers was definitely enjoying herself.

Well, hell.

Now what was he supposed to do? For someone who had planned on "mastering" Sizzle tonight, the roles had become rather blurred. He wasn't actually sure who was mastering who. Or whom. Where was Mrs. Farber when you needed her?

She brushed his cock with her cheek, slowly and caressingly.

That did it. She was definitely mastering him. This was not what he had intended. He would have to stop it. Immediately. In just an hour or two.

"Dylan?" Her breath was ruffling his short curls. God that felt good. He'd really have to keep control of things, or he was going to embarrass himself twice in a row. That would not be a good thing.

"Mmm?"

"I want to taste you."

His brain short-circuited. "Okay . . ."

"I've never actually . . . well that is, I don't know . . . I mean . . ."

"Susanna." The fact that his voice was still working had to rank as Miracle of the Week. "Just do what feels right."

She smiled, blue eyes glittering in the candlelight. She licked her lips, slowly, and dropped her gaze to his cock.

He trembled, he couldn't help it.

Her tongue reached out and lightly flicked at the bead of pre-cum that was oozing from the tip of his poor, suffering, aching cock.

He sucked in air.

She glanced up, a new knowledge flooding into her eyes. He'd just handed her control.

She licked him again, more forcefully this time.

He'd worry about control later.

Even with her hands cuffed behind her, Susanna was beginning to find her way around the idea of oral pleasure.

He bit back a moan as she plunged her mouth over a good portion of his length, teasing and tantalizing with flicks of her tongue as she pulled her head back.

He dropped his hands to her hair, brushing it back from her face so that he could clearly see her mouth as she took his cock in and out, and her eyes as they closed in concentration.

"I want to touch you," she breathed in mid-stroke.

"Nooo . . ." he groaned, knowing it would be all over but the screaming if she got her curious little hands on him as well.

"Dylan, let me touch you, please?" Her tongue traced up the underside of his cock and licked at the dribbles of moisture she was causing.

"No."

With an effort that practically burst blood vessels, Dylan backed away from her.

"Stand up." His voice was harsh with need and his cock, now a purplish red.

"Turn around." She did as she was bid.

Her hands were cuffed low on her back and he couldn't resist thrusting his cock into them.

She scrabbled for a hold, but he pushed past, seeking the insubstantial thong and the treasures that lay beyond.

He pulled the back of the thong to one side and rubbed himself up and down her cleft.

By this time, her hands were cupping his balls and he was pressed close against her.

They both moaned as his cock dug into her most private places.

"Dylan . . . Dylan, don't . . . I haven't . . ." She stuttered and froze as she felt the swollen head of his cock pressed against the tight ring of muscles between her cheeks.

Dylan just held himself there for a moment, knowing he'd go no farther but needing to wrench some control back from this fiery woman who threatened to devour him, body and soul.

He slid his hands down to her cuffs and stepped back.

Tugging her along, he sat on the bed and with a quick pull tumbled her facedown across his knees.

Finally, he had Sizzle Chalmers where he wanted her.

8

HIS QUICK MOVE SURPRISED her, and Susanna couldn't stop a squawk from bursting out of her throat as she fell, sprawling, across his lap.

Her breasts dangled toward the floor as he held her wrists tight with one hand and played with her thong with the other.

"Now, Dr. Chalmers. We are going to talk about a certain night eleven years ago."

Oh, no. This was not a good thing right now. Susanna wanted fucking, not discussing. This was not a time for soul baring or reminiscing. This was a time for getting out of her thong and getting his cock to where it would do the most good. Inside *her*.

Obviously Dylan understood the first part of her needs, at least.

His hand slid under the waistband of her thong and he

tugged, this way and that, knowing that the fabric would be pulling against her swollen labia.

"Pleeeeasssse . . ."

"Mmm. Yes. We certainly need to talk about that night."

How could he think, let alone talk? She could feel his cock like an iron bar against her side. She wanted him, he wanted her, what the hell was the holdup?

"No, we really don't, Dylan. Couldn't we just . . ."

"Just what, Sizzle?"

"Just . . . you know . . ."

"No. Tell me. Tell me what you want." His fingers trailed across her buttocks and eased the thong down past her hips. She realized with the small, still-sane portion of her mind that he was pretty damn dexterous with one hand. The other was still firmly holding her in place.

She writhed a little, to indicate her needs and also to help him rid her of that damned thong. After tonight she was seriously considering never wearing underwear again. It was nothing but trouble.

"You spied, Sizzle. You were a naughty girl." A hand smoothed her flesh, and dipped between her thighs, making her sigh.

"You know what happens to naughty girls, don't you?"

She shook her head.

A sudden sharp slap jerked her straight out across his knees.

"Ow. That stung."

"It was supposed to."

Another slap followed, this time in the center of one cheek.

She gasped, waiting for the sting and burn to follow. It was sharp, but warming, and she realized, incredibly, that it was heightening her arousal. Her clinical mind wanted to take notes and observe the physical reactions to the stimulation.

The rest of her just wanted more.

She got her wish.

"Naughty girls have to learn their lessons, Sizzle." The hand focused on the other cheek with a sharp blow.

"I . . . I . . ." she stuttered, wriggling beneath his hold.

"Oh my, what beautiful rosy cheeks." He bent forward and ran his tongue across her flesh.

She yelled at the feeling. "Dylan . . ." His warm wet tongue had passed over her newly sensitized skin like a lightning rod charged with electricity. She'd never imagined a tongue could feel like that.

Before she had a chance to fully examine the sensation, a flurry of smaller smacks warmed her upper thighs.

"Are you sorry you spied on me and the twins that night? Sorry you watched me come?"

"No," she grunted, gritting her teeth and desperately fighting her cuffs. She wanted. She *needed*. She was getting desperate to feel Dylan inside her. The memories he was recalling, along with the punishment he was administering to her backside, were turning her into a seething wriggling mass of lust. She might just be the first fatality recorded from unfulfilled desire.

Her bottom was burning now, and she knew it must be bright red beneath his palm. She was sweating, her heart was racing and she waited for the next blow almost eagerly.

It never came.

Instead, Dylan's fingers teased between her legs, pushing their way through her juices to her cunt.

She moaned as she felt him slide one and then two fingers into her body.

"Oh God, Dylan . . ."

Her back arched as he withdrew and then plunged his fingers back in again.

"Is that good, Sizzle?"

She was almost beyond rational thought. "Yesss," she hissed, struggling to open her thighs and get more of his touches against her needy flesh.

He pulled his hand out and smeared her moisture over the hot skin of her buttocks.

Then he smacked her again, quick and sharp.

She cried out and pressed her clit into his lap, trying desperately to seek relief from the terrible ache that was building inside her.

"Better than watching, Sizzle?" *Smack.*

"Uhhh . . ."

"Isn't it better to be a part of it? To feel someone else doing it to you? Rather than standing alone doing it to yourself?"

"Mmmm."

Smack.

"You didn't answer me."

"Yes!" The shriek of need erupted from her throat. "Yes. You're right. You win. I give in. I shouldn't have spied on you. Or I should have joined you. Or whatever. I don't care. Just let me come, damn you . . ."

She couldn't see the strain on Dylan's face as his lips curled in a tense grin. But she could hear it in his voice.

"That's my girl. Now you know what you want. And it's the same thing I want."

Smack.

"It's the same thing I wanted when I watched you eleven years ago, and the same thing I've wanted every time I fucked someone since. All I could see were your blue eyes staring . . ." *smack* " . . . at . . ." *smack* " . . . me."

Dylan's last smack brought tears to Susanna's eyes and she almost missed realizing her hands were free. The tension in her shoulders eased and with another lightning-quick move, Dylan had her on the bed.

He spread her legs apart and jabbed his cock against her. "You want me?"

She widened her legs even more, ignoring the pain in her backside, ignoring the cuffs dangling from her wrists. "Oh, god, *yes.*"

Her world had narrowed down to what was between his legs and how quickly she could get it between hers.

He plunged inside her in one forceful thrust.

Then he froze.

"I had a physical two months ago. I'm healthy. What about you?"

She gazed at him through a fog of need. What the hell was he talking about? Then she realized. His cock was buried deep in her body and they hadn't stopped for protection.

"I'm healthy too. My last physical was six months ago, but I haven't slept with anyone in ages . . ." She whispered the words through clenched teeth, knowing that if he moved one inch she'd disappear into the vortex of an orgasm to end all orgasms.

"I can tell." His response came through gritted teeth. "You're so tight around my cock. Tight and hot and silky . . . like a velvet fire."

"Oh God, Dylan . . . finish it."

She closed her eyes and bit her lip.

"Not until you look at me, Sizzle. Open your eyes." He moved slightly. "Look at me. This time, it'll be *me* making you come."

She obeyed him, helpless to refuse.

He moved with purpose, withdrawing until he was almost free, then ramming himself back into her welcoming heat.

She moaned at the feel of him rubbing her inner flesh.

She groaned as his hand found her clit and stroked it carefully in time with his thrusts.

She gasped as her buttocks tensed and his breathing grew ragged and his cock hardened inside her.

And she screamed as she finally, wonderfully, explosively, orgasmed under the pounding, sweating weight of Dylan Sinclair, her eyes staring straight into his.

By God, it might have taken her eleven years, but it had been worth the wait.

THE FEEL OF HER CUNT as it clutched at his cock in rhythmic contractions sent Dylan over the edge.

With a muffled roar he let himself go, pumping into her for what seemed like an eternity.

He couldn't remember an orgasm like it. Along with his cum, she must have gotten part of his spleen, one lung and quite possibly his tonsils.

And, incredibly, it wasn't enough.

Just watching her eyes as he filled her was a whole experience on its own, and no sooner had his cock stopped pulsing than his mind said "*again.*"

With a sigh he eased his cock free of her warmth.

His hand caressed her breast, watching her eyes as he smoothed the softness of her skin. She was tense, still shuddering slightly from the aftershocks of her orgasm.

He gently leaned down and brushed her nipple with his tongue, soothing, caressing, loving the taste of her and the feel of her.

She sighed as he touched her, the sound running through his loins to some place deep within him.

He lay next to her and ran his hands gently over her body. He freed her wrists from the dangling cuffs and kissed the inside of her arm, running his tongue gently along the soft skin to her armpit.

He nuzzled the warmth there, breathing in the salty-sweet scent of her body. She sighed as he kissed his way across her chest and down her cleavage.

Gently, he did as he'd promised some time ago. Rested his face on her ribs and gently nibbled on the underside of her breast.

She giggled, and wriggled.

"Ticklish, huh?"

She nodded.

He followed his determined path down to her navel, toying with her belly button and rimming it with his tongue.

Her hands went to his head, sifting his hair and stroking his neck.

Their movements were slow and gentle, as Dylan and Susanna learned each other all over again.

Dylan's head moved lower and he spread her legs wide apart.

"Dylan . . ." Susanna muttered. "Don't . . . you shouldn't . . ."

"Ssshh. You're beautiful." He took his finger and rubbed her juices gently from her pink folds. It was mixed with his cum and the sight and scent of their recent lovemaking was incredibly arousing.

He bent and touched her soft pussy with his tongue, smiling at her indrawn breath.

"If I recall our conversation correctly, this is an area where your counseling skills could use a little firsthand experience."

A gasp and a slight groan acknowledged his words.

"Now, Dr. Chalmers, I am about to demonstrate the Sinclair technique of oral gratification. First, we caress . . ."

He ran his tongue gently over the surface of her shining flesh, loving the shudder he caused.

"Then we flicker . . ." Suiting actions to words, he flicked his tongue carefully across her clit, listening to her body as it reacted. The clench of her hands on the sheets rustled loudly through the room, and her breathing ratcheted up several notches.

"Ah, yes. That seems effective." His breath fanned her moisture. "Then we go on a little voyage of discovery . . ."

"D-D-Dylan . . ." The stutter hissed between Susanna's teeth as her legs fidgeted next to his shoulders.

He firmed up his tongue and investigated several nooks and crannies. His movements brought a moan to her throat and a certain telltale flex to her muscles.

Her scent was strong, and getting stronger, and Dylan found his own body responding. He was amazed.

He continued his education of Susanna Chalmers. He licked some more, and poked and fluttered, and made sure to pay the proper amount of attention to her clit, which had obviously recovered from her earlier climax.

Her hips were now moving in response to his mouth and she was panting.

Slowly, he pressed kisses into her mound and pulled himself up onto her arms.

"Susanna . . . I want you again."

"Oh, Dylan. Dear God . . . please?"

This time their joining was slow, sensual and full of emotion. She needed no encouragement to watch Dylan's face as he slid his cock past her pink and glistening folds and into her warmth.

He sighed as he felt her surround him once more, the heat of her body burning into his unprotected flesh and making this an experience beyond imagination.

With a smooth twist of his hips, he rolled onto his back and pulled her on top of him.

"Now it's your turn to be on top." He grinned, enjoying the look of surprise on her face and noting the moment it changed to one of speculation.

He grunted as she wriggled herself into a comfortable position, experimenting with little moves this way and that.

Surprisingly, she didn't straddle him.

He sucked in a breath as she pressed her thighs together and fit herself between his legs, gripping his cock tightly within her and adding the extra friction of her firm muscles against his balls.

It was heaven. It was incredible. It was typical Sizzle. Her overriding curiosity, driving her to experiment, was resulting in sensations Dylan could not have guessed at before this moment.

She pulled her hips up and away, and he raised his head, pulling a pillow beneath his neck.

"Look at us, Sizzle. My God . . . look at us . . ."

She lowered her head to see and he pushed her hair aside. They both watched as her body slid over his cock, her red hair shining fiery against her creamy skin and his slick length. She eased back down and took him deep, so deep their hair tangled where their bodies met in a confusion of warmth and shadows.

She sobbed in a breath. "Dylan . . . dear heavens, Dylan . . . I had no idea . . ."

He was beyond words. Watching their bodies as they blended into one was the most arousing thing he could ever remember doing in his entire life.

He felt the surge begin low in his spine and his whole body tightened.

"Sizzle, I hope you don't mind . . . I think I'm going to . . ."

She raised her head and the firelight danced in her china blue eyes.

"Yes, Dylan Sinclair. Come. I want to feel you come. Inside me, deep inside me. Fill me again, Dylan, please?"

She rolled her hips as she plunged down onto his cock and ground her clit against his body.

Dylan reached for her breasts, cupping them in his hand and rolling the nipples firmly between his fingers.

She gasped with pleasure.

His body trembled and he pinched the delicate buds hard.

She sobbed and thrust even harder against him.

He couldn't help it, he shouted. Loud and long. His cock spurted his cum deep inside the body of the woman gyrating on top of him, and it took uncounted eons for the pulsating to ease.

She had helped. Her orgasm even now clenched his softening cock and milked the last drops from it.

Exhausted, she fell onto his chest, her hair tumbling onto his sweat-soaked skin.

"Oh God." It was about all he could manage in the way of post-coital conversation. Mentally, he chastised himself, promising to do better in the morning.

He pulled her up and tucked her into his body.

Sizzle Chalmers was sound asleep.

His shoulder was cold. Turning, he shrugged the covers up over his bare skin and let his senses slowly awaken.

He could still smell their loving.

Without any fuss or bother, his cock immediately swelled in response to her scent.

Sizzle. Susanna Chalmers. She'd been everything his mind had imagined for the past eleven years and then some.

They'd fucked like two people who'd been starved of sex for a lifetime or two. Which may well have been true for her, but he had no such excuse.

Nope. It was different with Sizzle. Wonderfully, enormously, terrifyingly different.

And he'd better do it again just to make sure. His cock throbbed in agreement. He hoped she wasn't too sore.

He slid his hand beneath the covers to Susanna's side of the bed.

There was nothing there.

Adrenaline flooded his nervous system and he sat up with a rush, ignoring the cool air that battered his flesh.

The fire was turned down low, the candles had gutted, and there was nothing, not one sign, to show that she'd ever been there.

All her clothes were gone, the cuffs were back on their hook, and his pants were folded neatly on a chair.

He leapt from the bed and started looking for a note. There had to be a note. Women always left a note, didn't they? At least they did in the movies.

There was nothing.

After a fruitless time spent hunting throughout the room for something, *anything*—he even checked the bathroom mirror to see if there was a lipstick message. Even though she wasn't a serial killer, she might have used that method. But once again, there was nothing.

Dylan was forced to a nasty realization.

His legs gave way and he collapsed onto the side of the bed, hands resting helplessly on his knees. He shook his head in denial, but his heart made him face the truth.

His Sizzle was gone.

"Susanna, Aurora Swann is on line two . . ." Sylvia's
face still registered a certain amount of awe at an-
nouncing that particular caller.

"Thanks, I'll take it."

Susanna sighed and straightened in her chair, reaching for
the phone. "Hi, Aurora, how was Venezuela?"

"Argentina."

"Whatever."

"It was fine. Hot and a lot of people spoke Spanish. What
else can I tell you?"

"How about what I can do for you. You did call me, you
know."

"Just figured I'd check and see if the bastard called you
yet."

Susanna sighed again. "Don't call him that, Aurora. I
walked out on him. You know that as well as I do."

Susanna could still remember the look on Aurora's face from that eventful weekend. It had taken her only moments to realize that the figure creeping stealthily down the Club's huge staircase at some ungodly hour was not a burglar, a rapist or a tabloid photographer, but Susanna.

They'd looked at each other, and a moment of feminine understanding had passed between them.

Aurora was on her way out too.

They'd shared a car and kept in touch ever since. "Did Jonas call you?"

There was silence for a moment. "Nah. Didn't expect him to."

"So, here we are. Great sex under our belts and no guys in sight."

"Wanna grab dinner someplace? Oh, I know—I have a new chef here at the Club, come on over early. We'll eat in my quarters and rent a movie. What do you say?"

"Hugh Grant?"

"How about Hugh Jackman?"

"Grrrrowl. How *about* Hugh Jackman. Yeah. It's a deal. See you around six."

"Cool." Aurora hung up.

"So you're dating Aurora now, huh?" Sylvia's ironic tones echoed across the office as she brought some invoices in for Susanna's signature.

"Sheesh, Syl. She's a really nice person. I like her a lot and we have stuff in common."

Sylvia raised an eyebrow.

"Well, as much as a five-foot-seven relationship counselor and a mega-rich six-foot heiress can possibly have in common."

"Yeah."

"Okay. So mostly we sit and bitch about guys. Isn't that what women are supposed to do when they spend time together?"

"*Women,*" said Sylvia firmly, "aren't supposed to lose those guys in the first place. Having hot sex with those guys is better than bitching about them. Trust me on this."

Susanna humphed. "Look, both Aurora and I got scared, okay? It's not that unusual. We recognized it, and we're dealing with it."

"Honey, the only reason you got scared is because you found a guy who made you *feel.*"

Susanna looked down at her hands that were tapping out a rhythm on her desktop. "I know."

"So why the hell aren't you out there beating the bushes for him?"

"Because."

"Because why?" Sylvia snorted. "Listen to me. High school all over again. But seriously, why haven't you tried to get in touch with him? It's been almost three weeks."

"Because . . ." Susanna bit her lip. "Because I need to figure out if it's worth the risk. Because I don't know if I can stand it if I get some sort of 'piss off and never darken my doorway again' type message from him."

Sylvia sat on the edge of Susanna's desk and looked down at her affectionately. "Boy, for a qualified relationship therapist you sure know how to fuck up your own love life."

Susanna choked out a laugh. "Hell, Sylvia, tell me how you really feel, why don't you?"

"Sweetie, love is a gamble. It's a risk. It's great sex that you want again and again, not just once. It's a person that you can fall asleep on and drool over as well as orgasm with. It's a guy whose cock drives you insane with lust and whose heart swamps you with tenderness. It's scary, overpowering, terrifying and magnificent. It's also warm, wonderful and unfortunately a lot rarer than it should be."

Susanna stared at Sylvia, trying to absorb her little speech.

"If you think that there's even a chance you could have that with Dylan, then damn it, girl, go find him. I'm tired of watching you moon around the office, having bitch-fests with mega-millionairesses and jumping every time the phone rings."

"That bad?"

"Worse."

"Oh hell."

SUSANNA'S MIND DRIFTED OVER Sylvia's words as she parked her car and went around the side of the Aurora Club mansion to Aurora Swann's private quarters.

A person that you can fall asleep on . . . . Well, she'd done that, not even realizing that it had happened until she'd woken with the steady sound of his heart beating in her ear. She didn't think she'd drooled, but they were both so sticky and sweaty, who could tell?

A guy whose cock drives you insane with lust. Hah. Yep. No question about it. Insane was probably the best term both clinically and personally. The woman she thought she was would never have allowed herself to be spanked, licked, sucked and fucked and then screamed out for more as soon as it was done.

She felt the heat of a blush creep over her cheeks as she remembered Dylan's touch.

Damn. She was trying so hard not to relive those moments. She was so afraid that the memories would be all she'd have for the next fifty years or so. What if she wore them out?

"Thinking about him again, aren't you?" Aurora's wry voice penetrated the fog around Susanna as she opened the door and pulled her inside.

"Urgh. Why does everyone always assume I'm thinking about him? Couldn't I be worrying about a case? Couldn't I be trying to figure out the best way to organize my office hours so that I can have time to do some clinical research?"

"No. Your face is flushed, your breathing is rapid, and your pupils are slightly dilated. Your palms are probably sweaty, and I'm not going to ask about the state of your underwear. Ergo, I deduce you are not doing anything like what you just said. You're having a severe attack of Dylan Sinclair."

"Well—shit."

Aurora grinned and Susanna grinned back. "C'mon, let's go see what the chef whipped up. And then we'll see what Hugh Jackman can whip up."

"Mmmm. Sounds good. Both of them."

The women shared a companionable meal, and did their level best to keep the conversation off men. They failed miserably of course.

"So no word from Jonas, huh?" Susanna regretfully dropped the last piece of pizza unfinished on her plate. "Good pizza, by the way. Compliments to the chef."

Aurora smiled crookedly. "If you can tell me why I've hired someone at an exorbitant salary to make something I can send out for, for a great deal less, I'd be very happy." She pushed away from the low coffee table and reached for her soda. "And no, no word from Jonas."

"Is he in town?"

"I don't know."

"Aurora. You have more money than God. You can find out these things, can't you?"

"Susanna. You have a telephone. You can call Dylan, can't you?"

"Touché."

The two women looked at each other.

"We're pretty poor excuses for twenty-first-century women, aren't we?" Susanna shook her head at their pathetic state. "Things haven't changed that much in the last couple hundred years. We're still waiting for the guy to come marching over our drawbridge on his white horse and announce his intentions of rescuing the damsel."

"Well, yeah. And I don't mind telling you that I'm in a fair amount of distress. Even *with* my Tubmate II. Although I'll be forever in your debt for telling me about it."

"This is so stupid. We're bright, intelligent, well educated, and in your case, filthy rich, women. We're not ugly, by any stretch of the imagination. Any man should be glad to know that we are interested in him."

"Right on."

"So what we should do is just pick up that damn phone and tell these guys that we want them. In our beds, hard, hot and ready to rock."

"Hoo-rah."

Susanna looked at Aurora. "You go first."

Aurora groaned and buried her head in her hands. "Yeah, sure."

The ping of Aurora's doorbell interrupted their conversation, and Aurora wore a puzzled look on her face as she came back with an oblong package in her hands.

Susanna looked up curiously. "Got an admirer?"

"No. Apparently you have."

Susanna sat up in a hurry.

"It's addressed to Dr. Chalmers, care of me. Now what's that about?"

"Haven't a clue." Susanna touched the delicate silver wrapping with one finger.

"I doubt it's a bomb. My security is better than that. How about you open it?"

"Think I should?"

"*Susanna . . .*"

"Okay, okay. Hold your horses . . ." Grinning, Susanna put the package on the coffee table and began to peel back the layers of tissue.

Opening the lid of the box inside, she tilted her head in bewilderment. "Well, what have we here?" She pulled out something that was soft and furry and leathery.

"Oh my. A flogger. Nice work too." Aurora's eyes sparkled.

"Yeah. Nice work . . ." Susanna held it up, admiring the woven leather that covered the handle and the intricate work at each end. It felt nicely balanced in her hand and she moved to let the streamers of fur-covered suede slide free. The black fur fell softly through her hands and she couldn't resist the urge to swing it slightly.

Aurora sighed. "Honey, let me show you . . ."

The hands of an artist took over, and Susanna watched as Aurora gently flipped her wrist, making the strands slap softly on the couch pillow.

"This is a soft flogger, Susanna."

"Oh. Yes. I figured that . . . fur and all."

"No, you misunderstand. The word 'soft' here means that it is used for light action. It won't leave a mark or cause much in the way of pain. It's really for beginners, and to be honest with you, I prefer to use it after some harder work. It's really good when brushed across skin that's already been warmed up a bit."

"Ah. Okay. And I need to know this because . . . ?"

"Because this is apparently only part of the gift." Aurora had given the flogger back to Susanna and was rummaging in the box. She held up a large iron key with a note attached.

Susanna took it with hands that were starting to shake. "This key will unlock the rest of the gift."

She raised her eyes and stared at Aurora. "Oh shit. He's here."

A smile crossed Aurora's face. "I'd say so."

"What am I going to do?"

"Looks like he's gone to a lot of trouble for you, Susanna. I guess I'd recommend that you at least hear him out. But do what your heart tells you, okay?" She reached out and lightly held Susanna's hand, squeezing it around the key. "Seems that you're gonna get to go first, after all."

The short walk from Aurora's apartments to the members' facilities seemed to take hours, and gave her plenty of time to develop an enormous case of the jitters.

Susanna didn't know what was trembling more, her knees

or her nerve. She stood outside the door with a huge key in her hand, knowing all too well that Dylan Sinclair was inside.

Knowing, hoping and perhaps some part of her wishing that he wasn't. The part that was scared to death he'd look at her and just want to fuck her again and then leave. The part that said she had nothing to offer a super-stud hot-body like Dylan Sinclair. The part that had run away from the prom all those years ago. The part that was screaming "don't go in there, you'll only make a fool of yourself."

The part that was afraid to admit that she'd fallen in love with Dylan Sinclair eleven years ago.

She watched as some other person raised her hand for her and put the key into the huge lock.

She watched that other woman turn it so that the little lights turned green. She heard the other woman's breathing hitch as the door unlatched, and she knew that other woman was getting aroused at the thought of a certain hot man and his hands and lips all over her body.

Susanna shook her head to clear it, drew in a deep breath and stepped into the darkened room.

For a moment her heart stopped.

She couldn't see anybody at all.

"OPEN YOUR EYES, SIZZLE."

Her eyes were pinched tightly shut, and Dylan wondered what the hell was going through her mind. Was the thought of seeing him that bad? His gut clenched.

She opened her eyes and blinked, as if surprised to find out they'd been shut in the first place. She looked around the now familiar room and finally her gaze came to rest on him.

She caught her breath.

Dear God, why didn't she say something? Did she think that he spent huge amounts of time hanging around in neo-Victorian bedrooms by his wrists without a stitch of clothing?

Her eyes fell to his crotch. Well all right. She'd noticed.

Noticed that his hard-on couldn't get much harder without requiring a zip code of its own. The fact that he'd been getting harder as he waited, chained to the four-poster, had become pretty obvious to him, and by the looks of things it was dawning on her too.

"Susanna . . ."

"Dylan, I . . ." She stopped, and flicked the flogger in agitation. "Dylan . . . I'm sorry."

Dylan raised an eyebrow in surprise. "For what?"

"For running out on you. For not saying thank you, at least, for such a lovely evening."

Dylan's head buzzed. The best sex he could ever remember having, in fact better sex than he'd thought it was humanly possible to survive, and she called it a *'lovely evening'*?

He growled.

She jumped a little.

"It wasn't a 'lovely evening,' as you so politely put it, Susanna."

He saw her wince at his words, and realized she'd taken them the wrong way. He sighed. "It was possibly the best night of my life."

That caught her attention and brought her gaze back up to his eyes. Not that he minded her staring at his crotch, but a guy had his pride.

"Really?"

"Oh yeah. You and I *burn* together, honey. I didn't know it could be like that with a woman. I also didn't know what it would be like to wake up and find you gone."

She drew in a breath, but he forestalled her. "Then I realized that I'd pushed you way too hard. That I'd probably terrified you and made you think I was some kind of sex fiend."

"Dylan . . ."

"Hush. Let me finish. I'm trying to apologize here, Susanna."

Susanna cleared her throat and moved nearer to him,

swishing the flogger absently as she closed the gap between them.

"I don't know what got into me that night. I've never spanked a woman before, but I do know that it was one of the most exciting things I've ever done. I can't decide if it was the spanking or the fact that it was your beautiful bottom beneath my hand. Perhaps we could have played cribbage and I'd have gotten that turned on. I don't know."

Dylan sure knew that this conversation was turning him on. His cock was now a statue of amazing rigidity and thinking of Susanna's buttocks as they glowed across his lap wasn't helping any.

"All I'm asking is another chance. I spent the whole of my trip to Washington trying to figure out a way to get another shot at making things work between us without scaring you. And so this is it."

He glanced up at the chains and rattled them.

"It's all yours. I'm all yours. You are in control, Susanna. I think I took that away from you that night, and I want you to know that I give it back. Please, just tell me you'll give me another chance?"

Dylan stared at Susanna, trying to read her expression. Her china blue eyes were lowered and she seemed to be concentrating on the strands of black fur as she pulled them across her hand.

"You've been in Washington?"

"Um, yeah. Engineering Society meeting and a few other things. I had to leave right after the party, but never got a chance to tell you. I got back a couple of days ago, set this up, and here I am."

"Hmm."

She moved around the room, slowly strolling from the fireplace to the side table, taking a leisurely tour, and turning out the electric lights as she passed the door.

Dylan's heart jumped.

"So you did want to see me again?"

Dylan barely suppressed a snort. "Oh yeah. Just like I wanted to keep breathing too."

She turned away, hiding her expression from his watchful eyes. "And you want me to know that now I'm in control?"

"Well, yeah. I want you to feel comfortable with me. I don't want you ever feeling afraid, and I was worried that you did. That *that* was the reason you ran away from me."

"Actually, it wasn't."

"It wasn't?"

"Nope."

Dylan was starting to sweat. He knew this conversation was incredibly important for both of them, but he was stark naked, seriously aroused and she was circling him like some kind of predator. And if she didn't stop playing with that damn flogger he was going to do something *really* embarrassing like come all over himself. Again.

"So why did you leave me?" He tried exceptionally hard to keep a whine out of his voice. "I was really pissed to wake up and find you gone." He failed. The whine was there, and he knew she heard it.

She crossed behind him and he almost dislocated a shoulder trying to keep his eyes on her.

He nearly dislocated both eyeballs when he saw her pull her sweater off over her head.

"It's getting hot in here, isn't it?"

She moved back into his line of vision, completely blasting his optic nerves into oblivion.

She was wearing a pair of low-slung jeans, and a bra that should have come with a government warning. It was deep emerald green, with little flutters of lace barely covering the nipples. In fact, they didn't quite cover her nipples. Oh God, he was in trouble now. He hoped.

Standing just far enough away from him, Susanna unsnapped her jeans and slid them slowly off her hips. A matching thong was revealed, and Dylan offered up a prayer of thanksgiving to whoever's "Secret" she was wearing.

"Not your usual lingerie choice, is it?" His voice was husky and she grinned.

"Aurora took me shopping."

"Remind me to give her a thank-you present. Think she'd like Iowa?"

"I think she's already got one."

"Yeah. Probably." Dylan licked his lips as Susanna pulled her hair free of its elastic and shook it out around her shoulders.

A moan echoed around the room, shocking Dylan as he realized it came from him.

Susanna was still staring at him, and now she began prowling again. This time she was less hesitant.

"So, what am I going to do with you, Dylan?"

He cleared his throat of the fourteen tons of asphalt that seemed to have suddenly clogged it.

"No, that's all right. Don't tell me. Let me think here . . ." Susanna wandered over to the fireplace and bent to the control, flaunting her backside with its teeny green dividing strip.

Dylan knew he wouldn't survive. Death would certainly be forthcoming very shortly. The coroner would probably have to do terrible things to his corpse to stop it from grinning.

The fire flared up, lighting the halo of hair around Susanna's head. For a few seconds he was blinded.

Then the soft sting of the flogger against his thigh jerked him out of his fantasies.

Sizzle had decided what to do with him.

Oh boy.

IT WAS RAPIDLY BECOMING clear to Susanna that "drooly" guys weren't just a feature of women's romance novels. Her salivary glands were starting to work overtime as she circled the man chained naked in front of her.

The firelight danced over his muscular body, highlighting his chest and the proud length of his cock as he struggled to turn and keep her in his line of sight.

The feel of the flogger in her hands, the brush of the air against her almost bare body, and Dylan ready to obey her every whim, was about the most erotic thing she could ever remember happening to her.

She closed the distance between them. "Turn away from me."

He reluctantly turned his back on her.

She came right up close, and pressed her breasts against his back, letting his buttocks rub across her thong.

A sound came from somebody, but Susanna would have been hard-pressed to identify whose throat had moaned.

She slipped her hands round his waist and stood on tiptoe,

peeking over his shoulder to watch as the tapered strips of fur dangled around his cock.

This time, there was no doubt. The groan was definitely his.

"God, Susanna."

"Yeah, Dylan. This is fun." She pulled back quickly, letting the streamers tug his cock as they moved away.

She circled around in front of him, a grin on her face. "Now. Let me see. I have a flogger, and you are chained to a large Victorian four-poster bed. Why, Lord Witherspoon. I do believe you've been a bad boy."

Devilish fire danced in her china blue eyes and she slid her hand behind her to the catch of her bra. The sound of the clasp opening made Dylan wince.

"No? Should I leave it on?" Her eyes widened as she asked the innocent question.

"No—please. I'm sorry, I just . . ." Dylan seemed to be having difficulty stringing words together. Well, well, well.

"Okay. It is getting quite warm in here, isn't it?" She teased him some more by turning her back and shrugging the straps down her arms to her elbows. Letting the bra fall to the floor, she raised her hands and glanced over her shoulder at the almost rigid Dylan. "Much better."

She turned and ran the fur lengths across her own breasts. "Wouldn't you say that was better, Dylan?"

Dylan fought for speech, Adam's apple bobbing helplessly.

"Mmm. This fur certainly feels nice against the skin. At least when it's stroked like this it does. Tell me, Dylan—oh, I beg your pardon, Lord Witherspoon, I meant to say. Does it feel good against your skin, too?"

With amazingly accurate aim, Susanna flicked the flogger across the top of Dylan's thigh, just catching his buttock with the tips as they wrapped around his body.

He gasped. "Oh, shit."

"Bad? Oh dear. Poor Lord Witherspoon."

Seeing as "Lord Witherspoon's" cock was dribbling moisture from a massively engorged head, and sweat was filming his chest, Susanna felt reasonably sure that she had inflicted no lasting injury.

She repeated the move on the other side just to make sure, but this time she was less accurate. A couple of tails flicked his balls.

"Ouch. Careful, woman." Dylan's eyes flashed open in surprise.

"Still okay with this? Shouldn't we have a safe word or something?" Susanna dredged up the details of bondage scenarios from the two courses she'd taken in "Things You Might Not Consider Recommending During Therapy, But That Have Their Place in Relationship Counseling" (BDSM 103/104). It had been two quite enlightening semesters, but she'd never imagined actually participating in games like these.

She was a little shocked to find that she was really enjoying it. No, too mild an expression. She was *really* getting turned on by it.

"If you want. Safe word is . . . uh . . ."

Susanna picked that moment to stroke her breasts again with the flogger. Dylan made a very physically obvious effort to drag his brain off her nipples.

"Yes, Dylan? Safe word is . . . ?" she prompted.

"Um—God—er—how about Iowa?" Dylan had obviously grabbed for the first word that came to mind. "Fuck" had clearly been dismissed as a viable option.

"Very well. Iowa it is. If, at any time, I damage you, or cause you pain in any way, or you are uncomfortable with what I'm doing, then all you have to do is say 'Iowa,' and I will immediately stop what I'm doing."

Dylan dredged up a tight smile. "Don't expect to hear it, babe. If you can dish it out, I can take it."

"Oh, Lord Witherspoon . . ." Susanna chuckled, running the flogger around his neck and over his shoulders. "You are such a . . . a . . . *guy!*"

"Glad you noticed," Dylan said, shivering. "Gonna do anything about it?"

"In time, in time. Your Daisy has to enjoy herself too, don't you think?"

"Yeah, well, *Daisy*, you're gonna get more than you bargained for if you don't stop flicking my cock with that damn thing."

"Really?" The drawled word surprised Susanna, who had no idea that she could even drawl at all, let alone produce a sexy sound while she did so.

She circled Dylan once again, stopping just out of arm's length in front of him.

"Hmm. So no more cock flicking. Oh darn. And I was just getting the hang of it. Well, I'll just have to try something else."

She moved nearer and thrust her hips forward, letting his cock slide across the emerald green silk of her thong. It left a trail of moisture behind, and a man with seriously clenched teeth.

"Oh, I like that. Let's try that again."

"Let's not and say we did," muttered Dylan, seemingly unable to take his eyes off her body.

"Only it wasn't *quite* right. Hmm. Let me see . . ." Susanna tugged at her lip as if in deep contemplation. She snapped her fingers. "I've got it."

She stuck her thumbs in the waistband of her thong and slid it down her hips, letting the flogger trail across her skin as she did so.

Dylan groaned.

"Oh, now that's much better." The fur strands stood out in sharp relief against the white of her belly as she stepped out of her thong, widened her stance and let them dangle between her legs.

"Oh my. Yes, I see why people like these things." She moved the flogger, lightly flipping the streamers between her own legs.

Dylan groaned again. "Sweet mercy, woman . . ." he hissed.

"So sorry. I got distracted." Susanna was not only distracted, she was damn near an orgasm to end all orgasms. This was way too arousing and she wasn't sure if she was ready to let Dylan watch as she climaxed on her own.

A small part of her was shocked that she was even thinking that way, but the new enlightened Sizzle Chalmers took that small part by the scruff of the neck and locked it away in a closet. The coast was clear.

"Dylan. Face the bed." The order was sharp, but instantly obeyed. Dylan had obviously recognized the wisdom of following the orders of an aroused naked redhead with a flogger.

She quickly lashed out as she'd seen Aurora do, laying the strands across Dylan's buttocks. A satisfying slap resulted.

"Are you all right?" Okay, so a little part of her professional conscience was still lurking.

"Yeah." The word was a bit husky, but clear nonetheless.

"Good." She lashed again, and this time relished the sound and the feel of the fur landing on his solid backside.

She followed her two hard strokes with a soft teasing flick, making him writhe a little.

Then she surprised herself. She moved in behind him, bent down and rubbed her breasts across his glowing buttocks.

"Oh shit, Sizzle . . ."

"Was that an 'Iowa'?"

"No, *God*, no. That was just a plain 'oh shit.'"

"Good."

"I don't suppose you'd consider letting my chains down."

"Not a chance." She turned him around, feeling his damp flesh beneath her fingers. His face was flushed and a muscle was twitching in his cheek. His eyes, ah yes. His eyes.

He was looking at her like she was his every dream, his every fantasy. As if he could devour her with his eyes.

She shut her own for a second, shocked by the intensity she'd seen in his hazel depths.

Attracted by his scent, she swayed toward him, opened her eyes and leaned in to his chest. Gently, she settled her mouth around his nipple, teasing it with her tongue.

She let her breasts brush his body, and when he slid a thigh between hers, she welcomed it, letting her clit rub lightly over his muscles.

She sighed around his flesh, and felt him shiver.

"Honey, I want you so bad I'm dying here." The words were strangled out of Dylan's throat.

"How bad do you want me, Dylan? Tell me." She dragged her lips to his other nipple and treated it to similar suckling. The flogger was behind his back, and she made sure the fur was rubbing against his buttocks.

"I'll die if I don't have you. My life depends on getting my cock into your wet heat. And I know you're wet, I can smell the excitement on you." He bent his head and licked her shoulder, her neck, anyplace his tongue could reach.

"You want me that bad, huh?"

"That bad and more. I need to be inside you. I need to have you shaking around me, grabbing onto my cock with your cunt as you come apart. I need to suck your clit until you explode into my mouth a dozen times in a row. I need to fuck you for days. And then do it all over again. And again."

"Wow." Susanna rested her head against his chest, weakened by his words.

"I need you, Susanna, Sizzle, Daisy, whatever. I need all of you. Now. Please?"

D YLAN HELD HIS BREATH as Susanna's blue eyes met his. She seemed to be looking for something from him, some expression, a gesture maybe. He didn't know. All he could do was gaze at her, letting his desire and his need show in his eyes.

She sighed, dropped the flogger and reached for his chains. "I want you too," she breathed as their faces drew closer.

Her fingers fumbled with the catch as Dylan brushed his lips across hers.

After agonizing moments of almost touching, almost kissing, one arm was free. With a grunt that combined relief and pain, Dylan immediately pulled her body against his and kissed her with every iota of skill he possessed.

It must have had some effect because she gave up trying to open the second cuff. It clanked awkwardly to the floor behind her as he flipped the final buckle open.

He was free and she was his.

Her tongue dueled for supremacy inside his mouth as his forced it back so he could plunge into her sweet depths.

He swung her around and lifted her onto the bed. Without a murmur her legs spread wide, welcoming him between.

"I can't wait," he muttered.

"Me neither. Oh God, Dylan, now, please?" She was all but sobbing, fingernails gouging his shoulders and back as she struggled to get him closer.

His hands fell to her hips and without another thought he plunged himself deep into her heat.

They both sighed in relief.

Dylan could never ever remember feeling like this when he was inside a woman. Her fiery flesh was burning him, but pulling him even farther into her secret places. He pushed her hips tight against his, swearing he could feel her swollen clit against his cock as he withdrew and thrust again.

She moaned and her head fell back, hair tumbling behind her and catching the light from the fire.

She was magnificent.

She was his.

He knew at that moment, as sure as if he'd received instructions from Heaven itself, that this woman was his.

Their rhythm increased, and he slid his hand between them. She reached around and grabbed his buttocks.

She squeezed as he pressed.

Their bodies slammed together in an explosion of desire, lust and passion. Within seconds his cock was pumping, her cunt was squeezing and they were both sobbing.

Their orgasm left them both limp and voiceless, sprawled in an awkward tangle of limbs, half on and half off the bed.

Dylan tugged them both into a more comfortable position, realizing to his astonishment that he was still half hard inside her.

"Dylan," she whispered, finally focusing on him. "Dylan."

He knew how she felt. His voice hadn't returned yet. He let his hips move slowly, watching her response.

"*Dylan.*"

It was unmistakable. She was ready for him again. This mind-blowing sexual experience was doing the same thing to her as it was to him, making them both insatiable.

"I've got to have you again, Sizzle," he whispered. "Slow this time, slow and easy."

Suiting words to action, Dylan rested his arms beside her body and slowly plundered the treasure that was Sizzle Chalmers.

Stroking his cock against her slick silk was the most incredible feeling, and Dylan knew he could never tire of it. He allowed one hand to gently tease her clit, watching, gauging her response and the level of her arousal.

She was coming along very nicely too. He could feel the juices inside her bathing his cock. His arms trembled.

"Dylan, let me." Susanna pushed at his shoulders, turning him.

Willingly, he rolled, letting her settle on top of him.

This time, she straddled him, rubbing her clit against his hardness.

He reached for her breasts, so temptingly near, and raised his mouth, loving the way she leaned forward to make it easy for him.

Endless moments of time passed as they slowly made their way up to the fiery heights, each discovering new places to touch, new movements to bring pleasure, new expressions on the face of the person loving them.

But before long, their bodies let them know that eruption was imminent. Susanna's thighs began to tighten, and the cords in Dylan's neck were strung taut.

Susanna began her last ride toward orgasm.

Dylan caught her hips in his hands. "Iowa."

She struggled against her own body. "What?"

"Iowa."

"Dylan." She sobbed out the word. "You want me to stop? *Now?*" Her movements seemed to be almost out of control as he could feel her urge to push down on him against his hands.

"Just answer one question."

"Dylan, God. Not. Now." She tried to push down and force his hands out of the way.

His muscles damn near cracked but he held on, keeping them both suspended, seconds from orgasm.

"Now, Sizzle. *Iowa.* It's *Iowa* until you answer a question."

"What?" she nearly screamed at him.

"Marry me?"

"Huh?" Susanna had no idea whose dream she was in but it couldn't have been hers. In this dream Dylan Sinclair had just asked her to marry him seconds before giving her the second climax of the night.

Definitely a dream.

"I mean it, Sizzle. I can't imagine fucking anyone else like this. Ever. I don't think I'd want to. And the thought of you and someone . . ." Dylan shook his head. "Well, we won't even go there."

Susanna stared at him.

"But it's more than that."

"It is?" She was finding this whole thing very hard to understand, mostly because her brain was pointing at her clit and screaming loudly at her. *Excuse me? Impending orgasm here, level seven-point-three on the Richter scale. Get the fuck on with it.*

"You want to marry me? You want us, you and me, to get married?"

"I want us to get married, yes. I want us to have babies, a mortgage and a lawn mower. Possibly even a dog. I want to go to sleep holding you every night for the next fifty years or so at least. I love you, Sizzle Chalmers. Please, fill my life like you've filled my heart."

Susanna's eyes flooded with tears. She gulped. "Oh *Dylan*, my God. I love you too. More than life."

"Is that a yes?"

"Yes, I . . ."

No sooner had the words left her lips than Dylan released her hips and thrust upward with his own. The circle was complete. Her orgasm exploded in a fireball behind her eyes, and she was only dimly aware of Dylan's answering shout as his cock flooded her womb with warm cum.

Hah. That was an eight-point-one, if ever I saw one.

Once again, Dylan and Susanna collapsed, this time boneless, exhausted, completely soaked and unable to lift an eyelash.

"Hey, Sizzle, think we'll survive, 'til the wedding?"

Susanna grinned with the few muscles that were left functioning. "Oh yeah." She snuggled into the rather sweaty armpit of her dream man and put her arms around him. "Of course, there are no guarantees when it comes to the honeymoon. Especially if we pack the flogger . . ."